Abigail, Vampire Outcast

Mountain Warriors Book 6

R.J. Burle

Pier House Books

Copyright © 2025 by R.J. Burle

All rights reserved.

No portion of this book may be reproduced in any form without written permission from the publisher or author, except as permitted by U.S. copyright law.

For Brandon Zaner

He was a distant cousin I didn't meet until I was in my twenties, but he shared my quirky sense of humor. We soon became close friends, and although we'd only see each other every few years that friendship remained strong. Unfortunately he was shot in a case of random and senseless violence just before Christmas 2024. His heart was as big as his smile. Until we meet again.

As a side note, the good vampire, Brandon, in the story wasn't named after him, but they share a similar heart. I believe that I unconsciously used his name because it was fitting.

Chapter One

"We'll get you into the tent shortly, Abigail," I said.

"OK Eric," she answered with exhaustion but still a classy touch of patience.

We sat in the dead leaves of the forest, bundled up against the bleak winter night on a hill overlooking the village of the Mountain Warriors's camp, but despite my fatigue, I couldn't sleep. It wasn't just the razor cold gusts that easily sliced through my layers of jackets and the light blanket that I had wrapped around the two of us. Yes, the wind, that was like the blades of sharpened icicles, but what kept me awake the most was my worry. My goal on this dark night was to wait for the moments before daylight before sneaking Abigail into the camp. Usually the guards were the most lax in their attention at that time.

Fifty meters below us sat about thirty teepees made of thread bare tarps. A few had smoke rising from the holes in the tops. The scent of woodsmoke gave me a homely feeling and a desire to wrap up in my sleeping bag.

But I had to put nostalgia aside because I would face immediate execution if I was caught in the act of sneaking Abigail, the vampiress, into the camp. I had been warned by the chiefs of the camp not to have any more vampires visit me as if I had planned the unexpected visit

I had received just yesterday warning me about Abigail's impending execution.

I had managed to save her, but she needed a place to find safety. I hoped that I might find leniency if she was discovered in the camp after sneaking her in. I was hoping that the danger would be in the initial act and afterwards, when they realized that she wasn't a threat, everything would be OK. In reality, I needed a safe place for her to recover and I had no other options available.

Bryan, the second in command of the Mountain Warrior tribe, owed both his life and the life of his son to her intervention not long ago, not to mention many members of the tribe as well, but regardless, her presence would invoke great fear in most of the people in the group. I couldn't blame them. Many people had lost family and friends to the "wingless mosquitoes," as that smartass Scott called the vampires.

The day before, I had rescued Abigail from crucifixion and saved her at the point of her death. I had even fed her my blood from the veins of my own wrist that I intentionally cut to revive her, but even after drinking my blood she still hovered near death. She then drank the blood of a deer that she had hypnotized. After that, she had recovered some more of her strength, but she needed a place to hole up to heal from the grievous wounds. Even vampires had their limits.

It also warmed my heart that after she had her fill of the deer's blood, she let it go, pretty much unharmed other than a loss of a negligible amount of blood. She indeed had a kind heart. She wasn't just a good vampire, she was the kindest hearted person I had ever met. Period. I owed her everything.

On the hill above the camp, she leaned against me in an exhausted sleep. I could feel her body heat from her fresh consumption of blood. Just before her blood feast, her body temperature felt near the freezing mark in tune with the frigid winter air around us. At that point she had been unnaturally cold as if she was already dead. I had been curious if the vampiric virus had turned her cold blooded. I wondered if her blood warmed with the heat of the blood consumed. She was still very warm to the touch as if the imbibement turned on an intrinsic furnace. I wanted to ask more about it, however, our friendship, although intense to me, still felt too fragile to ask more personal questions about vampiric physiology.

I wrapped my arm around her and rested my cheek on the soft hair of her head. The feminine scent of her relaxed me. It was a natural scent that my nose could barely detect, but I loved it, and I drifted off into a quick nap despite my worry.

The vampiric virus that she was infected with was originally an experimental pathogen to give people heightened psionic abilities but it also gave the recipient the classic symptoms of vampirism. Abigail had been an expert at telepathy and hypnotic suggestion. She saw it as nothing spiritual but rather like Wifi, tapping into someone's neuronal bioelectronics and either reading them or in some cases actually controlling them, but all that had changed. After we killed The Mind, her power was pretty much gone except when drawing wild game to her for their blood.

While we waited in the dark, I relied on Abigail's innate sense of the approaching daylight. She could only venture out in daylight with a hooded cloak and sunglasses. No one was one hundred percent sure if sunlight was fatal for them. No vampire had tested it other than retracting from the burning rays of sunlight when it contacted their skin.

However, in her exhausted condition, I worried that she might not awaken in time, but just as I was about to shake her awake, her head lifted, eyes bright with awareness as she took in the dreary winter's night sky. I could tell that her nocturnal eyes saw things that I couldn't imagine.

She looked at me with concern and said, "We have forty-five minutes until daybreak."

I nodded back as I looked at the horizon, only to see the dark night as it had looked for the past hours. However, I knew that she could see the spectrum of the sun rays that no human could even dream of with her cat-like vision. I was sure that it was breathtaking to her.

We backtracked away from the precipice and I found a slim defile that a seasonal spring had chiseled in the steep stoney cliff. I knew that the bottom of the cliff was not seriously guarded. Abigail assured me that she could psychically take care of a guard if we ran into one, but I wasn't sure in her weakened state.

We followed the series of dry water falls down that were like stairsteps for a twenty foot tall giant such as The Mind. The defile leveled and I knew we were almost to the edge of the ville. I led the way and stopped at a blind corner in the ravine and felt Abigail bump into me.

"Sorry," she muttered quietly. "I am not quite myself."

I nodded, holding a finger to my lips and looked ahead as I slowly rounded the bend. I saw another corner ahead. I continued and when I reached the next corner, I stopped suddenly and again she bumped into me. I held a finger to my lips again. She nodded and weakly lowered her gaze to the ground. Usually she had a strong, confidently straight posture. Now it seemed that her head was too heavy to hold up with her graceful willow-like neck. In my mind, I cursed The Specter for nearly killing her.

In the camp, I saw a guard stare into the darkness just to the left of us. He was tired, cold, and bored from the watch through the dead of night. I saw his head bow down as if resting it. Two other guards stood their posts on the opposite side of the small camp. Nervously, I placed my hand on her as if afraid that the guards would hear our thoughts.

I nearly panicked as she gently nudged past me.

She looked and nodded at me as if saying, "I got this."

For a moment, I stood frozen as she walked into the camp, and then I followed. The black hooded cloak, the tell tale sign of a vampire, billowed lightly in her wake. I swore under my breath as she walked straight past, within a few feet of the armed guard. I couldn't tell who he was in the darkness, but I could easily see his form and knew he should see us. Instead he kept his head down as if sleeping while standing.

Abigail walked past, in front of him, as if she didn't see him and I wondered if he was under her control. I nervously shuffled past him as well and saw the blank look in his eyes as if he was staring through me. It was some sixteen-year-old kid. I didn't know his name, but I recognized him. Polite instinct gave me the desire to greet his blank face and unseeing open eyes, but Abigail shot me a sharp look under her tired brows as if reading my thoughts.

I then led the way to my hootch. It was a small tent made of saplings wrapped with three different colored threadbare tarps. They were the ugliest teepees that you could imagine, but they allowed for a small fire inside which was great for cold nights in the dead of winter.

I felt a little more confident now that we were in the center of the camp. Entering from the outskirts was where the danger had been. It was common for people to wake up to relieve themselves. Standing outside the tent wouldn't attract much attention.

I paused with curiosity at the tarp flap that served as my door. I wondered if one vampire legend was true. I whispered, "Here is my tent," as I held the flap open for her to enter first.

Abigail knew what I was doing. She gave me a weary smile, "Invite me inside, please."

"I welcome you into my tent, oh lady," I whispered with a light smile. I lifted the flap of tarp even higher for her.

I had heard varying rumors about vampires needing an invitation to cross a threshold that ranged from a lack of an invite would stop them like a solid wall. Others claimed that it would slightly discombobulate them. Abigail was my friend, and I needed her senses at full alert.

Before she entered, she gave the guard a casual glance and his awareness returned. He stared confused at the rock wall of the cliff and shook it off as if he had simply suspected himself of falling asleep on the job. He nervously looked around to see if anyone noticed his brief inattention as I followed Abigail inside. I was sure that we weren't spotted by anyone due to the lack of uproar.

Before closing the flap, I looked at the ground to be sure that I didn't leave any footprints. This was a new camp and had leaf litter everywhere rather than worn and dusty paths between the tents. Although I didn't see anything, I worried that Critter, the tribe's tracker, would see signs that I couldn't imagine. I told myself it was just paranoia, but I had every right to feel that way. After what we pulled off in Craigsville, Abigail and I had death warrants on our heads, and the Mountain Warriors would probably kill me for what I was doing now.

Once inside, Abigail collapsed on my sleeping pad.

I stood above her as she bundled up in my blankets and sleeping bag. "How did you control him?" I asked.

She opened her weary eyes. Questions filled the pools of her pupils.

"I mean," I clarified, "as tired as you were, and with The Mind destroyed, I didn't think that you would be able to use your abilities."

"I am pretty good when tired. I don't have self doubt or overthink things. Also I can still work on the minds of animals like deer and even sleepy people like the sentries at the end of their shift. His mind wasn't strong this morning."

I nodded. I thought of some of her contemporaries who would hold their hands up, straining like claws, as their faces contorted with effort when using their psychic powers. She always looked so natural as if she didn't even have to think about it. She was by far their most successful vampire when it came to psionic powers. She would have been highly valued by her former bosses if she didn't have her firm moral compass and a rebellious spirit.

"I think you'll master it, even without turning into a vampire," she said.

I nodded back, still standing in awkwardness above her. She had taught me some tricks in our short time together, but I had only the most rudimentary of skills, mostly geared toward blocking other vampires from obtaining the ability to control me, and preventing them from smelling my blood.

I could tell she was moments from succumbing to the sleep that vampires needed in the daytime, but she looked at me.

"What?" I asked.

"Are you going to sleep?" she asked. "You've been awake for two nights and have been through hell these past few days."

That was an understatement, I thought.

"I—" I could not say anything more.

She smiled slightly, "I won't bite, nor will you turn into a vampire just lying beside me, and I could also use your warmth to heal."

Despite my innate repulsion for vampires in general, there was something very alluring about her, and we were both fully clothed. She had many opportunities to kill or turn me, but she never made an attempt other than our first meeting and then she hesitated. Then she had been under orders enforced by a death sentence to kill me. I stared at her for another moment and then got down on my knees and burrowed into the blanket and unzipped a sleeping bag next to her to cover us both.

"So did you really need an invitation? Could I really hide from vampires in my tent if I didn't invite them but told them to go away instead?" I asked.

"Maybe if you petulantly stomped your foot," she said.

"Really?" I asked, sensing her humor.

She smiled, "No. However, we are psychic beings. I could have entered without an invite, but this is your place. It is similar to the way faith works against evil spirits. If I came in without an invitation, I would be slightly… off, especially if I was up to no good. Mostly, I was being polite, but a threshold is like faith. If strong, it interferes with our psychic and mental powers. Light from a fire would help as well for protection, but a pack of failed vampires could overcome a home as quickly as a raging grizzly bear."

I nodded and laid down beside her.

In the close confines, we naturally spooned together with my arm around her and my nose in her hair at the top of her head. Having been away from the caverns of the vampires, she no longer had that earthy smell of the dank recesses of the earth. My head swam with distant thoughts of that twisted maze of crystal passages of the Caverns of the Vampires and entered into a realm of endless dreams with the light of the sunrise seeping through the tarps and sweet natural feminine scent of Abigail.

***

A few hundred miles from the quarantined Forbidden Zone, Tommy Laurens stumbled slightly as he made his way through his office to his desk. He held onto leather chairs, grabbed one of his many video screens, or anything that came into reach to steady his feet as he walked through his office. His mind reeled and his vision blurred. He even sent a computer crashing to the floor as he blindly grasped for it. The noise of the splintering plastic and glass barely penetrated through his spinning consciousness as he worked his way to his office chair and plopped down into it with a gasp, only trusting gravity to get his butt into the cushioned seat. The so-called Safe Zone was now as deadly as the Forbidden Zone. At least for Tommy.

The blood that had been streaming from his broken nose and had run down his neck had started to dry. It stained his crisp white shirt and disappeared under his Armani coat. The blood was then camouflaged in his darkly mottled necktie. Trying to forget his nose, he focused on getting back onto his computer. Tommy's balance was off when he came to after Don Renton/The Specter had beaten him unconscious.

He looked at his clock and squinted at it. He guessed that he had been knocked out for at least thirty minutes, and the big man who did it was long gone.

His friend and star reporter for his hit reality show, Eric Hildebrande, now had a death warrant on his head inside the quarantined Forbidden Zone. This knowledge had shot a bolt of urgency through

Tommy's veins despite his instinctive desire to lay on the floor for a few moments where he had been felled. Walking the short distance to the desk had brought back more balance and lucidity with each step. Although a splitting headache raged in his skull, his mental cobwebs started to clear. Tommy sat down at his desk and rested his eyes for a moment while he got his wits back.

If Eric would be terminated in the next few days, Tommy's number one concern, besides saving Eric, was that he needed a new revenue generator for a reality show, and he thought he had found the perfect crew to both boost his ratings and possibly take the heat off of Eric.

It may sound superficial, but Tommy's life depended upon him bringing in more revenue through entertainment. Although he once considered this his dream job, he despised it now. His ally, Eric's adopted father and uncle, Governor Daniel Hildebrande had been overthrown in a nearly bloodless coup d'etat, and Tommy had to show his worth or the new Governor would simply discard him, most likely with a death sentence.

With the nation in the Safe Zone in a seemingly endless economic depression, his job was to pull in revenue for the tyrannical government through subscribers to his "reality shows." As the Director of the Entertainment wing of the Intelligence department, he had fulfilled that quite well. So far from the video footage that he had acquired from drones and reporters, specifically Eric in the zombie infested Forbidden Zone that covered the entire Southeastern region of the U.S. from the coast to most of Texas did just that.

For now, to cover for Eric, Tommy told his superiors that Eric's video from body cams were inaccessible due to an unknown technical difficulty. With the hunt on for his friend, he had to keep him hidden and put the public's and the government's attention on something else.

Tommy clicked on a link at his computer and brought up a screen with a glowing radioactive green that slowly shifted to other spooky colors with the same radioactive appearance. "BEYOND CLASSIFIED," was officially stamped on a virtual folder.

Tommy clicked it. He had designed the graphics himself. He clicked a few more buttons and entered more passwords going past the so-called dark web. So many of his subscribers thought they had access to a completely top secret site. These idiots, the government's customers, shelled out two hundred fifty bucks a month to see footage that was supposedly denied to the general public. However, these weren't as top secret as the membership believed. The videos were indeed generally too gory for the general public to have easy access to and were simply hidden under a few layers.

However, Tommy hired a bot company that spread the site's address across the internet as well as the "closely guarded passwords." People swarmed to his website and gave him access to their credit cards. Tommy had made a mental note to talk to some geeks with loose enough morals, to see if he could siphon money from the accounts, but that was for later. Right now he wanted to see how his up-and-coming stars were doing.

Feeling more clear-headed now, he checked out a "secret" chat room. Tommy quickly scrolled and scanned over most of the posts, and stopped when one caught his eye. The poster seemed to put up a facade of being a nuanced and slightly snobby movie critic. Tommy was about to skip over the long winded review when he saw a reference to the movie, *Goodfellas*, in the post. Tommy scanned the post because that was one of his favorite movies ever.

He read the post and nodded to himself as he read. Although a bit wordy, it described what Tommy had been thinking, except he never equated the video of this crew of vampires to the movie that the poster referenced. The gist of the post described these vampires, specifically one named Gog.

This group of vampires consisted of barely functional failed vampires. They weren't very intelligent, however they were idiot savants when it came to hunting others and using psionic powers to take control over people, zombies and especially over other vampires. This crew had everything the viewing public wanted: bloodlust, internal fighting, internal rutting, physical attractiveness, serial killers, and pure psychopathy. They hunted everything: humans, zombies, animals, and other vampires in the Forbidden Zone. This crew of vamps hunted not for food, but for the sheer joy of killing everything they could.

They were under the command of a mysterious rogue vampire who called himself King Sadazar and lived in an impenetrable castle. The King was a growing army of a few hundred vampires. They were so insidious that the government desired to take out the mysterious king, but helicopters could not approach his stronghold. The King could disrupt the electronics of the warbirds that attempted to bomb him with his psionic powers. He could even disable the rockets that were fired at his castle. Too many multimillion dollar aircraft had crashed before they could get within killing distance. Usually the government left the monstrosities alone in the quarantined area of the Forbidden Zone alone, but these guys were above and beyond in evil and it was feared that King Sadazar was looking to expand his Kingdom beyond the boundaries into the Safe Zone.

In the meantime, Tommy meant to milk the situation for all he could. He had a reality show to produce, afterall, and his life depended on him generating revenue. As the Senior Director of the Entertainment Wing of the Intelligence gathering branch, his job was to bring in that revenue, and this group was turning out to be a cash tree that all he needed to do was shake it. People gladly paid their taxes if they were entertained, and his shows were now bringing in the bulk of the nation's taxes.

The online post that had grabbed his attention compared this crew of vampires as a version of *Goodfellas* and the poster was correct. As in the gangster movies, you did find yourself rooting for the bad guys, the difference was that these were vampires rather than wiseguys, and without the civilizing force of law and order to channel their behavior, these vamps were exponentially more violent than Henry, Tommy, and Jimmy from the Goodfellas movie.

The sun had just set, so Tommy Laurens clicked the incoming drone video, and watched the scene unfold. It was awesome in its gory extravagance. It was just what he needed to get and keep his viewers.

Chapter Two

Tommy had just released the video. In just seconds, it registered a half-million viewers and grew exponentially.

The scene was in the bleak Appalachian winter forest of brown and grays by day that slowly faded into shadows and pockets of darkness that gradually overtook the land. Then everything darkened more until all the drab hues were limited to shades of blackness. The exception to this rule was the stark white body of the naked man that was tied to a wooden stake stained with a little of his own blood.

No one else was around. He was uninjured other than a fingernail scratch that started at his right cheek and trailed down his bare chest and into his lower abdominal area. The scratch had been inflicted on him by a sexy vampiress who had run her red nail down his face and body with slow, seductive violence. His pale skin seemed to glow in contrast to the Stygian gloom surrounding him as the blood leaked slowly like black ochre.

He was barely conscious of the drone that buzzed around him filming everything.

Terror bulged his eyes as he strained and pulled against his bonds. His breath heaved in ragged pants. His chest suddenly, almost violently, inflated as if he wanted to scream for help, but he knew the only thing to approach his screams wouldn't come to rescue him but rather devour him. However, if not the creeps of the night, then the cold would surely kill him before daylight.

Vapor left his mouth in a cloud and then dissipated as he whimpered slightly and then uncontrollably screamed anyway. "Oh my God! Help me!"

His teeth slammed together as he shut his mouth. Violently, he wrenched his head to look around to see if his uncontrolled outburst attracted any monsters of the night. He whimpered again. He craned his neck to look behind the stake, from one side to the other, but his vision could only penetrate about ten meters into the nighttime forest.

He then heard the sound of a steady tread of heavy footsteps in the dry leaves in front of him and to his left. The noise was faint at first, but gradually increased in volume as the person or thing approached. He whipped his head in that direction and saw nothing beyond the ten yards of darkness. He again whimpered uncontrollably for a few seconds as he heard the footsteps cease. His whimpering also ceased as well and his breath quickened. He opened his mouth to call out for help, but swiftly changed his mind and desperately held his breath for fear a cry would escape his bluing lips. He shivered in both fear and cold.

Off to his right he heard maniacal but muffled giggling, slightly quieter than the buzzing of the drone that spied upon him.

It was too much. Terror and near insanity temporarily overwhelmed him and he let loose a scream laced with curses, blasphemies, and insults. He came to his senses and closed his mouth, straining on his bonds and fearfully looked around him.

An hour before he was tied to the stake at sunset, while trying to make it back to his village, he had seen a figure approaching him. It was a beautiful woman in a black hooded cloak. He had heard that this was the uniform of the vampires, but her smile was so full of warmth. He lost sight of the forest around him. Only the deep pools of her eyes were in his vision as he walked to her smile so warm it would melt the pockets of snow that still remained from the last storm.

Her smile then turned seductively wicked with amusement. He stopped walking toward her immediately realizing he was within arm's reach. He shook his head realizing that he had been in a trance. He screamed as she flashed her fangs. Her face was monstrous for a split second. Her fangs were enlarged incisors that gave her a hideous bucked tooth appearance. Then her face reverted back to its angelic nature as she smiled with amusement at his terror.

He suddenly noticed that he was surrounded by five other vampires. They were filthy, smelly and had ragged faces where their victims had clawed at them. They were horrid with hungry eyes, not just for his blood but for his pain. Yes. He could read it plainly in their faces almost as if shouted at him, "We want your suffering. We want your soul."

A vampire who he could only describe as a horror with eyes almost glowing with demoniac insanity rushed to his face. His visage was ragged from the nails and teeth of his victims. He was far more torn up than the others. The man could smell its rancid breath and knew that the demoniac vampire had drunk the rotted fluids of zombies within the last hour.

To the man's right he heard a male vampire say, "I say, Gog." The voice was brutal in its gutural deep yet occasionally screeching quality, but the speaker forced the worst fake British accent that the man had ever heard. "Gog, I say ol' chap. No kill man."

"Gog hung-wy," the one called Gog shouted with excitement. The man guessed that he meant to say, "hungry."

Then the man blanked out under their spell. When he came too, he was bound, and stripped naked to the stake. He could hear the other vampires giggling behind him. The female vampire who had initially attracted him ran her nails sensually down his cheek, drawing a slight line of blood and then she leaned in, licking her crimson lips as she enjoyed the scent of his blood. She would have been beautiful had not the madness roiling in her eyes not made her so repulsive at the moment.

Smiling suggestively at him, she ran her nails down his chest down to his lower abdominal area, drawing a line of his blood as she went. She seductively licked his blood from her fingernails and then walked away and disappeared into the night with a sensuous sway of her slim but shapely hips that even the cloak couldn't hide. That was fifteen minutes ago.

His eyes shot forth to the path in front of him as he waited in terror for whatever thing was approaching him. There was nothing in sight within the ten yard range of his limited vision, yet he heard the steps of someone again. The clomp-crush sound of a person approaching in the brown fallen oak leaves. The rhythm was steady and assured, not the shuffling sound of a zombie. Nor was it the hesitant sounding steps of a person afraid of the dark. It was a warrior's confident stride.

His own confidence welled up just a bit. "Help," he said in a soft voice.

"Relax, I am coming," the strong male voice reassured. It was fluent and not raggedly guttural like those of the vampires.

The bound man sighed in relief, "Thank you. Thank you." He peered into the darkness and saw a dark approaching form take human shape in the night. "Those vampires caught me," the bound man added.

Then the man saw what the potential rescuer was.

He screamed in horror as the black form in the flowing hooded cloak solidified in his vision. It was another vampire. Even beneath the billowing cloak he could see that it was a well built and strong one.

The vampire brought a finger up under its hood into the black cavernous maw that formed around the unseen face.

The bound man complied with the signal for silence, but whimpered again knowing that his time was now measured in seconds.

The vampire brought down his hood, exposing a strong, handsome, and confident face. The vampire calmly said, "Relax. I will do you no harm, but why are you in this situation?"

The bound man stared at the vampire's face as more features were more noticeable with each step that brought him closer. It was clean, chiseled, intelligent, flawlessly rugged, and held no hint of malice or hunger. There was only curiosity and more importantly compassion in his gaze.

"Other vampires!" the man gasped out. "They are crazy. Dirty. Horrible." The man paused and added, "Please don't."

The vampire reassured the man, "I have already fed this evening. I will not harm you." When the vampire saw the eyes of the bound man widen, he added, "It was a rabbit. I only dine on animals. I leave human's be. I was once a human myself," he said with an odd touch of weariness, mixed with compassion and a bit of irony. The vampire smiled slightly and he could see his fangs were enlarged canines. This vampire overall looked better than the bucked tooth vampires who had captured him.

"Untie me, please," the man begged desperately.

"I will, but promise me one thing," the vampire requested, looking him in the eyes. The vampire paused in his movement letting the man know that any chance at freedom depended upon his agreement.

"Yes?" the man asked fearfully as if suspecting a fatal catch in the deal.

"Please don't attack me once you're unbound. I've nothing to do with those who did this to you."

"Sure. Sure. Of course," the bound man exploded in relief. "I promise. Just untie me. Please!"

"I am Brandon, by the way," the vampire said in an amicable tone, "and you, my friend?"

"Reggie," the bound man blurted. The more he studied Brandon, the more that Reggie doubted that his rescuer was a vampire. His face looked fully human and his eyes were filled with compassion, something the other vampires had no ability to ever hold, but Brandon was still dressed as one of them and had a comfortable relation with the darkness of night.

"Good to meet you, Reggie," said Brandon the vampire. "Now relax. I'll untie you, and we'll go our separate ways."

Reggie didn't relax as he wrenched his neck, nervously watching the vampire walk behind the stake, still not trusting but he offered, "Thank you. I knew that all vampires weren't bad." He didn't really mean it, but he wasn't going to insult his potential rescuer.

As the vampire started to untie Reggie's hands, Brandon stood and worked at Reggie's side so that he could see his face, just to put the bound man at ease. Brandon paused as concern touched his face. He asked, "Why did the other vampires do this to you? If they're crazy, they would've simply dined on you."

"I– I don't know," Reggie stuttered.

The vampire quit untying the rope. "Oh crap," Brandon muttered as he looked in the distance, seeing something that Reggie couldn't, lacking the nocturnal vision of the vampire.

"What?" asked Reggie.

"I believe that you're bait," he said.

"Bait?" asked Reggie.

"Bait for me or another vampire."

"Please, keep untying me," Reggie begged, as one of his arms came loose. He desperately tried to yank the other one free of the stake but couldn't.

"Stand back!" Brandon yelled at someone or something in the distance.

Reggie heard the razor hiss of a sword withdrawn from Brandon's sheath.

Reggie looked around in terror. He heard six footfalls approaching in front. He heard the giggling with no attempt to muffle it this time, and then he heard a psychotic cackling of the demoniac vampire named Gog.

"No, no, no," Reggie pleaded.

Brandon walked around to stand defensively in front of the bound man. His sword pointed toward the unseen cackling group. The six vampires appeared from the gloom with their eyes hungrily on Brandon. Reggie screamed again and then quickly fumbled at the knot that bound his other hand.

"Brothers and sisters, how are you this evening?" Brandon greeted in a genial tone to quell a bad situation. It was the tone of an adult trying to calm wayward children.

"I say, ol' chap. Lower sword, brother Brandon. I, Jim. This my mate Misty and friends Mary, Tony, Cindy, and--"

"And Gog! Me Gog," Gog said as he laughed hysterically. His massive muscles rippled beneath his shredded and stained clothing.

Brandon slowly lowered his sword, but only slightly as the six vamps aggressively surrounded him.

"You look like you just fed," Brandon said in a friendly tone. "There is no need for further bloodshed."

"Fun! Blood fun," Gog hissed and laughed maniacally.

"Why release cattle, Brandon? Is good food," Jim said.

"I don't dine on people," Brandon said.

"Traitor!" the vampiress named Cindy hissed through her beautifully full lips.

"I say, relax old boy," said Jim. "Relax."

Brandon stood hypnotically still. He almost mechanically let his sword lower from his guarded position and held it with just one hand. His eyes glazed from whatever psionic power the rogue vampires had over him, and as he stood, his muscle tone seemed to drop like lead into the sea. His head and shoulders slumped as if he slept on his feet.

And in a streak of black robes and feral shrieks, the six failed vampires were on Brandon, yellowed and red streaked fangs flashed in the night light from the slender sliver of the moon. Brandon's dark blood flowed and splashed on Reggie.

Reggie caught a glimpse of Brandon's eyes, dulled under a form of hypnosis despite the savage attack that he didn't fight. The big vampire was quickly knocked off his feet.

"Brandon!" Reggie screamed.

The lights blinked on in Brandon's eyes as calling his name seemed to pull him out like a lifesaver thrown from a ship. On his knees, Brandon savagely swung his sword grasped in both hands. His eyes suddenly lit with the flames of vampirism and he bared his fangs with a monstrous growl at the others. Brandon's swing just missed Jim. Brandon brought the blade back sharply and then he plunged the tip into Misty's heart. Her scream was cut short as his blade slashed and decapitated her.

Jim, the vamp with the horribly fake British accent, screamed in fury and then yelled, "Misty! My mate! No die to death! No succumb!."

Brandon attempted another swing but Gog leapt into him, and instead of his dripping sword slicing Gog, only Brandon's elbows struck the psychotic vampire's head. The vampires piled on top of Brandon.

Jim screamed, "Gog, no drink Brandon's blood. He must suffer torture for killing Misty."

But it was no use. The four other vampires led by Gog's fury inundated Brandon, draining him of everything. Unable to contain himself, Jim shrieked and jumped in with his fellows and they ravaged the vampire, grunting and growling like fiends and slurping up any of the big vampire's blood they could get.

As they were occupied, Reggie was able to free himself of his final knotted bond. He rushed into the night, hearing the growling of the occupied vampires in the distance. He sprinted naked, bouncing off of trees, running headlong without pause through brambles whose thorns ripped at the skin of his arms, legs, and torso as well as stabbing into the soles of his feet. He didn't even hesitate as one thorn stuck into his eyeball before he could protectively blink. Driven by mad terror, he pushed onward in a panicked flight.

After a half mile, he stopped and listened, hearing nothing but his own ragged breath and the whir of a drone. Then, not far behind, he heard an inhuman vampiric shriek that curdled his fluids. With a gasp and whimper of horror, he began to run into the night once more, only to run headlong into an unmoving muscular bulk. He bounced off and crashed to the ground and looked up into the horrid face of Gog, who laughingly bared his fangs.

Reggie shot to his feet and turned the way he came and ran into Mary, the sensual one who had run a long red fingernail down his cheek. Even the female vampires withstood the shock and impact of his running form like a stout steel post that had been pounded and cemented into the ground. Reggie bounced off a few other vamps who laughed at his terror before he found an open direction. He pushed through them.

He ran another few hundred meters unmindful of his direction other than to simply get away, until he bounced off Gog again. This chase went on with the demoniac screams of his pursuers howling in the night. The toying continued for another hour or so until Reggie ran into Jim and fell at his feet. Exhausted, bleeding, and half blind from a thorn that ripped his eye on his run through a blackberry patch, he gave up fighting his fate, but Jim calmed him slightly with a pat on his bare shoulder.

Reggie looked and saw that it wasn't just the original vampires. He was surrounded by hundreds of drooling idiot vampires. Even more dull of intelligence than the original group, yet just as fiery.

Jim said, "No worry, ol' boy. We drink your blood and then you'll join our army, brother."

Reggie screamed one last time before he was drained of blood, turned into a vampire, and was assimilated into the horrible group, but before Reggie blacked out, the last thing he heard was Jim plead the name, "Ab-by-gail!" to the night sky above.

Chapter Three

I awoke with the vampiress' mouth at my throat. It didn't bother me in the slightest. Her head rested on the pillow, eyes and lips closed in peaceful repose. Her chin was placed on my shoulder. My nose buried into her hair at the top of her head. Her faint womanly scent placed my mind at ease. I shifted slightly and she opened her eyes and looked at me.

Her eyes were always so deep that I could lose myself in them. They also seemed to stare into my soul with a knowingness that I found attractive. A faint smile graced her face and she snuggled into my chest.

We weren't lovers but we were definitely close friends at this point and in the tight confines of my cold tent on the small camp pad we cuddled naturally. That happens easily when two people have no one else they can truly trust, but we weren't sure if the virus could be transferred to me with a mere kiss on the lips. Even laying next to her made me wonder if I might catch her vampiric virus just from breathing the same air like you would a cold or flu.

I had been covered with vampire blood before and didn't turn, so intellectually, I knew it was most likely impossible to catch it through breathing, but deep inside, my instincts worried me.

We jolted as a knocking drummed on the tight fabric of the tent and I heard Critter's voice, that was an oddly cheerful, call to me, "You there, Eric?"

I hesitated as I got my bearings. I instinctively wrapped my arm tighter around Abigail. Her slightly pursed lips that perfectly concealed her two inch fangs were near my throat. I oddly felt both nervous and aroused now, especially when she lightly kissed me on the neck. It was playful despite the tension. I was glad to see her spirit back.

"Uh, yeah man," I replied to Critter.

I could sense him leaning in closer to the tent as he said, "I see a smaller set of footprints with your own tread. Did you find yourself a little sweetie?"

My eyes widened as I looked at Abigail. She looked back with the same worry. I couldn't completely lie. The keen-eyed tracker knew there was someone besides me in the hootch simply by reading our trail.

"Be a gentleman," Abigail whispered in my ear with a wink.

I nodded back with an awkward smile. The sensation of her breath on my ear tickled slightly. She seemed a bit punchy after the escape and good day's sleep.

I said out loud to Critter, "A gentleman doesn't speak of such things."

There was a long pause. I worried about Critter's jealousy. He had lost his family in the zombie apocalypse. I knew that he was running the list of women in the camp through his head. The male to female ratio tilted heavily towards the male members and was the source of occasional fights and tensions between the fellows. I worried for a moment longer when he suddenly laughed in good nature, "I hear you, brother."

Again there was a pause as if he was waiting for me to say something. Eventually, he said with a chuckle, "You still need to be looked over for bites, you know. Both of you."

I was a bit relieved when I heard his laugh, and I replied, "Yeah, yeah. Hey man. What time is it?"

"A little after 4:30. Almost dark. I know you have had a rough few days, but we need to see you both while the sun is out. People get suspicious of those who hide from the sunlight," he said.

"Yeah, yeah, we're getting up," I said, trying to sound both casual and sleepy.

"But you need to get moving. Adam is up and has a hard on for you ever since you knocked him out and for breaking protocol the last time you graced us with your presence."

"I will be up in a minute," I said, not responding to the cajoling sarcasm in his tone. He was usually taciturn by nature, but I suspected that he respected me for my rebellious outburst last time I was here. He was a wildman at heart and respected that wildfire that blazed and yearned for freedom in others.

"The girl you're with will need to be inspected as well, you know," he needlessly added again.

"Yeah." I cringed as I spoke that. I could not hide the dread from slipping in my voice.

Adam was in his early seventies and was something like the head chieftain in this herd of cats. In times of emergency, such as battle, he and his warchiefs like Critter and Bryan held absolute control. Adam was also the main instructor in charge of teaching any combative arts. Although he had a lot of power over the tribe, it was still somewhat of a democracy, with the individual power of each member to be considered during a peaceful period such as today. However, everybody had to follow established protocol. The proverbial rules in stone held more power than any one person or group in this tribe, because the rules were agreed upon and enforced by every person of the tribe.

The last time I was here, I was slow to follow the protocol of getting checked for zombie and vampire bites. Afterall, I was pissed off after they abandoned me in the Caverns of the Vampires. I had insulted Adam as well. He had tried to slay me with his sword, but to everyone's shock, I had read every one of his moves. I had continued to bob and weave, further frustrating the sword master. After almost toying with him for a minute, I eventually laid out the chief with a merciful blow to his skull from the dull aspect of the back of my sword.

The fragile balance of power in the camp was shaken. I was the new guy and seen as weak, but had destroyed that with a single blow. I wasn't sure how I would be greeted after that. Would I be respected and treated with a higher regard for finally standing up for myself, or would I be feared, hated, and taken down with the back stabbing that happens in any group of people?

Critter said with finality, "Come to Shelley's tent before dark, as in right now."

"You got it," I replied. "I'll just get dressed."

Critter lingered a moment. I guessed he was waiting to hear Abigail speak to get a clue as to who the mysterious girl was who I had slept with.

As his catlike footsteps faded, Abigail asked, "What do we do?"

"First you lose the vampire cloak. They will definitely know you in that, but they only saw you at night with a hooded cloak so they might not recognize you in civvies," I said this as I reached over and grabbed some of my clothes out of my backpack. "This red hoodie and sweatpants should protect you from the last sun rays of the day."

Before she took off her cloak, I looked at her wrist where The Specter had nailed her to the cross. Even though it was to be expected, I was still surprised to see that the nail hole in the wrist had healed to a small scar that I knew would be gone in another couple days or so. I felt a pang of jealousy at her regeneration abilities. The life of a vampire had its temptations.

I simply said, "I'm glad to see you healing so fast."

With distant, worrying eyes, she said in a quietly anxious voice affirming what I had told her, "At night, I think I could pass for human. I don't think they will recognize me without my vampire's garb." She bit her lower lip, keeping her fangs hidden as if she doubted her own reassurance.

"Don't worry," I said looking her in the eyes and admiring her beautiful, fully human face, "you look great,"

"Thanks," she said, taking it as reassurance rather than a complement.

She then took off her cloak and the black paramilitary pants that all the vampires and military in the Forbidden Zone wore. We faced away from each other as she removed her clothes and put on some of my clothes. She undressed so quickly that the clothes sounded like a flag flapping in a stiff breeze.

"Let's get this over with," she said when she finished changing.

"Can you hypnotize? Like hypnotize the whole camp? So that they don't check you too intensely?" I asked.

"No and certainly not with The Mind killed. I can only focus on a person or two if that, and I am weakened during the day. The guard last night was sleepy, and I was too tired to have any self doubt."

I nodded at her as I considered our strategy. I finally said, "So here's our story, in case they interview us separately… You're simply a human girl who I rescued from Craigsville." I thought and added, "We knew each other well in college at Miskatonic University. Let me do most of the answering if we're together and just pretend you are too shy to speak."

She nodded back and said, "Lead. I'll follow."

I nodded and then I stared at her.

"What?" she asked.

"When will you need to...?" I could not finish.

"Need to what?" she asked, looking at me with her eyes that were sometimes sedating, but now they were sharp as swords under slitted eyelids. She knew what I was asking.

"Feed," I said. "Drink blood?"

"Not for a day or more. That deer has sated me. Blood is a very pure fuel. We vamps don't need regular feeding. I may need to sneak out tomorrow or the next night and attract wild game."

"What about your vampire's sword?" I asked about the sword on her hip. Her holstered handgun at her appendix and the M-16 slung over her shoulder wouldn't draw attention as anyone who wished to survive a full day in The Forbidden Zone was well armed, but a sword used by vampires?

"I will lie the same way you did. I'll claim that I achieved it by slaying a vampire. Although in this case, I actually did slay some vampires before I got the sword, not after," she said with a smile knowing that I lied about how I'd killed her to get the sword at my hip. In reality, she had gifted it to me when I needed the sword. I touched the hilt thinking of all we had been through since then. Sometimes I used the sword as we stood back to back, shoulder to shoulder, fighting as a team. Other times, I had aimed this sword at her heart as the Mountain Warriors and

I squared off against her and her coven. It was nice that we were now firmly allies. I never wanted to point a sword at her again.

In some ways I felt foolish. She had implied that the sword had a degree of magical abilities that helped me slip through a pack of vampires once, but I was beginning to suspect that I got through, not with magic from the sword, but rather due to her psychic control over the other vampires.

I exited the hootch, and she followed with her red hood up. In the mountainous winter, it looked natural to wear the hoodie. Even so, I noticed that every eye was on us. Part of it was curiosity of what would happen to me after assaulting Adam, the chief. The other aspect of curiosity was, what girl would hook up with an outsider?

I saw some kids playing soccer with an old basketball that was discolored as if it had been in the river for a few years. Indeed the river provided almost every essential for this camp, I could see how waterways were valued as deities in ancient cultures.

The squeals of delight from those playing soccer were subdued due to the camp's need to keep a low profile. With literal monsters prowling the hills, these were some of the most well trained, disciplined kids I'd ever seen.

As I led the way to Shelley's hootch, I noticed Abigail squinting in the fading light. The bulk of the sun's body had set behind the trees of a distant hill. In another fifteen minutes it would be completely gone for the day. It was one of the few times that I longed for night in this vampire haunted land.

I was grateful that I didn't see Bryan. He was the second in command. I was certain that if anyone would recognize Abigail, it would be him.

I nodded to people who returned the friendly greeting with a tilt of their heads, but their eyes looked past me as if into some mystery that couldn't be probed.

I knocked on Shelley's tarp with the knuckles of my pointer and middle fingers. The rap on the taut plastic resounded sharply, louder than I expected, like a small caliber gunshot.

"Come in," Shelley said sweetly.

The older woman had an indomitable energy that went with her abilities as the camp's herbalist and healer. Her voice and inner vibrance suggested a woman forty years younger than her actual seventy years of age.

I held the tarp for Abigail to enter and then I followed. A small fire lit the interior. Critter sat close to the fire, sipping a hot tea made of locally gathered herbs. My heart sank, however, as I stared into the opaque, reflecting glasses of Adam. All I could see were the reflected sparks from the small fire in his lenses. As for the rest of his face, I couldn't read anything. His jaw was set as hard as the granite cliffs that surrounded us. My eyes made their way to the bruise on the side of his head that I had given him on our last encounter.

"Don't worry," the tribal elder said in a neutral tone. "I hold no grudge and give my due respect to a valued warrior."

I nodded and said nothing. I had already apologized for my actions yesterday. I noticed that all the eyes were on the vampiress.

"And who is this 'friend' of yours who you spent the night with?" Adam asked as he stood up. He did so gingerly, but I felt that his old age act was just that, an act. He had the grace and fluidity of a man half his age when the chips were down. I suspected that he moved stiffly so that others would underestimate his speed and power. Either that or he was just tough as nails and his body worked well despite his age. Regardless, he had my respect despite our altercation yesterday.

Abigail started to tell them her name, "A—"

"Ashlyn," I blurted out a quick alias. "She is my girlfriend. My partner, mate--" I verbally stumbled as I searched for the correct word. Surprisingly, "mate" was commonly used to describe lasting romantic partnerships in the Forbidden Zone, but it still felt weird to use it. It sounded animalistic rather than romantic. I continued with the rehearsed story, "We actually met back in college. We rekindled that spark quickly. It was quite a coincidence that we met again, back in Craigsville."

"Quite a coincidence, indeed," Adam said overly agreeable.

I felt like he was suspicious. Him taking a friendly approach after I knocked him out wasn't what I was expecting. I lamely agreed with him, "We just hit it off really well."

Abigail had looked at me with some surprise when I called her my "mate," but in the post apocalypse world, relationships happened very quickly. To say she was just my friend would have invited more questions. Friendship holds more thought and rationality, rather than the rush of passion. I couldn't just say we were friends.

"Yes, quite a coincidence," Adam calmly agreed again as Abigail and I just stood there. "You know the routine," he added.

When we didn't undress, Adam said, "If she is indeed your girlfriend-- 'mate,' as you put it, I am sure you have seen each other. People don't follow the more ritualized courtship of the 1950s these days."

"Just to your underwear, uh, Ashlyn," I instructed Abigail, hoping that she didn't wear anything too vampy-like underneath. I hadn't thought about what she wore for undergarments.

We both stripped, and I couldn't help but take a side glance at Abigail's body. She was beautiful, strong, and shapely. The black bra and panties that she wore stood out against her pale skin that wasn't completely vampiric nor was her underwear overly vampy. Somehow her lingerie stirred more in me than if she stood before me completely nude.

I scolded myself. To entertain such desires for an infected being no matter how gorgeous or friendly was the first step to suicide.

I noticed her gaze was on my body as well and we made eye contact. She stared at me, lips slightly opened and pursed, both innocently and as if waiting, inviting a kiss, but any lustful thoughts were instantly gone. Any hint that she was a vampire would be instantly deadly for both of us, but I don't think they had any suspicions of me being brazen enough to sneak a vampire into the camp. They were mostly looking for zombie bites.

Shelley examined Abigail and laughed, saying, "Well, she definitely isn't a vampire."

Adam noticed my surprised look as my eyes darted in the womens' direction.

I watched as Shelley reached for the silver necklace around Abigail's neck. She palmed the small cross that rested on Abigail's bosom and studied it.

"I am a Christian," Abigail said.

Shelley nodded and gently placed the cross back against Abigail's heart between her breast and continued her inspection.

Adam still looked at her with suspicion and asked, "Did anything bite either of you?"

Abigail and I replied in the negative.

Adam, who had been a veterinarian and now the camp's doctor, approached me after giving me a cursory look over. He quickly looked over the wound on my wrist from where I fed Abigail my blood. I had removed the bandage earlier for this inspection. The wound was obviously a cut and he paid it little attention.

"Excuse me," he said as he pulled the waistband of my plaid boxers forward and quickly looked down the front of my underwear, the sides, and then the back with medical professionalism. As creepy as it may sound, everybody had a story of a seemingly healthy stranger or even a loved one who returned from a solitary excursion into the woods, only to turn into a zombie from a hidden bite and attack the members of the camp. People naturally hated admitting to receiving a bite. It held a stigma worse than leprosy in biblical times. In many instances, friends instantly killed bitten friends before they even had a chance to turn. That was usually done out of mercy as well as panic. Bitten victims usually begged for a quick death or ended their lives themselves.

I caught a glimpse of Shelley doing the same, peeking under Abigail's bra and panties. I sighed when I saw the healer relax. I also noticed that Critter had relaxed as he sat sipping his tea. His posture had been deceptively restful, but I could see his legs, though seemingly relaxed, had been coiled under him, ready to pounce. His fingertips also lowered from his sword handle, and then he crossed his legs. I guessed that he was there to apprehend or kill us if we were suspected of infection.

Adam and Shelley nodded to each other and then to Critter. Critter relaxed even more.

"She's clean," Shelley announced.

"So is he," Adam replied.

As Abigail redressed, Shelley stopped Abigail and held her arm looking at the crucifixion scar on her wrist.

"If I may ask, how'd you get this odd scar?" Shelley asked as she turned Abigail's arm over and saw there was also a similar scar on the other side of her wrist where the nail went all the way through just last night.

Abigail hesitated for a second and then said, "It's something stupid that I did as a teenager. It makes a better campfire story for later." She said that with such class and a shy smile that everyone in the tent just laughed lightly.

The tension truly felt gone and Adam said, "Dinner'll be ready shortly at the communal fire."

I nodded and said, "Thanks."

We finished dressing and left the hootch. In some ways that was the easy part. The next obstacle was worrying if Abigail would fit in around the campfire, and even more worrying to me, would Bryan recognize her?

As I wondered where Bryan was, we headed to the communal campfire. As if on cue, I saw Bryan, the warchief, limp toward us.

Damn, I swore to myself.

***

The internet chatroom buzzed with posts that recounted the chase after poor Reggie until the next horror of drone footage appeared. Tommy's headache from his prior beating disappeared as he enjoyed watching the view count rise. His only regret was the attack on Brandon. The good vampire had been interesting in his own right, but life was cheap in the Forbidden Zone. Indeed, 90% of the population had died in the last two years, and life expectancy was minimal for anyone. However, Brandon was a rare polished diamond in that rough land.

Tommy continued his monitoring of the videos with the knowledge that his new show had bought him some time to live.

He then looked at random drone footage. Abigail and Eric were still avoiding detection. No one had bothered looking at the Mountain Warrior's camp for them. Abigail would definitely not be welcomed there, and after Tommy had talked to Eric over the phone in Craigsville, Tommy knew that his friend was madly in love with her. Although Eric didn't say that he loved her, Tommy had never heard Eric speak of a woman with anywhere near that passion that he spoke about Abigail. Although it was insane for a human to travel with a vampire, Tommy knew his friend well enough to know that they were together somewhere.

With the authorities keen to capture or kill Eric and Abigail, Tommy had no choice but to attempt to find them. That was also part of his job. Without being able to find them anywhere else, Tommy sent a couple drones to spy on the Mountain Warriors' camp.

It would've been an audacious and deadly plot for Eric to bring Abigail to that wild encampment, but Tommy's friend had thoroughly shattered the mode of a mild mannered reporter a few weeks ago. Tommy originally didn't expect Eric to live a few days, but at this point, Tommy believed Eric was capable of anything. Also, Tommy avoided looking at Eric's body cam videos. Currently, Tommy claimed it was inaccessible due to a glitch, but if he clicked on it, it would be a dead giveaway that Tommy was hiding Eric's whereabouts. Many in power wanted Eric dead, immediately, and if it was known that Tommy was withholding the information, he would be just as subject to termination despite his rank as Senior Director.

Chapter Four

On a crutch, Bryan limped toward us and nodded to me, but I could tell he was in a hurry to get somewhere else. However he did make quick eye contact with Abigail and gave her a curt but gentlemanly nod. There was no recognition of her on his face. Her change of attire had been enough to make her seem like any other woman we might encounter in the Forbidden Zone. Later, I was sure that he would inundate her with questions or at least someone else would. It was his nature and duty as second in command to vet newcomers, but for now, he didn't seem suspicious and appeared to have something urgent on his mind besides us.

As we passed him, I was surprised when I felt Abigail's fingers touch my hand and slowly explore as her digits laced around mine. She spoke into my ear, "To avoid suspicion, we should play the part."

I gripped her hand wishing it could be true. She smiled at the strength and passion of my grip. Hand in hand, I led her to the communal fire. It was dinner time.

We sat together side by side on a log. There were forty or so people gathered around the fire giving us side glances as they spoke quietly among themselves.

I watched Scott, the camp's resident smart ass, help with the cooking. He was a chubby man in his fifties with a mouth of a sixteen year old snot. I could smell oily bear meat grilling and could feel my stomach growling in anticipation as Scott poked at the feast with a tong.

The scent of oily meat might have once turned my stomach, but surviving in the winter wilderness changed things, and my body instinctively knew what was best for it. I longed for the fatty insulation to line my skin. The smell of the juices dripping into the open fire from the seared fresh meat set me drooling like a Pavlovian experiment.

The people engaged in polite conversation around us and gradually brought us in. The residents of the camp were friendly but curious about Abigail/Ashlyn, the new visitor.

"May I lean against you?" Abigail asked.

I nodded and we leaned into each other for support. Her head rested on my shoulder and my cheek in her soft hair.

I wasn't sure if she had an introverted spirit or if she was really just nervous about being in the company of humans for the first time in years but Abigail slowly opened up and began to speak to those around us. Despite the winter chill, the camaraderie was warm and the fire was hot. Someone suggested that Abigail take off her hood.

She looked at me as if uncertain how to behave around people. As far as I was concerned, as long as she didn't bite peoples' throats, which I knew that she wouldn't, she should be OK.

The sun had set and I nodded to her. She let the hood of my red jacket fall over her shoulders and she brought out her luscious long hair that had been tucked under the collar. She gave it a light toss and it spilled down her back, shoulders, and bosom like a silky waterfall. I heard people whisper around me about how beautiful she was and how I was a lucky man. I wasn't fully sure if I heard them actually speak or if I was reading their minds. It had been a really weird few weeks since I had entered the Forbidden Zone, and despite the sleep, I was still exhausted.

"Dinner's ready!" Scott yelled.

I excused myself and ran back to my hootch and got some plates and utensils for Abigail and myself. When I returned and handed her a plate, she looked at me with crinkled eyebrows. She couldn't stomach solid foods, of course. Before we could communicate, Scott appeared before us with a large platter of steaming bear meat.

He plopped down a chunk on my plate surprisingly before delivering a smartass comment. It was a raggedly hacked off piece. What part of the bear did it come from? I had no clue. Nor did I care. A muscle that propels the back leg or the blood through the heart was the same thing in my opinion. In my famished state, I was just glad that it was a big chunk. I tore into it with my cutlery. I was dimly aware that the way I engorged myself was far more savage than the way Abigail had drunk the blood from the deer just last night.

As I ate, Scott stood over me and I ignored his usual silly taunts as I ate. Sometimes I found him hilarious and loved him. Other times I found him to be too much and had even exchanged shoves with him before others intervened on more than one angry occasion in the past when his jokes were too personal. At this point I was too on edge and famished to appreciate his humor.

He stepped in front of Abigail, who held her plate in an oddly confused manner.

"You want some of my meat, honey?" Scott asked. When I glared at him for the innuendo that was clear in his tone, he winked at me.

I then softened my anger against him as I realized that Abigail was about to be outed for avoiding human food.

"I'm really not that hungry," she said.

Scott nodded, "If you're one one of those wussy vegetarians that Eric used to be, we got an economy sized can of corn simmering on the fire."

"I'm just not hungry right now, and I'm not a vegetarian," she replied.

That's an understatement, I thought.

Scott looked at her. Suspicion clouded his brow. In this time of scarcity, where everyone seemed to be a day away from starvation, no one ever passed up a chance to eat.

"She just had an MRE in my tent and it didn't sit well with her belly," I said.

His curious face relaxed and I let go of a breath.

"I'd love to have a beer or a sip of whiskey to settle my belly," she said as she eyed a stack of beer cans and a whiskey bottle recently liberated from an abandoned town nearby.

"We can arrange that," Scott said. Then he added jovially, "Maybe if you've enough liquor, ole Eric might get lucky for once in his life."

She laughed politely. The beautiful light tinkling sound of her laugh calmed the fire burning in my eyes as I glared at Scott, and I managed a smile, despite him pushing it.

"Hey Robert. Toss this beautiful young lady a beer!" Scott yelled. "We're on a mission here against Eric's virginity!"

Robert, the wiry teenager, tossed him a beer, which Scott caught and handed to Abigail. She cracked it open with a thanks and took a long draught catching the drops with her lips as the foam threatened to bubble over.

I remembered that she could indeed drink alcohol. The vampires were on a strict liquid diet to say the least. Solids irritated them for some reason. If I were confined to a cave all day and lived by liquids alone, I was sure that I would turn back into a raging alcoholic.

"You want one Eric?" Scott asked me.

"Not today, man."

I wanted a beer, but I could never stick with just one drink or just one twelve pack for that matter in stressful situations such as introducing a vampire to a crowd of people. Stone cold sobriety was the best bet for me at the time, needless to say.

"Watch it, Ashlyn," Scott warned. "You should have a little meat. You're looking as pale as your friend. People will think you're both vampires."

I stopped chewing on the grizzled bear meat and locked eyes with Scott. I wasn't sure if it was a joke or an accusation. If it was a joke, it went beyond the point of good taste, not that Scott was aware of those boundaries. We held eye contact until he laughed and slapped me on the shoulder.

"Give her a small chunk of meat," I said. "A little more vittles would do her well."

"Okey dokey," said Scott.

He plunked a piece on her metal plate that made a sound that combined the meaty smack of a slap across the face with the ringing sound of a crashing cymbal as Abigail's knife and fork jangled.

Scott immediately started to joke with the next person. It was a middle aged man who looked irritated that Scott spent too much time clowning around and not enough time serving.

I leaned in and whispered in Abigail's ear that I would eat her bear meat later. It was odd, but I was worried about getting caught communicating with her telepathically, when in fact that would have been an impossibility, but I also reasoned that it wouldn't be out of the ordinary for a newly reunited couple to whisper intimate dispatches back and forth.

I looked around to see if anyone was looking and switched plates with her after I finished my meat, and I began to dig into hers.

When Scott saw her empty plate he commented something about how she still wanted his meat.

"Scott. You're going a bit too far tonight," I said.

"Brother, he goes too far every night," Critter said from across the campfire.

"You got that right," Scott laughed.

I looked at Abigail as she laughed and I joined in the laughter. It was a genuine laugh as I began to relax after Abigail passed that hurdle.

Critter then asked, "What happened to Abigail? Did they?" He left the question hanging.

"Yeah. She died on that cross," I lied as I felt myself stiffen again. "There was nothing I could do against that odds. The only good news is that I think Josh Righter is in charge of Craigsville."

I was fortunate that my rescue attempt happened during the middle of a coup d'etat in Craigsville. With me attacking The Specter and Critter shooting down some helicopter gunships with a rocket launcher, Craig was deposed and a friend of Critter's, Josh Righter, took control of the town. In the mass violent confusion of the town's civil war, I escaped, carrying Abigail on my shoulder.

"That's good. About Josh," he quickly added, "but I'm sorry about Abigail. She seemed to be a genuinely good vampire."

"Hell yeah!" Scott agreed from across the fire. "She saved my fatass in those caves. I owed her and I usually like to pay back on my dues."

I nodded and continued to eat. Critter's kind words and Scott's passion bode well for the future, I thought, and I was starting to enjoy the meal rather than eating to simply nourish myself.

It was then that I noticed that there were no drones buzzing around. I was sure that they were focused on the civil war in Craigsville, and searching distantly for Abigail and me. I had no doubt that we were number one on the kill list, but no one would expect me to sneak a vampire into this tribe.

As I began to eat the bear flesh slower and actually savored it, we engaged in polite conversation with the people around us. I didn't know everyone personally well, but I now recognized everyone's face. However I still felt like a stranger in this tight knit group.

People were rightly suspicious of outsiders. Compassion was unfortunately seen as a virtue of the foolish and the dead these days. I didn't blame them. It was a rough land. I was still getting used to the intensity of it, but Abigail was a class act. The people seemed to open up to her in the few minutes with her more than they had with me in the last few weeks. As she started on her second beer, she relaxed out of her introverted state. She flitted in witty words of both wisdom and frivolity with the grace of a bird flying through the trees. Were she not a vamp, I would definitely see her as a keeper. I dismally wondered how long we would stay together. Likely days at the most and months if I was lucky, I reasoned. As much as I loved her, we were technically separate species. I just hoped that we would part ways later rather than sooner.

A few kids played at her feet with a few old plastic toys, cracked and paled with age. The elements definitely took a toll on the cheap replaceable plastic world that we had unwittingly left behind. Abigail occasionally moved a toy car with her foot or joked with the children to their delight. Their peeling squeals of laughter intermingled with the pleasant conversation. It had a homely feel lit by the bright fire.

This will work, I thought optimistically. If she could win their trust, I was sure the camp would accept her despite being a vampire. Eventually, I knew they would find out that she was a vamp. I knew that Bryan would most likely recognize her eventually. He'd only been around her in the height of battle or under a spell but I knew he'd seen her face even for just a moment. Hopefully, this costume change would get us by for a while and their belief that Abigail was dead could go a long way. I knew we as people saw what we wanted, and I was sure they would see the good hearted woman who she was when it all came down to it.

Everyone seemed to believe me when I said that Abigail/Ashlyn was just an old flame from "the before," as people referred to the time before the zombies. Outside of the Caverns of the Vampires and out of her black robe especially after the sunset, she was any other woman and a beautiful, classy one at that.

I figured that as soon as they realized that her dietary needs were different and that she liked to sleep all day, that they would have already accepted her and let her have the blood of wild game. She was a natural night watchwoman with her nocturnal eyes and could protect us from night attacks from other vampires. She also had the psionic power to bring wild game to camp which would really help the camp that always bordered on starvation. Once they realized that she wasn't after human blood, there was no doubt in my mind that they would accept her as a vampire into the tribe. All we needed to do was hide her true nature for a short time to build their trust.

My thoughts were pleasantly interrupted as I heard the most joyous scream of delight from a child.

"Abigail!" the young boy screamed with the pure, excited love only a kid can muster for a favorite aunt.

For a split second the joyous cry warmed my heart.

Then in horror, I watched as Bryan's young son, Bradley, launched himself into Abigail's arms with a bear hug, almost knocking her over the log where we sat. I had to reach out and grab her shoulder to keep her upright against the unbridled enthusiasm.

I had forgotten about Bradley. Abigail had rescued the boy when he was kidnapped and held prisoner in the Caverns of the Vampires. I didn't realize they had bonded so well.

Before I could react, I saw Critter's sword drawn and pointed at Abigail's heart, after he had bounded over the fire like a panther.

"It's Abigail! The vampiress!" The woodsman swore.

Everyone stared at us wide eyed, not sure of what was happening in the shock of the moment.

Critter looked around at the people of the camp, his sword never wavering from Abigail's heart. He angled himself so as not to impale Bryan's oldest son when he delivered the expected fatal stab.

"She's the vampire!" he accused again. "A vampire!"

Instantly, plates and cups were dropped and at least forty swords and firearms were aimed at us. That is no exaggeration. Everyone except the smallest child carried some weapon on their person.

Even eight year old Bradley always had a combat knife on him, but he saw no reason to use it on his rescuer from the Caverns of the Vampires. Bradley, on Abigail's lap, kept his arms wrapped around her neck. The two other children looked up curiously from her feet. Maybe it was their jadedness that came from growing up in the Forbidden Zone, but none of the kids had any fear of her and only wonder creased their brows at the display of weaponry as well as the change of the mood.

I was sure that her close proximity to the children was the only reason why she wasn't run through and torn apart with steely blades and lead bullets. However it also caused panic to mount with those who were pointing their weapons in our direction. They acted as if the children were held hostage. At any second I expected to be ripped apart.

I watched as Bryan, supported by a crutch, limped forward from his tent. The sword wound at the Cavern of the Vampires still pained his leg. Recognition now lit his eyes as he looked straight at Abigail. Then, I saw raw anger seared by betrayal as his eyes bore into mine. His path took him front and center and he brushed the pointed weapons and rifle barrels away from our direction as if the gleaming blades and black barrels were mere toothpicks. I was even more fearful. His judgment would decide our fates.

"Bryan. She saved our lives and Bradley's too," I protested from my seated position. I dared not stand nor make any sudden movement for fear of drawing an attack from the gleaming blades and darkened barrels surrounding us. I even kept my hands in front of my chest and avoided any sudden hand gestures for fear of the nervous hair triggers.

He stopped and glared down at me as he said, "And that's the only reason you two still draw breath." He paused dramatically and then added, "For now."

The ominous gravity of his words weighed heavily on my shoulders.

"I did not betray the settlement." I protested. "She was marked for death by the other vampires and The Specter's military, because not only does she refuse to eat people, but because she saved us. We owe her. You owe her. She has nowhere else to go. She needed a place to rest and recover from injuries she sustained for us. For everyone here."

"Maybe, but my son is sitting in her lap with her mouth inches from his throat."

Abigail set Bradley on the ground and pushed him towards Bryan. "Go to your father," she said.

The boy obeyed her with a confused look on his innocent features. Anna, Bradley's mother, swooped in and grabbed him in her arms and rushed him away.

Abigail then looked up at Bryan and held her hands up, palms facing him in a bit of a plea, but her eyes were both strong and calm.

Abigail started to say, "Listen, I know—"

"Shut up, witch!" a woman yelled from across the fire.

Abigail clenched her jaw shut.

I instinctively wanted to say that she was a vampire, not a witch, but I feared that we were nearing the combustible point of an all consuming inferno.

"She wants to help us," I said. "She can protect us from both zombies and vampires, especially at night."

"Cobras help with rat infestations," Bryan said as his face wrenched with disgust. "but I would not have one underfoot where my children play. She may be an ally, but..."

"Oh man!" bellowed Scott as if something vitally important dawned on him. "You screwed a blood sucker? Is it like sexually transmitted? I hope you used protection of some sort. Like a flame retard suit or something."

I have never seen such a look of disgust on anyone's face.

"An abomination!" a man yelled from across the fire.

I looked away from Scott and appealed to the camp as a whole, rapidly spitting out her defense in fear someone would silence me, "She shared my tent, that's all. I did actually save her from the crucifixion she was sentenced to. For saving us, by the way. Saving Bryan's son. Her ribcage was also crushed when we killed The Mind. That's why the vampires don't have psychic control over us, because of her. She needed a place to hole up and heal. She was too weak to sleep in the woods with everything that creeps out there. I hoped you could learn to trust her. She has a good heart. She'll be our night time protector and can lure in wild game. She saved Bryan's son," I kept repeating.

"She's a vampire!" someone yelled from the dark.

"She saved Bryan's son!" I shot right back.

"You said that already," Bryan said.

"She was with the monsters who kidnapped him in the first place!" the woman who called Abigail a witch yelled from the other side of the fire.

"Most of those monsters are gone, dead, because of her," I said. "David, Richard, the others... They won't torment us anymore, because of her."

I had helped with killing some of them, and Richard had given his life for me as I saved Abigail, but I wanted Abigail to get full credit.

I saw the cold reflective stare of Adam's glasses on the edge of the campfire's light. Although I feared him the most, he seemed to be staying out of it and letting his second in command handle this situation.

I looked at Bryan and saw that the fiery sting of rage and betrayal had left his eyes. That flame had cooled dangerously and all that was left was cold sober judgment. That scared me more. There was nothing more that I could say. I knew that our fates had been decided right then. I looked at him as I waited to hear his pronouncement.

Bryan delivered his judgment in a searingly cold tone, "I owe both of you more than my life. However, that debt has been paid this evening by not cutting you down where you sit. After an hour goes by, the two of you are to be killed on sight. I suggest that you do not linger. Leave the camp. Now." He violently jerked his thumb so it pointed away from camp, in the direction of anywhere, but here.

The coldness of his tone froze his words from entering my conscious mind for a moment. I blinked a few times before I fully understood.

Suddenly, I was on my feet with a hand on the pistol at my hip. I wouldn't survive a shootout. However, guns were only used as a last resort. Zombies had a way of following a report for days. No one wanted to face a horde, but I could tell at this instant, that this moment was almost considered a last resort. Because of their almost mythological psionic abilities, one vampiress was feared more than a legion of zombies. Despite leveling their guns at Abigail earlier, once Bryan took charge, everyone lowered the barrels slightly, but still at the ready. I was now safe to make my verbal stand, and I did so boldly with my hand on my weapon for emphasis, but I made absolutely no attempt to draw it. Mine was a show of strength and passion, not a threat.

"You can't send us into the night," I stated, looking for sympathy. I was genuinely scared of leaving the camp at night.

Most people who were exiled were sent out first thing in the morning. No matter their crime or grudge in a matter. It was unheard of to sentence a person to zombism. Someone sent into exile was given a chance to find a place to hole up to defend themselves from the terrors of the darkness. They were usually discharged first thing the next morning. Not just after nightfall.

No one said a thing so I repeated my plea, "You would send us into the night?"

It was deadly silent for too many seconds.

"That vampiress is the night," Critter retorted.

***

With seemingly every weapon of the camp aimed, directed, or pointed at us the whole time, Abigail and I quickly packed. She defiantly donned her black flowing, hooded cloak of her vampiric coven. I didn't think it was tasteful, everything considered. However, it seemed to be her way of accepting her outcast status and I couldn't blame her. With our weapons and backpacks in tow we walked to exit the camp.

Everyone followed us at a distance as we walked past the tents. A few feet away I heard Scott call to us. He was the only one gutsy enough to get that close to us. His tone was like a friend just making casual conversation. It pissed me off even more. "Hey, I'm sorry. But you know... I mean I see you're happy with her..."

I glared at him letting him know that I was far from happy.

"I mean, you know, she's a nice girl..." He struggled for words and then went with what he thought was light hearted humor, "You know, dating a hot vampire girl...It's like the comfort of sitting on a warm toilet seat in a public restroom. Yeah it's comfortable sitting there, but you know that some stranger's bare ass warmed it for you."

That was the stupidest and most senseless analogy I had ever heard, but it was the way he was. I just gritted my teeth and glared at him.

He didn't seem to notice my glare. He never did. He continued, "I do wish you luck. I think you're both good people at heart, but damn, people are just scared. I ain't scared. I know she's good people, but people are just scared. Not me. I know you're good people..."

I was about to tell him to shut up as he let his final repeated sentence trail off, but he was the only one who offered any hint of sympathy or friendliness in his own off color way. Instead, I just shook my head, glared at him, and thankfully, he finally saw the look on my face and he stepped back and shut up. I think of all of them, he was actually trying to be nice, but that old smartass had the quickness of words like a teen but the ramblings of a half senile old coot. It was his nature to give a compliment with a sarcastic dig. I took it as his fear of showing emotion, especially love. His heart was too big for this heartless land and he tried to hide it in sarcasm.

As we neared the edge of the camp, Bryan sidled up beside us and seemed somewhat apologetic. I saw Bryan's wife holding back her teary eyed son Bradley far behind the mob of people. She told him to "shush," and I guessed he was saying something nice about Abigail. It was just the kid and the old smartass Scott who were the only ones to give any support for the woman who had saved many in this tribe on more than one occasion.

Bryan kept up with me for a few steps. I could tell he wanted to say something and I could see a hint of regret on his face. I slowed to make Bryan's limping stride more bearable for him. Abigail only slowed slightly and was a few steps ahead of us. Her head was held up regally with her eyes longing for the night ahead. The night held less terrors for her than this ville.

"I may have overreacted, man," Bryan said. "I thought that I lost my kid in the vampires' cavern." He raised his voice slightly to speak more to Abigail. "To see him returned to me and then see him in the lap of a vampire, even if you saved him, ma'am. It was too much. I—"

"You're welcome anyway," Abigail grumbled quietly over her shoulder as we walked. Her eyes looked to the comforting night ahead, that held nothing but abysmal terror for me.

Two nights ago, I feared nothing. I couldn't account for my sudden change other than back then I thought that I had a home in this camp, a safe zone where I could always return. Now I was going into hell with my only companion, a denizen of the night, and despite her powers at night, she was still in a weakened state from getting crushed by a giant two nights ago. Then she had been drained of her blood and half crucified last night.

With my mind worrying about the possible short life ahead of me, I found that I barely heard Bryan say, "I'm sorry and wish you both well."

After a moment, I replied bitterly, "Yeah..." but I could think of nothing more to say to Bryan.

"Give it sometime," he said, trying to reassure me. "If you survive a few weeks out there, I will see if I can get them to welcome you back."

Abigail glared at him and he looked down. I could tell that she knew that she would never get a welcome, but rather her death by the swords and guns of the mob. Both Abigail and I knew that his invitation applied only to me and I felt as equally insulted as she did.

I had a lot to think about, but in the moment all I could focus on was that I was no longer welcome among my friends whether inside or outside the Forbidden Zone. Tommy, my childhood friend, and Daniel Hildebrande, the Governor and my uncle and adopted father, banished me from civilization and all I loved as well as my past. Now in this wild land, the few friends that I managed to make had exiled me from the safety of their camp. The only companion I had was a vampire whose vampirism still slightly scared me. However, she also stirred a longing for her in me. Aside from vampirism, I really loved her although I couldn't admit it, barely even to myself except in moments of life and death situations.

"...Eric. Abigail," Bryan said.

I suddenly realized that he had been talking quietly as if in fear of his tribe over hearing him say words of encouragement to us. It infuriated me even more.

"Shut up, Bryan." I muttered.

Without a further word, I angrily looked away from Bryan and marched faster leaving him behind with his sore leg until he was swallowed up by the mob. I jogged to catch up with Abigail who continued to yearn for the night beyond the light of the campfire. As I quickened my pace, a stone flew past my head, and it cracked against the back of Abigail's skull. I wheeled around with her, and stood ready to stand my ground, if anyone tried to attack us.

Abigail took a single aggressive step toward them with her shoulders up, and flashed her fangs with a terrifying vampiric snarl like a giant hissing cat. A human is not able to sound half as terrifying as a vampire. Something changes in their throats with the turning process.

I cringed as the campfolk quit following us with gasps of horror as they retreated a few steps back from her.

"Let them go!" Bryan ordered. "And dammit! Don't throw another stone!"

I saw Critter backhand the guard who Abigail had hypnotized just this morning. I guessed that he was the one who threw the rock.

Despite Bryan's order, I still expected a hail of gunfire to crash into us any moment. However, all I saw was terror on the faces of the campers as if they feared that a barrage of bullets would only stir Abigail's wrath, and with each step we took away from the mob, I felt an odd relief to enter the night.

No one in the camp would miss me.

It was with this knowledge that I felt my mind turn from regret to a raging resolve as tough as the steel of my sword. To hell with them, I thought. Now, I looked into the night with as much determination as my vampiress companion. I swore off the camp as I would a bad addiction on the floor of rock bottom degeneracy.

It was only when I could no longer see the camp's fires lighting my path that I looked back one more time. With the flickering light of the torches and campfire behind the villagers, I knew that they could no longer even see us even as black shadows. However their figures, silhouetted by the fires, stood guard like phantom sentinels of hell, defending the gates against the unseen of the night.

Abigail followed my look. I could see the camp through her eyes. The black armed figures stood at rigid attention, weapons bristling, defying the sky above. One figure even held a pitchfork. The distant fires of torchlights and campfires blazed like the flames of hell as seen from the top of an abysmal pit.

Yes, I saw civilization, shattered though it was, from her vampire's point of view. It was no longer my home and never would be. I was with her. I hated them and the rage in my resolve blazed furiously.

We continued and after they were no longer in my sight, she removed her hood and looked into my eyes.

"I'm sorry," she said. The anger had left her and only the deep comforting pools of her eyes greeted me. "I really am."

She was my only companion simply because we had helped each other when no one else was there. However, together, we would be welcomed into no other group but despite being as independent minded as both of us were, you needed a group to survive out here.

A flash of emotion stabbed me with a pang of guilt mixed with hatred for everyone. If only our circumstances could have been different. That was what I really hated, the circumstance. I loved her, but I had trouble admitting it to even myself, because I didn't want to be a vampire, nor at that point did I want to be human. I just didn't want to be in this world, period.

"No. I'm sorry," I said, meaning every word of my apology as my rage subsided. I had no right to the rage that I felt, especially toward her. There was no facade over her heart. She was pure, a far better person than me.

She nodded her head and took my words at face value. I was grateful she didn't probe my mind deeper. I was apologizing for the flash of hatred that I momentarily held for her as well as the rest of the world from my fear of banishment. Now I accepted it all and peace began to fill the void left by the rage.

We walked deeper into the night, not just into the terrors, but also away from everyone who I had mistook for a friend. As we entered a steep ravine, I heard the whir of a few drones high over the ridge. They were rushing to the Mountain Warrior tribe. I guessed that they ran out of places to search for Abigail and me.

On a positive note, our banishment probably saved our lives as well as the entire Mountain Warrior tribe. I hadn't really thought it through before because I was mostly set on getting Abigail to safety, but if the drones had found us there, Blackhawk helicopters would have strafed every man, woman, and child to get Abigail and me.

Chapter Five

I walked beside her, but yielded when the path occasionally narrowed. I instinctively trusted her guidance. She had much better vision for the dark and the night was her realm. She never stumbled, and she nimbly walked as surefooted as a tourist on a boardwalk in the midday sun. When faced with logs that would trip me in the dark, she lightly hopped upon and ran along them like a cat even with her heavy pack and weaponry.

The night wore heavy on my shoulders as the march stretched into the late evening and early morning hours, and my exhaustion compelled me to wonder when this journey would end for the night.

"Where are we going?" I finally asked as I realized she had no intention of stopping until morning light.

"To find a safe place to sleep."

"Not the Caverns," I said thinking of her former coven's headquarters.

"No," she smiled graciously at me in the moonlight. "I am considering you as well. I am looking for a safe place to camp where we are both safe from people and vamps."

"Where're we going, ultimately?"

"To Asheville," she said.

"What?" I exclaimed and then lowered my voice as I nervously looked around the dark woods. "I've heard nothing but horror stories about that place."

She smiled sardonically and said, "Nowadays, horror stories include just daily living out here."

"True, but I heard that the whole population had been changed, turned into zombies."

"I want to kill The Mind of Asheville," she said.

I swore, I had temporarily forgotten that there were more than one Mind. The one at Shining Rock had almost killed us. Facing another one was not what I wanted to do. They were literally twenty foot tall monsters that ate humans and even vampires.

Abigail nodded in commiseration, "Yeah, I'm not looking forward to that either."

I sighed and said, "It must be done."

"Abigail brightened slightly as she said, "but even better, there's a major hospital in town. I'm hoping to find a cure for vampirism," she said with such hope in her voice that I couldn't help but feel the same way. I oddly wasn't too fazed yet with the decision to kill The Mind, a monster with psychic abilities beyond my understanding. Asheville was a long way away and I was more concerned with immediate survival, but to really cut down on the power of the enemies, we had to kill them all eventually.

"Really?" I asked about a potential cure for my friend.

"Yes. I want to fulfill other desires in life rather than satisfying the bloodlust."

"Like what?" I asked, hoping that I wasn't probing too deeply.

We stopped walking and she looked at me. "Many things of course, but I want to be able to eat brussel sprouts." A whimsical but sad smile tugged at her lips.

"You like brussel sprouts?"

"No! Never," she said like a curse.

We both chuckled and she continued, "but for some odd reason, I find myself craving them even though solid food causes intense sickness. I just miss being human. I figure that if I could stomach brussel sprouts, I can handle anything, and ironically, my least favorite food is what I crave the most."

"Is there another reason why you want to go back to being fully human?"

She looked deep in my eyes and a sadness filled her face. We held the gaze that bore the weight of what we both thought but didn't dare speak out loud at this point. She finally said, "Let's go."

I could tell she had more to say. Both of us did. With the strain of the barrage of emotions that was as heavy as gunfire against our minds, we were speechless. Emotions neither of us could make sense of yet. Because of that, silence was all that was between us and it manifested with that longing stare for each other in our eyes. She started to walk.

"Wait," I said.

She stopped and looked at me with slight irritation as if knowing what my next question would be.

"When are we stopping for the night?"

"I thought we would stop for the day, at sunrise," she replied.

"I need to sleep at night," I protested. I was tired and besides, tripping over every object that she nimbly leapt over was really wearing thin.

"The night may tire you, but sunlight weakens me. Even The Specter wasn't cruel enough to torture me in the light of day," she said.

"You have the cloak, sunglasses, and sunscreen, and among vampires, you're relatively compatible with daylight. You can pretty much pass as human in the day."

She made no attempt to hide the irritation in her voice when she replied, "Well the daylight is rough on me, and I can protect you from the night creatures."

I retorted, sarcastically using her tone and inflections, "Well, the night is rough on me, and I can protect you from the day creatures."

We argued for a moment, and Abigail finally said, "Listen, if we can't appreciate each other for what we are, we should split up now and go our own ways."

After saying that, we were both quiet and looked at each other with almost an expression of shock.

We were incompatible on so many levels. She had the same misgivings as me, but the shock from her blunt words caused her mouth to open then close in pursed lip speechlessness. Mine as well. We continued to stare with the longing in our looks at each other for the desires we felt for each other that we could not admit yet.

Our faces hardened with the reality of the situation.

I said, "I know we haven't known each other long, but you're the best friend that I have ever had. I don't say that lightly."

"I know," she replied. "I feel the same about you. However there is a 'but' in your statement. I have always sensed it."

I nodded and finally said, "You're right. We inevitably have to split up. From what we've experienced, you will eventually have to live with other vampires and me with people, and vampires are as hostile to me as people are to you, and I hate that."

"I agree," she said. "You rescued me against all odds in Craigsville. I even told you to run. I still can't believe you did what you did. The world had abandoned me, both people and vampires, but you came through. I will always be grateful to you."

"You did the same for me when I was in the vampires' lair," I said. "I'm also grateful beyond words."

"Me too."

We spontaneously embraced and held each other as we spoke. The embrace happened so quickly that I could only feel her warmth of affection for the moment and relief that we wouldn't split up that night, but we clung to each other.

I continued, "But it's dangerous for both of us right now if we split up."

She nodded and then went on, "I agree. So what do you suggest?"

I replied, "That we should stick together for now, but we need to take advantage of our strengths. In the future, I propose we hike until midnight, make camp, and then break camp at midday. Just to make it fair."

It was already well after midnight now, but I didn't say anything because we did need to cover some ground. The drones would be searching for us in this area.

"Sticking together for now is wise," she agreed.

"For now…" I said, hiding my reluctance to say what I wanted to say to her. I wanted to appear stronger than the way I felt, but deep inside I was waging a battle. I knew we would have to split up, yet, I never wanted to leave her side. Although we were technically different species, I was in love with her, but it was a feeling I didn't think that I could ever act on. That war in my heart felt like a knife wound.

Still in the embrace, we held each other tighter for a moment.

She frowned and said, "Let's find a safe place to shelter, and we'll talk more, but I really don't want to separate now either. I'm sorry I said that. I have a lot on my mind."

I nodded my agreement and said, "I feel the same. Let's go."

We embraced tighter for another moment. Initially it had been spontaneous and now the embrace felt more warmth, so warm that we seemed to melt into each other and I could feel that she was as reluctant to let go of me as I was reluctant to let go of her, but eventually we did disengage.

We continued and walked for another hour when I felt the palm of her hand rest upon my chest, stopping me.

I heard her say, "Shhhh." She wore a look of utter disgust at something she saw ahead of us in what was unfathomable darkness to me.

I could hear something rooting though the dead leaves on the forest floor like a wild boar. I continued to peer into the darkness, but couldn't see what repulsed her.

"What is it?" I asked.

"Just an example of a vampire that makes me embarrassed to be a vampire. Let's go around that thing," she said.

I was grateful for the suggestion and started to back track. For her to call a vampire a "thing" told me this beast was horrible. However she suddenly stopped and stood rigidly in place.

"Abigail?" I whispered.

She held up a finger to me as she continued to look in the direction of the thing that disgusted her. I stepped up to her and whispered, "Abigail. Let's go."

"Wait," she said. "You stay here."

"What is it?" I asked, seeing the horror etched in her face.

"Just stay here. Don't follow me. I will be right back. No matter what you do, do not follow me."

After she said that, she stared at me to reinforce her words.

"I hear you," I replied.

I quietly drew my sword as she stalked forward in the direction of the growling, muttering thing. I heard the thing curse and thrash in the dry leaves as she whispered to it in a calming tone, assuring the thing that it was safe. Her spoken voice was as soothing as a lullaby as she approached it.

Curiosity overtook my mind, and I soon followed, eager to see what could turn the stomach of a vampiress. As I drew near, I could see a form in a vampire's hooded cloak on all fours like an animal. I could see that its leg was tied to a tree. It didn't appear to have the intelligence to untie the rope.

Once close enough, Abigail said in a pleasant tone to the grotesque shadowy form, "Greetings brother," and raised her hand at chest level in a salute shared between vampires.

The creature growled savagely and lunged at her, but the rope on its leg restrained it.

I was surprised to see her step forward instead of retreat. Compassion filled her voice as she said, "Brandon. It's me, Abigail. Brandon?"

The thing stopped its attack and made a growl that sounded like a question.

She went to her knees beside the horrid thing and ran a hand over its head as she cooed in a consoling tone, "Brandon, what happened to you, my dear?"

"Ab-by-gail? Sister?" the vampire asked in a guttural tone of dull recognition.

"Yes, it's me, Brandon," she said, almost choking in tears. I was surprised. We had seen all forms of diseased human degeneracy. I didn't understand why she was so shaken. In an almost mesmerized state of curiosity, I kept walking forward. The vampire she spoke to was ripped up and bloody like he had been mauled by a pack of wolves.

From all fours, the thing she now called Brandon lifted its head in the air catching my scent. It growled the word, "blood," and lunged at me.

Abigail stopped it by the collar of its cloak. She shook him and tried to stand him up, but I could see the femur on its right leg was shattered and would not support him. His leg was bent painfully at mid thigh and I could see the white bone poking through the pant leg. He howled in agony as he collapsed back down, but his hungry eyes were fixed on me. Despite the obvious pain that he should've been feeling in his ruined leg, his focus was on my blood scent.

She squatted down and held his face in her two hands and said, "Brandon. What happened to you, my dear?"

The vampiric man/animal seemed to come to his senses. I watched in horror as the man went back and forth between insanity and lucidity, but he told a story of vampires from King Sadazar's bloodline in a choppy voice riddled with psychopathy and idiocy and occasional lucidity. His delivery ranged back and forth between friendship for her and bloodlust for me, and I had to write a summation of what he told us, because his tale went all over the place.

I noticed Abigail shuddered at the mere mention of the Vampire King Sadazar. Both vampires were near tears when Brandon told her of Sadazar's army of failed vampires turning both humans and good vampires into bloodlusting faileds, and they even drank the fluids of zombies in their path. He told of how they caught him as he sought to free a human the night before. Brandon was now suffering great anguish because he knew in a few nights he would seek to join them as a member. Each minute, I could hear his voice strain more and more as his mind seemed to get progressively more and more deranged.

Abigail cursed when she heard that they drank his blood. Vampiric blood wasn't nourishing to other vampires, at least not as good as human or even animals. It was usually done to shame the other vampire. There was a stigma to treating another vampire like an animal such as a human. They saw uninfected people as inferior and it was strictly done as an act of domination. To a vampire, being drained of blood was similair in nature to the violent act of a sexual assault.

He finished his tale. A bit of lucidity returned and he apologized for trying to attack me, and then begged to borrow Abigail's sword.

"Why," she asked suspiciously.

He hesitated and said, "So I can cut this rope that binds me to the tree."

She studied the situation and said, "I'll cut it for you, but let me look at your leg first."

"Abigail, are you sure?" I asked.

Brandon looked at me and said in a moment of forced coherence, "I understand your uncertainty, both of you, but let me cut my bonds myself."

She considered and instead said, "Let me look at your broken leg, Brandon."

An odd gleam fired up his eyes as he looked Abigail over and then looked in the area of her belt.

"OK," Brandon finally said and seemed to relax.

As Abigail bent down to attend to his broken leg, he suddenly reached for her. She jumped back and easily escaped his grasp. Then she stared in horror as he had pulled the handgun from her appendix holster at her belt and gripped it in his hands.

"Brandon," she pleaded.

He held a calming hand up as the other held her handgun and said, "Know now that I am of sane mind for this brief moment. I love all the world so I must do this deed, but don't let them bite either one of you, or... This," he let that warning hang in the air as he pointed the handgun at his head.

"No!" Abigail cried.

Brandon paused for a moment and then brought the handgun from his head and pressed the barrel to his mid chest, just left of his sternum and pulled the trigger. His eyes widened with the shock of the bullet tearing through his heart. Abigail bent over as if she felt the pain of a bullet through her own heart. Brandon then placed the gun in his mouth but stopped. He removed the handgun and offered it to her.

"I don't believe in suicide. Finish me, sister, as I say my final prayer," he said this surprisingly calmly as blood began to leak from his mouth.

With a sob, Abigail took her handgun back, and as Brandon stared at a distant mountain and muttered a silent prayer, she completed the job. She dropped her gun as it recoiled. The strange vampire collapsed at our feet and was dead after a few twitches.

"I'm sorry," she sobbed to the twitching form of her friend.

I was shaken at his determination never to rise again. Abigail and I stood there in stunned silence. I finally picked up her handgun where she had dropped it and cleaned it on Brandon's black robes before handing it to her. She inspected it further and numbly wiped off some gore that I could not see before she holstered it. It dawned on me that he originally asked for the sword to kill himself, but once the handgun was within easy reach, he went for that quicker end.

Instinctively I placed an arm around her shoulder. She buried her head in my chest and wept. I rubbed her head. It was rumored that vampires were incapable of tears. Although my heart ripped for her, I still liked seeing her dispel the myths, simply by her being a gracious person. In fact she was the most good hearted human I knew despite being a vampire.

I held her as she talked about who Brandon had been. She paused sometimes for close to a minute between some of the sobs and sentences. She was in a state of shock and she slowly came out of it as she accepted the reality of having just killed her friend.

She said, "He's the most moral vampire, most moral man I've ever known, far better than me. He refused to drink the blood of people, even from the communal chalice. He was a good man. I drank from the chalice for fear of execution, but he refused. I told myself that it was OK to drink from the chalice because I didn't kill the person myself. The person was already dead, but Brandon was a better vampire than me. He was so strong. Under the threat of death, he refused. I was supposed to be his mate. They paired us up before I was supposed to mate with David, but he refused to be a part of our coven. I loved him and envied his courage. I wished to join him in exile, but I was scared. I've been meaning to find him. Now, it's too late. He was a good man," she kept repeating that last sentence.

I could see her regret turning into paralyzing depression so I steered the conversation back to the fight, "What's this King Sadazar? Killing other vampires?"

She glared at me because I couldn't keep the optimism from my voice at the thought of a vampire killing other vampires.

She said, "King Sadazar was from a different bloodline. His line is pure evil. He was supposed to be killed by The Specter."

That surprised me. Any vampire too evil for The Specter had to be evil incarnate, or maybe good. I still wanted to admire anything that angered the wrath of The Specter and other vampires, regardless of what I had just witnessed.

Basically, I was in denial. Deep inside, I didn't want to think that there was anything worse than The Specter. That was just too terrifying for me at the moment.

She continued, "Sadazar is genuinely a monster. He was rumored to have been asleep for the last millenia. Rumored to be a vampire of the antediluvian age, before the Great Flood."

"Great Flood?" I asked. I had an idea what she meant, but it sounded too crazy.

"Noah," she said and when my eyes widened, she confirmed. "Yeah, Noah and the arc. We can't let Sadazar nor his minions turn anyone else. His bloodline turns good vampires into failures like poor Brandon."

I nervously cleared my throat. I wanted to give her more time to mourn, but spending any more time in this spot was dangerous.

"I hate to do this but we need to get out of here, like now," I said. "The gunshots will attract everything that we don't want–"

"No," she said in a determined tone that resembled a she-wolf's growl.

"What?"

"We need to bury Brandon. We can't leave him like this."

I nodded my head in agreement, but deep inside, it felt absurd to bury a monster. Really, I wouldn't have wanted to bury a human at that moment. Whether he was good or not, I still didn't trust any vampires other than Abigail, of course, but more importantly, standing in the middle of the woods at night after a firearm was discharged twice was stupid. Anything could be attracted to it, and nothing good. A gunshot advertised a wounded and easy meal for too many evil creatures. We needed to make some miles under our boots and fast, but I knew that Abigail was determined and needed to accomplish this for closure. Sometimes a man must risk his life not just for the life of a loved one, but their piece of mind as well. I could see that she needed this. I couldn't imagine what shooting a friend did to her.

It was a hastily dug, shallow grave in the rocky soil with a camp shovel from our pack, and she said a brief prayer and a eulogy once Brandon was covered. When that was accomplished, I could see she had some semblance of closure in her mind and the reality of our situation brought grim determination to her face.

"We need to move out, now," she said as she nervously scanned the forest.

"Yes," I agreed.

We hiked a few miles at a blistering pace before finding a place to camp. The site was on rocky ground and at an uncomfortable angle on a hillside, but it was far off the beaten path and we were relatively sure that we'd be safe. I climbed into the tent as soon as it was pitched and fell asleep almost instantly. Despite the worry, there was no fighting the exhaustion.

The sun was just peeking over the horizon before Abigail came into sleep. I was concerned for her when I saw the worry lines on her face. I gave her a quick hug and although I went back to sleep almost immediately, I was aware of her tossing and turning. I could only imagine the worries that kept her awake in the morning hours.

***

I woke up a little after noon. I wanted to wake her up and hit the trail so that we would not hike too late into the coming night, but I decided that she needed more sleep. Seeing her friend in such a state and assisting him in suicide understandably rattled her nerves. At that moment, my heart really broke for her. When it had happened, I had only been concerned with getting out of that area, but now in relative safety, I had nothing but concern for her.

Killing an enemy was bad enough for PTSD. On top of that, I couldn't imagine what the mercy killing of a close friend could do. When she was being crucified, I had failed in an attempt to mercy kill her with a gunshot, even as her vampiric father tried to psychically force me to pull the trigger. I tried to go along with his influence, but simply couldn't kill her. Now I was glad, of course, but at the time it had seemed appropriate.

Outside of the tent, I saw that she had spread a blanket over the tent and covered it with leaves and branches. I guessed it was for both camouflage and insulation as well as keeping the sun from penetrating the thin fabric for her daytime slumber.

I walked and sat fifty feet away from the tent overlooking a small creek beneath our camp. I ate some cold remains of the bear meat that the Mountain Warriors let me take.

Although I found myself missing the electronic distractions, I found that I could watch a creek flow with almost the same intent that I would watch a movie. The difference was that with the creek, I couldn't hide from the inner demons that plagued me, and as time went on in the Forbidden Zone, I was glad to get a chance where I was forced to face these demons without distraction. I found that I could conquer them easier. Although some demons seemed insurmountable. The worst of them were my extreme and conflicting feelings for Abigail. Someday we would have to go our separate ways, but as much as I knew the necessity of parting ways, I really didn't want to. I knew that she was torn as well, but after her facing her death from people in Craigsville and the supposedly friendly tribe of the Mountain Warriors, not to mention, groups of vampires that would see me as food, I saw no other future for us.

I began tossing rocks into the creek with a sling, the same weapon with which David slew Goliath. I was getting pretty accurate with it. After I hit a rock the size of a head from fifteen yards three times in a row, I heard the rustle of the tent opening. Abigail exitted in her hooded cloak. The tarnished dime-sized sun was bright for winter and she kept her head down with the hood up so that all I saw was a black hole where her face was hidden.

She said, "I know it's a good distraction, but the sound of the stones hitting your targets could give away our position."

I was mid-throw and I stopped, hanging onto the rock. I didn't think it was that big of a give away. We were deep in the woods, in daylight, and far from anyone else. Instead of arguing, I hung my head and chuckled.

"What's so funny?" she asked.

"I thought I found something to replace my habit of scrolling through my cellphone. Who knew slinging rocks could, well, rock?" I replied.

A chuckle emitted from the black maw of the vampiric hood at my poor pun.

I smiled and said, "Thanks for laughing with me. I, uh--"

"What?" she asked.

"It's just weird speaking to a hooded specter. I can't see your facial expressions. It was just eerie seeing you emerge from the tent."

She sat beside me and said with a laugh, "Please don't compare me to The Specter."

"Oh sorry. I didn't think."

She grimly laughed, "When someone nails one's arm to a beam in an attempted crucifixion, it doesn't sit well."

She said that with a smile that displayed more humor than I would have shown if I suffered what she had suffered the last few nights.

"You got it," I replied.

She asked, "May I lean on you?"

"Yes," I said.

She leaned on me and I leaned against her with my arm around her back. Despite her chuckling at my poor pun of "slinging rocks, rocks," and then talking about The Specter, I knew she was hurting deep inside from shooting her friend, Brandon. Loyalty to those she loved was such a powerful driving force in her, that I knew it tore her up even though he had already shot himself in the heart.

Although she didn't have to ask if she could lean on me, I found it endearing when she did. I squeezed her lightly. When she didn't react negatively to the pressure on the ribs that had been crushed a few days ago, I hugged her tighter.

"Thanks," she said.

"No problem."

"No," she said. "Thanks for a lot of things. For letting me sleep in. For going with me when exiled from your friends. For helping me bury Brandon, when it was smarter to run. For-- For everything."

"Thank you, too. For all that you have done for me," I said, my voice trailed off. I had too much to thank her for. Abigail leaned into me more. As my arm was across her upper chest she gave my low back an affectionate squeezed with her arm across my waist.

"By the way," she began, "I know we talked about going our separate ways eventually, but I really think we should get to Asheville first, kill The Mind, look for a cure for my vampirism... Then decide."

"Yes. To be honest, I really never want to leave your side. It's just..."

"I know," she said. "I don't want to split up either, but..."

I looked at her black form. I was sure that it looked like I was cuddling with the grim reaper. I held back a joke. I had known some people who liked the vampire culture back in Washington DC, who loved the darkness for the sake of darkness. Abigail only sought darkness because the light would actually hurt her. I suspected that she potentially had a mental complex about her dark appearance.

She said, "I know you don't like vampires." As I inhaled to make a retort, she cut me off by saying, "I know you make an exception for me. I know you may come to accept others, but last night, helping me bury Brandon, meant a lot. I know you wanted to get out of there. That was the smart thing to do. I insisted on the emotional thing, but I had to do it or it would have driven me to madness."

"I know," I said. "I also know that you would have stuck around for me in a similar situation. I can't imagine what you are going through right now. He was a good man."

She looked at me with the hood drawn back just enough so I could see the sincerity in her face. "We're not all bad, you know. Brandon deserved a proper burial."

I pulled her tighter to me. The sincerity in her face really got to me and I felt a tightness in my throat as well as a warmth in my heart. "I know," I said. "Not all of us humans are monsters either."

We both quietly chuckled.

She sobered and said, "Seriously, if I get bitten by one of Sadazar's minions, please kill me before I revert to the state that Brandon was in. I wish you knew Brandon before that change."

I nodded and said, "I can tell he was a great man." I paused and added, "and kill me too." I paused and added, "If I ever was to become a vampire, I want to be like you... and Brandon. Not like them."

She nodded and we embraced tighter for a moment, sealing the fatal deal with a tight mutual squeeze. We then sat in comfortable silence, just enjoying each others' company for the moment despite our grim pact.

She spoke up, "Hey, we're going to have to be careful. You couldn't see what I saw in the dark, but I saw their tracks all last night. There are literally hundreds of those vampires traveling together. The ones who ruined Brandon. That's why I cautioned you about slinging those rocks."

I nodded, remembering her worry when she came to bed last night.

"Should we warn people-- and vampires around here?" I asked. I had quickly added vampires although deep inside, I still kind of admired vampires who killed other vamps. They were the enemy of my enemy, other than Abigail, of course.

"I am not sure. I am an outlaw among vampires. You're not too popular yourself. The two of us traveling together, we would not be welcomed anywhere, even to warn others."

"That's an understatement," I said. "So do we avoid this coven, or try to stop them?"

"I don't know," said Abigail. "These vamps don't have quite the psionic control over people like my coven did, but they can use those tricks on other vampires, maybe more so over vampires. They scare me. They really do."

"I thought that all the vampires lost their psionic powers when the Nunnehi cut you off and then we killed The Mind..." The Mind had some genetic modification that made him grow twenty to thirty feet tall and his head had been the size of a small car so his brain could interface psychically with people and computers. He was terrifying indeed.

Abigail ruefully shook her head, "There are other Minds, like the one in Asheville that we need to kill. Also there are other vampire bloodlines. The virus that turned me, was just one of many strains. Other strains were experimented with. Sadazar's was one of the most sinister. His viral bloodline is ancient and horrible."

"How so?"

"It has changed him physically and mentally over thousands of years. I have only heard stories without knowing what is right, wrong, propaganda, conspiracy theory, science fact or fiction, like every other bit of gossip these days... but everything that I heard was bad, very bad. Almost like vampire versions of campfire stories. Really horrible stories. We need to avoid them at all costs."

She said nothing more, but I could see in her eyes that she thought that we couldn't possibly avoid them.

"What's wrong?" I asked.

She hesitated and said, "They know about us and are actively looking for us. I feel them probing my mind."

"Us in particular?" I asked, worried.

"I don't know for sure, but we crossed their trail many times last night. They are performing grid patrols, probably for us. I hope that I am just paranoid."

"Why do you think they are after us if they are outlaws and we are outlaws?" I asked, expecting to hear some archaic psionic power linking her into some cosmic collective vampiric knowledge.

She pointed to a high knob as she said, "They are trailing us. I saw a scout watching us from that ridgeline just before the sun rose as you slept."

I nervously looked around. Although I knew that it was daylight and they were asleep. Also, the more evil vampires tended to have less tolerance of the light. Abigail was a rarity in the way that she explored the world in the daylight despite her slightly weakened state. Still, they knew where we camped, I thought with worry.

"Let's go," I said, wanting to put as many miles between us and the pursuers, but deep inside, I felt that anywhere that we headed was into a trap. Like Abigail, I could feel the tendrils of their psychic powers getting into my mind and it worried me when she had said they had greater power over vampires.

I worried more as I looked at her. Abigail's usually sharp eyes had a slightly glassy appearance.

Chapter Six

I wanted to run immediately, but Abigail took her time packing her gear and getting dressed in my red hoodie to pass as human by day. We worked in silence, but I was agitated and I carelessly stuffed things in my pack when I should have packed more carefully, and that carelessness would come back to bite me. I thought that her slow movements may have been depression from having to kill her friend last night, but her apathy was starting to infuriate me.

I stood over her with my arms crossed over my chest. All my gear was ready. I didn't attempt to hide the agitation from my face nor in my shifting as she slowly packed her stuff. We needed to get the hell out of there.

I finally asked, "Why'd you let me sleep if you saw them watching us?"

"I didn't want to arouse their suspicions by suddenly leaving. They won't be watching us during the day and they probably don't believe that I will attempt to travel during the light. Besides, we needed rest. I'm still weakened from the ordeal in Craigsville and the crushing of my ribcage by The Mind."

That was true. If she'd been a mortal woman, The Mind would have killed her instantly with what she had suffered, but although I cared for her, the panic that drove me to move was making me less sympathetic than I should have been, no matter how valid the reason.

"Then we need to move now," I said looking at the mid afternoon sky, "Or we will face a death worse than what we have already faced." I added thinking about Brandon's fate.

"Agreed," she finally said.

She began to work faster, but I wondered if she was affected mentally in some way by this strange coven simply through their psychic powers. I felt something that resembled static in my head as if something was trying to influence me, but it was all new to me. Her apathy seemed to go beyond depression, and I suspected that she didn't want to worry me by admitting that these evil vampires were psychically affecting her in a way I couldn't understand.

We were finally back on the trail. With the sun above, I felt strong and optimistic but the lower the sun settled and the longer the shadows grew, the more worried I became.

As a child, I remembered going to bed, worried after watching something scary on TV. I'd sleep in the doorway of my room, and kept a fearful eye on the light emitting from the crack under my adopted parents' door. As long as I saw the light, I had hope that they would rescue me if something horrific happened based on whatever I had seen on TV that evening. Once they turned off their bedroom light, I felt that deep dread of being alone in the dark with my nighttime imagination. I felt the same dread now as I watched the sun recede behind the mountains behind me, and it left me feeling without protection. Watching the shadows ever elongating as if catching up with me, made me feel like the night itself was creeping in on us. I wanted to run from the growing shadows of twilight that seemed to reach for me. The shadow branches of trees were like clawed hands ever growing. The difference between now versus my fear of my parents' lights going out was that my terror of the night was actually warranted this time.

During the day, I had been leading the way and Abigail followed. Once the sun had set, she took off my hoodie and donned her black hooded cloak. To be traveling with a night creature should have given me confidence, but even she was terrified of what lay ahead in the dark and I felt like she was hiding her true terror from me. If a vampire was scared of what lurked in the dark...

However it stayed pretty uneventful until an hour before midnight.

We were walking along a slim, narrow trail. A cliff rose high to my left side. The rock face disappeared into the darkness of the night above me. I could usually see further in the night, but a cold mist had been moving in, slowly saturating the air. Even Abigail's night vision was limited. I looked up at the cliff above and had a sense that it went up quite a ways but I lost sight a mere ten feet above me. I walked with the fingertips of my left hand gliding over the wet sandpaper feel of the granite, as there was a steep drop off a mere foot away on my right.

My mind was wandering when Abigail said, "You are lucky that your human eyes can't see what's to your right."

Even in the night with her vampiric hood down, I could see a slight smile on her lips and awe in her eyes as she tilted her head forward as her body pressed against the cliff to our left to see over the precipice on the right.

I flattened myself against the natural wall and peered down. Again, my vision ended less than ten feet from my eyes. I muttered a curse as I could hear water surging and tumbling far below. It had been a distant white noise, that at first I thought was a small chuckling creek just a few feet away, but now I realized that it was the torrent of a raging river far below us.

"I imagine that the sight is quite breathtaking," I said in good humor.

"It is worthy of a postcard. Just be careful of your step. It could be your last," she needlessly advised with a nervous laugh.

After traveling another forty feet the trail slightly widened and I walked beside her to the left, closer to the natural rock wall, for the companionship of being together but also to try to see what she was seeing ahead. I could still hear the rage of the river below, but it was slightly muffled due to the largeness of the platform. The drop off was now about ten feet or fifteen away from the cliff.

She took in a harsh but quiet intake of air.

"We're surrounded, but play it cool," she said in a surprisingly calm voice. "These are failed vampires. I think I can talk our way out of this."

I swore silently.

She used her hand to nudge me behind her and took a few bold steps forward.

I peered into the blackened gloom of the night to see what startled her. For a moment I saw impenetrable foggy blackness as we were deep in a cove on a starless night. Then it appeared that the very night air broke apart to form dark shapes. With horror, I saw that the blackened forms were five cloaked and hooded vampires.

They stopped and stared at her in surprise when they spotted her.

"Greetings, brothers and sisters," she said in a friendly voice.

"Greetings, sister, brother," a male replied in a grating voice. He continued on in chopped up English with a roughness of a high functioning but failed vampire. However his tone of voice seemed to imply that he tried hard to sound intelligent. It took me a moment to realize what he was doing. He was using the worst fake British accent that I have ever heard beneath his fragmented grammar. His mind seemed to wander back and forth between different subjects as he said, "You different strain, I say. My name is Jim. Are you not different blood strain, sister, brother?"

I noticed that under his black hood, he wore a cooking pot like a helmet as well as other forms of impromptu armor like cut up tires for shoulder gauntlets. The others in his coven looked equally ridiculous but also deadly.

"Yes, brother," Abigail replied. "I'd heard there were others, but you're the first I have met outside my own coven."

"Coven, I say, sister. Witches we not. Virologist pretend be folklorist, name us." He laughed gutturally. That was a common joke, but vampires did indeed congregate in covens. A group of vampires is also called clutch, brood, pack, or clan. I think coven sounded more mystical and classy to them. Although vampires call a herd of failed vampires a pack, they despised being called a horde. That's reserved for the undead zombies, and vampires tended to hate zombies as much as people did.

Abigail's tinkling laughter joined in. Her laughter actually endeared me to her because she sounded so human. By now, I did tend to see her as a normal woman when I wasn't paying attention, it was only when her dietary needs or nocturnal cadences jarred me back to reality.

Jim laughed and then the remaining four vampires laughed loudly building upon each other. I had the distinct feeling that they laughed only because they heard Abigail laugh rather than understanding the humor. As I gazed upon their faces, I realized that they were really bad off as far as faileds go. The one who led and spoke for them seemed to be the only one with a dim spark of intelligence in his eyes. One of them in particular had a demoniac gleam to his hideously scabbed face. It looked like he fed on the throats, oblivious to his victims tearing at his face with tooth and claw. Both of his nostrils hung like flaps to the side of his nasal bridge before the inherent healing of the vampiric strain could fuse the flaps back together. I had a feeling that he reveled in the pain he received from the flailing, dying, and futile resistance of his victims.

As they laughed I saw that their fanged smiles were hideously repulsive. Abigail's covens had two inch long canine teeth. Their fangs were slender and at the sides of their smiles and easily concealed. I actually thought that Abigail's fangs added to her beauty. This coven had enlarged lateral incisors rather than canines. Instead of having slim fangs, they appeared to be horribly buck-toothed with a large gap.

Even worse than their snaggle toothed fangs, I was more unnerved by the violent desire burning in their eyes. I had originally thought that the demoniac had been staring at me and was focused on getting at me, but then I realized he was staring one thousand yards past me as if focused on an insane goal far beyond anyone else's perception.

I stayed behind Abigail and could sense that she used her remaining psionic abilities to hide me. I knew that she was shielding me from their sense of smell by focusing on their noses and the part of their brains where it registered the scent of human blood. She had taught me how to do that and I had limited success. Now I relied on her powers as I tried to aid her as well with my own mind, but obviously, I was nowhere near as good as a vampire was. Although Abigail and I lost our ability to have communication with our brains, we still had abilities to jam the probing of other vampires depending upon their powers. I was hoping her shield defended me against them smelling my blood along with my own feeble help. It seemed to be working. So far I hadn't attracted unwarranted attention.

Abigail and the bad English accented vampire spoke a little longer and I could tell that Abigail had some connection and was able to get the faileds to understand things that went beyond verbal speech. All except the demoniac. He seemed only keen for devouring something unseen in the distance.

"What name?" Jim finally asked. He stared at her with an odd hunger that I didn't quite understand at first. He scared me.

"Ashlyn," Abigail answered.

"Pretty name, gorgeous," he nodded and pointed at his companions. "Her Cindy. He Tony. Her Mary, and this guy," Jim said as he motioned to the demoniac, "we not know name, but call Gog. He cool. Very cool. You like him. He crazy cool."

"I Gog!" The demoniac exclaimed his name far louder than needed.

The faileds laughed raucously. Especially the one called Gog.

"Hung-wy," Gog shouted enthusiastically. I guessed he meant to say, "hungry." However, even in the dark, I could see by the flush of his face that he had very recently consumed his fill of blood. This scared me because I realized that he was a psychopath who just wanted to kill for fun, not just for blood.

"He hungry. Always hungry, I say," said Jim, causing the faileds to growl a guttural laugh. "Humans your way?"

"No," Abigail said. "Me heading Asheville."

I noticed Abigail clipped off useless words to communicate with these failed vampires.

Jim spat in disgust. "Nothing there. Just flesh eaters. Rotter zombies. Taste bad, but easy to catch. Fill belly easy, I say."

Abigail's nose wrinkled in disgust at the thought of anyone, even a failed vampire, trying to eat a zombie or consume its rancid fluids. A person or an intelligent vampire could smell the stench of decay a mile away if the wind was blowing to your misfortune. Besides, a zombie bite could turn a vampire into a failed. A very bad one, like Gog, for instance.

"Business in Asheville, official, and I need go. Now," she said in her adapted version of failed vampire clipped English. The longer she spoke with them, the more pronounced her chopped up language became.

Abigail siddled me behind her even more with her hand and tried to scoot past them on the narrow trail, but Jim's hand shot out and grabbed her wrist stopping her.

"Pretty," he said, staring longingly and predatorial at her face..

"Excuse me?" Abigail said with an edge in her voice as if trying to still be polite despite the violation. She tried but failed to remove her arm from his clamp-like, insistent grip. Her nose wrinkled with repulsion at his smell. I caught the scent of decay as if he had indeed fed on a zombie recently. I also detected the stench of atrocious hygiene.

"You very pretty. Be mine mate. My last mate was killed by evil vamp named Brandon." He stared intensely at Abigail. There was a hunger in his eyes that went far beyond just bloodlust. In fact, it was pure lust. He then stated loudly with a sense of entitlement, "Mine. Mine have it," he said looking at Abigail with ever growing lustful and possessive hunger. In his passion, I noticed that he dropped the horrible attempt at a fake British accent.

The grasp on her arm broke Abigail's concentration as well as my own for masking my human scent, and the eyes of the demoniac Gog now narrowed in focus. He no longer stared a thousand yards away. He looked straight at me with the black holes of eyes as his ripped up nostrils flapped and flared as he sniffed the air. I knew he could smell human blood. I just hoped that they didn't figure out that it was me.

"Gog smell hu-man," Jim said as if explaining the actions and baying of a hunting hound.

"We fed earlier. Scent still on us–" Abigail started to say but her voice was cut off.

Suddenly, with a ferocity that scared me, Gog shrieked a scream of the demons as he stared into my eyes. There was no point in denying. They knew.

I drew my sword as I was instantly the center of all of their attention. They stared through Abigail as if she became as ephemeral as the fog around us. Abigail kept her sword sheathed as if in the belief that she could still talk our way out of this.

"Put sword down, cattle." Jim said to me. "Your Ashlyn needs to share. It is etiquette for all vampires to share cattle." I noticed in his urgent command that he no longer attempted the fake accent.

"Go to hell, bloodsucker," I snarled.

"Cattle" was a term that vampires called people who were kept alive to occasionally feed on. The vampires used a slim dagger to draw blood without infecting the person with a bite. The "cattle" were sickly in appearance and appeared as pale as a starving vampire. They stuck with the vampire either out of brute psychic force or the promise of achieving immortality that a bite would deliver. Besides the obvious threat, I, as well as Abigail, found the term extremely offensive. I always thought the terms, "fighting words," were overly dramatic. My uncle had drilled in me the "Sticks and stones," axiom, but it was true in this case. I wanted to fight beyond just defending my life.

Jim was about to say something back to me when he noticed that Gog now only had eyes for Abigail. "What is it Gog?" Jim asked. "Why stare at Ashlyn?"

"Ab-by-gail," Gog muttered.

"Ab-by-gail," Jim said dully as the name slowly sank into his shattered mind. His horrible faux accent was back in full force, "I say, It is dear Ab-by-gail, most beautiful. Attractive as bloody beating heart pulled from human cattle."

My stomach turned at what he considered sensuous and beautiful language to woo a love interest.

The focus of all of them came back to Abigail. Somehow her outlaw status was known to all vampires. I can only describe the stare as a mix of awe, love, and maybe even hunger.

"Ab-by-gail, Ab-by-gail, Ab-by-gail," all the faileds chanted with longing stares.

As the other vampires focused on Abigail, Gog's eyes slipped from her and he gazed unblinkingly at me. I nervously shifted my feet and gripped my sword tighter.

Then all of their ravenous eyes were focused on me again.

"You not have Eric. He friend. Not cattle." Abigail said in clipped English.

"Traitor! I say, Ab-by-gail, dear girl," said Jim. "Be mine mate and you live. We dine on your human cattle pet together."

"Eric my friend. I kill and die before you have him," Abigail said right back, sounding like a failed vampire. However, her normally sharp eyes almost appeared glassy to me in the dim, almost nonexistent light. At that point, I wasn't sure if she was using the clipped dialogue to communicate or if they were starting to psychically influence and dominate her.

Gog screamed and ran straight at me as if Abigail vanished and he planned to go straight through her as if she was a wisp of fog.

"Abigail!" I screamed.

Her light returned to her eyes as I shouted her name. In one motion, she stepped aside, drew, and swung her sword. Gog ran, clotheslined by her blade. His head flew off his neck as his body continued past her and slammed into me as my blade penetrated his heart and thrusted out his back. His decapitated head lay on the ground but his eyes still hungrily followed my every movement.

I twisted the blade savagely and removed it. It was overkill, but I had seen a beheaded vampire brought back to life. A shredded heart would ensure that Gog would remain dead even if his head would be conscious until dawn. His body bonelessly sank to the ground as I removed my sword with a wicked twist and kicked his body away from me.

Although vampires were harder to kill than zombies, I preferred slaying vampires to zombies. Vampires were still alive and didn't smell of deathly decay. It took days to get the zombie stench off you if their goo got on your clothes or skin. The scent of a slain vampire lasted as long as the scent of a slain man, but Gog reeked of the zombies that he consumed. It went far beyond the stench of the poor hygiene of a failed vampire or even the rot of a dead uninfected person. Zombies smelled worse than anything that I had encountered before. Gog reeked just as bad.

I tried to stand side by side with Abigail but she stepped so that she stayed in front to protect me from her brethren. I felt like I needed to stand shoulder to shoulder with her, but I trusted her instinct. She was better at dealing with other vampires.

The vampires started to sing, "Ab-by-gail. Ab-by-gail. Ab-by-gail," repeatedly in a slow growling like chant. They slowly circled us on the narrow path and continued to walk around us. They looked at her pleadingly. I could tell that they were enamored by her outlaw status.

They occasionally looked at me hungrily as they chanted at her, as the two of us stood back to back, swords out, to protect each other.

"Ab-by-gail, Ab-by-gail, Ab-by-gail. We love outlaw Ab-by-gail," the sickening sing-song quality of the chant was driving me crazy. It was getting into my head and I felt dizzy, but by far, it affected Abigail worse, I soon discovered..

"Ab-by-gail, Ab-by-gail, Ab-by-gail. Join us. Be Jim's mate," they sang together as if they planned the song in advance. I wasn't sure if it was pre rehearsed or if they were connected by some form of hive-mind.

Jim spoke over the chant of the others as they continued to chant her name, "Come back with us. Don't be traitor. Be mate, ole girl. Give us your cattle. We share his blood."

Abigail's voice cracked with emotional strain. It was rumored among people that it was supposed to be impossible for a vampire to cry, but she seemed on the verge of tears, but despite the wavering tone, she said firmly, "Eric. Press your back to my back. Don't lose contact. If I turn towards you, kill me immediately."

"What?" I exclaimed.

"Ab-by-gail, Ab-by-gail, Ab-by-gail," the chant continued. "Don't kill self. Join us and live. Truly live as vampire."

"Call me back, Eric. They are from a different strain. They are getting in my head," a desperation welled up in her voice that I had never heard from her.

"What?" I asked again at a loss for words. It confused me that these idiot failed vampires had any means to control her. She was one of the strongest people, human or vampire, who I had ever met.

"Call my name Eric, please," she said with growing desperation. "They're taking control of my mind. Calling my names brings me out of their control."

My veins felt like a coolant line chilled my body with icy liquid fear. "Abigail!" I screamed louder than the faileds chanted.

"Thank you. Keep calling me back. They have psionic powers that I haven't experienced. They are like idiot savants with their powers. Brandon was right." she said with her voice cracking with weakening resolve.

"We not idiots," said Jim. "King Sadazar say we special."

I held back on an obvious insult to his self proclaimed, "special," status.

Instead, I kept calling Abigail's name as we stood pressing our backs against each other and swords pointing outward as the coven of failed vampires continually circled us. It reminded me of when Abigail's coven had Bryan, Critter, and me surrounded. They convinced Critter and Bryan to attack each other with blades. Only Abigail's intervention saved us that night.

Now they had us both ensnared in their mental webs as they circled us on the narrow path, but it was Abigail's mind that they were winning. I don't know if they were more specialized with influencing other vampires, or if they wanted to win her first and then attack me.

Our swords pointed out as they chanted over and over "Ab-by-gail, Ab-by-gail, Abi-by-gail..." All their attention was on my partner. They took me for a regular person who had no means to resist their psionic abilities, but still they influenced my mind to the point where I was feeling that they would get full control of me. I prayed, The Our Father, with a bit of guilt as I said it more like a magical incantation than an actual prayer, but it did seem to strengthen my resolve. I wasn't religious, but with my death looming, I was grasping for anything.

I could feel the muscles of Abigail's back writhing like serpents beneath her skin under her cloak. She made eye contact with me with eyes that blazed with inhuman lust for my blood. It was like making eye contact with a great white shark making a reconnaissance pass by a diver before delivering a fatal attack.

I elbowed her ribcage sharply. I screamed her name. Her rib fractures had healed but I guessed that there was still some lingering soreness from her breaks.

She grunted with surprise and said, "Thanks, Eric. Keep talking to me. Call my name, please. Don't let them...."

I desperately screamed, "Abigail!," as I attacked the vampire known as Mary. Mary shrieked and her drool flecked my face, but she could wield a blade. She fought back, blocking my slash and swinging at me. Out of the corner of my eye, I saw a blade descending towards my head. I ducked, blocking it, and saw it was wielded by Jim.

I retreated, trying to press into Abigail's back, but she wasn't there anymore. I attempted to keep my peripheral vision open to see side attacks. Critter and Bryan drilled into me to avoid the tunnel vision inspired by fear. Peripheral vision also gave better night vision. Nowhere near what vampires were capable, but I needed every edge I could seize. Unfortunately the vampires kept attacking and I was separated from Abigail.

Three vampires pressed on me with their swords as the fourth one, Cindy, stood inches from Abigail, staring straight into her eyes. I feared my companion was theirs. Abigail's two handed katana hung harmlessly at her side in her right hand. Cindy stepped closer so that their foreheads were touching. Their eyes were locked on each others'. I thought that Abigail was gone, gone into the abyss of their mental webs. I feared that she was theirs as she stared blankly back into Cindy's eyes.

I screamed her name but it had little effect, only causing her catatonic eyes to blink.

I slashed at Jim's head. It was a feint. Without looking at Mary, I sliced a backhand through her throat, sending a shower of her blood everywhere, and then, I penetrated her heart with a quick thrust and a twist.

The vampires screeched cat-like yowls as Mary collapsed to the ground, cursing me viciously until the blood clogged her throat and spilled down her chin.

I looked and saw Cindy had her forehead touching Abigail's and her hands were on the back of Abigail's head, bracing her in place, but that was unnecessary. Abigail was catatonic. Abigail was Cindy's. I could see their eyes locked as if becoming one being, one mind.

As Jim attacked me, I ducked and launched myself at Abigail in an attempt to push her away from Cindy, but Jim and his sword blocked my way. Abigail glared at me with the eyes of a stranger. The fire of blood craziness lit her eyes, and she saw me as her prey. She held the same savagery in her countenance as Bryan and Critter held against each other as the vampires convinced them to attack each other. If two men who viewed each other as brothers could be so manipulated, I knew it wouldn't be hard to turn a vampire against a human, even an ally. If she forgot who I was, the scent of my blood would be her only guide.

I charged Jim, knocked his sword out of my way and hurtled at Abigail. My shoulder impacted her chest and we both rolled on the ground where my head painfully crashed into a rock. I didn't dwell on that as we both shot to our feet facing each other with our swords pointed at each other's face.

I screamed out her name, "Abigail!"

I stood and was surrounded by three vampires who kept the infernal chanting of "Ab-by-gail, Ab-by-gail, Ab-by-gail."

My blade pointed at their heart level as I moved my sword back and forth between the three.

"No," I screamed as I saw Abigail's point her sword at my heart with her vampiric brethren coming up beside her.

With my back against the cliff, I faced off against the three vampires.

No, I quickly corrected myself: I was now facing four vampires. I had to include Abigail as my enemy as she stared at me hungrily with her sword aimed at me. I hoped that I could kill the others without having to fight Abigail. Maybe then I could snap her out of it. However, I wasn't sure if there was a way to use non-lethal force against her. She was as deadly with a sword as anyone I had encountered. To go lenient on her was to invite death to myself.

I screamed, "Abigail!"

The four vampires walked at me with an ominously confident and unstoppable gait. Some other failed vampires outside the original group of the five closed in around us. I had not been aware of them until now. I could count at least 10 newcomers who stood on the periphery letting Jim, the obvious leader and his immediate crew have first dibs on me, but I didn't know how long they would hold back. I could hear more growling and shrieking outside of my night vision, and knew there were at least a few dozen more.

The failed vampires began to press in on me and stood shoulder to shoulder with the original four, including Abigail. I stepped backwards until my back was against the cliff wall. Swords wouldn't work at this point as they all converged. As I sheathed my sword, a vamp charged me. I barely pulled my handgun and pumped a round in its chest and another in the head. It collapsed on me as the other vamps charged.

The gunfire caused them all to shriek and the vampires on the periphery charged as well.

"Abigail!" I screamed as I opened fire into the advancing horde.

I wasn't sure if it was my scream or the gunfire, but she yelled back, "I am with you Eric!" and I watched as vampires fell around her under my gunfire and her sword slashes.

However, I had little hope. We were horribly outnumbered on the narrow ledge, and I wasn't sure if I could count on Abigail to keep her wits. I worried about this as my handgun clicked empty. I holstered it and removed my sword because I had no time to reload a magazine. They were inconveniently in a lower cargo pocket, but seven vampires lay dead at my feet. The chant of Ab-by-gail had ceased after the gunfire. That gave me a shred of hope that she would stay with me.

I steadied myself for a royal battle, maybe my last, as the full mist seemed to suddenly move in. With the already dark night, I found that my sight was down to practically zero because of the fog. I felt as if I were fighting under a wool blanket pulled from an icy creek. The humidity of the suddenly cold fog was so dense that I felt as if I had a wet plastic bag over my face as I breathed.

"Abigail! I can't see a thing." I called.

I could hear her sword striking flesh and heard her full vampiric warcries twenty feet away from me.

She yelled back, "None of us can see. The fog is too thick. I can only scent your blood. Keep calling my name and kill anything that comes near you. I think that I knocked out Jim and wounded Cindy. I am slightly free of their mental control."

"OK Abigail! Stay with me."

"OK Eric!"

With my back against the cliff, I heard the scrambling of the vampires around us, their snarls, curses and feral growls. Abigail seemed to be making the most vocalizations. I could hear the screams as her sword slashed them down. Her own vampiric shrieks were equally horrifying. Because of the change, vampires can make a shriek louder and more terrifying that any human, man or woman, should be able to make. Hearing those cries come from Abigail's sweet face terrified me at times, but I was glad that she was on my side. Very glad.

Without thinking, I whirled and slashed at the scuff of feet on the rocks to my right. My sword sunk into the flesh of a vampire where the base of the neck met the shoulders. I heard a savage male voice scream at me with an inarticulate curse. His voice was cut off in a bloody gurgle. I swung at a few other vampires and was forced to leave the cliff at my back, and as I whirled, they came upon me. The dark rock of the cliff was now lost in the mist. I wasn't sure where I was.

"Abigail," I screamed desperately.

"Eric! Back against the cliff!" Abigail commanded, followed by the sound of her sword sinking into flesh and a snarl from her effort.

Her command caught me mid stride and I stepped into nothing. I fell back away from the abyss, just in time and rolled back onto the path and into the body of a dead vampire. I jumped away, tripped over another body that might have been Gog's, and slammed into the wall of the cliff. I blindly held my sword in front of me like a talisman, not able to see anything or anyone. I feared both the vampires and the fall from the cliff that I couldn't see.

Again I heard Abigail snarl. It was vampiric, barely human nor female in nature, but communicated her savage desire to live, to defeat the enemy, to protect me in my night blindness.

A dark figure rushed past me from Abigail's direction, and I could smell the stench of human/vampiric fecal waste. It growled as its feet skidded on the trail and I could hear it coming back to attack me. It was guided by its sense of smell. I blindly sliced into the night and felt my sword cleave the skull and sink into the soft brain matter beneath.

I heard the pounding of running feet and a panicked scream that dissipated as that vampire plummeted down the cliff. The scream eventually ceased, but I never heard the body hit water or rock over the din of combat.

I heard another scuffle of hurried feet. I raised the sword but instinctively hesitated. I could smell Abigail's sweet and wild scent over the horrid stench of the failed. I saw her black shape within inches of me.

"I almost swung at you," I told her.

"There are hundreds of these failed," she said in panting breaths, worn out from the combat. I was as exhausted as she was.

A terror touched my spine. I was more fearful of these beast of mankind than I was of the unseen abyss beneath me. "What do we do?" I asked.

"Hold my hand and do as I say. Trust me, Eric."

"I have no choice, I fear," I said as I let go of my sword with my left hand, holding it firmly in my right. I blindly reached for her hand, but couldn't find hers as I heard her snarl and heard the whistle of her sword and the wet impact of her screeching target.

I retracted my hand not sure of where she was. I then felt someone grasp it with such confidence that I knew it was her black form.

"Run!" she exclaimed.

I was pulled by her and I followed blindly, and we both quickly achieved a full sprint. A black form suddenly appeared coming at me. I shouldered passed it without breaking stride, knocking it over. Something about vampires made them more solid than people, but my shoulder hit him square in the chest.

"Jump, Eric!" she screamed as I felt her hand tug at me with her own leap.

I pistoned my foot against the ground and felt a rock slip from under my foot, a sharp pain lanced up my twisted ankle, but I still successfully leapt. I let go of her hand and plummeted a few feet before I realized that she had literally led me off a cliff, and a very high one.

Chapter Seven

Heavy with heartbreak and overpowering desire, Jim watched as his prize, Ab-by-gail, plummeted down the cliff as he shook off the concussion that the spirited vixen of his desires delivered to his head. His makeshift stewpot helmet had spared him the cleaving that she had given him.

"Ab-by-gail. Ab-by-gail. Ab-by-gail," he repeatedly whined with a growing intensity. Each time he said her name, his leg muscles coiled to leap after her off the cliff.

He watched with jealousy as other vampires from his coven followed Abigail along with Eric off the cliff.

"Eric," he growled the name angrily. Then he said optimistically, "King Sadazar."

Jim knew that he wasn't the brightest vampire in the world, but he also knew that he was the smartest in this coven, besides King Sadazar of course. He loved repeating the King's name to himself like a mantra. That was why King Sadazar placed him in charge of finding Abigail, and also Eric. Jim was smart. Smart enough, he reassured himself. If King Sadazar trusted him, it had to be true.

As much as Jim loved Abigail, he hated Eric, but the Vampire King Sadazar wanted them both alive in his army. King Sadazar was smart and that was why he ruled. He was big, tall, strong, so he ruled. Nine feet tall and winged! The Vampire King had ruled since before Noah built the ark, probably almost a hundred years ago by Jim's faulty mathematical reckoning. King Sadazar said he was one of the giants in the Bible that the flood was supposed to destroy. Nephilim was the word that Jim thought he was looking for. The king had used it. King Sadazar told Jim that not even God could kill him.

Jim had faith in his king because anyone who could live all those decades (or was it centuries, math wasn't Jim's strong point,) was near to being a God. Especially if Sadazar was powerful enough to live when a God wanted him dead, Jim thought as he believed every word of his king. The King was God!

Now those who commanded helicopters and drones wanted King Sadazar and all his minions dead as well.

But King Sadazar was immortal. He could make choppers crash with just a thought. Such power! Jim had seen it himself. Helicopters crashed into beautiful, blinding fireballs at his whim.

King Sadazar is God. King Sadazar knew everything that Jim thought and could control him and all the others in the coven. If the King was the smartest in the world, and Jim's mind was under the King's control, Jim was also the smartest man alive.

"King Sadazar is God," Jim repeated out loud as he looked down the cliff.

He had heard the distant splashes that was possibly Ab-by-gail and others hitting the icy river, but couldn't see because of the sheer drop. He also heard wet splats and screams as many, maybe even sweet Abigail, hit the boulders and the cliff as well.

Jim backed away from the precipice. He was too smart to jump down there despite desire. He communicated mentally with his coven, stopping anyone else from taking the foolish leap as he screamed, "Stop! Stop, I say. We walk down there. Catch my sweet Ab-by-gail."

King Sadazar spoke in Jim's head. He now told him that precious Ab-by-gail still lived, but barely. Although Ab-by-gail rebelled, Jim was now connected to her after Cindy did that mind thing with her. Jim had to rescue Abigail from Eric and bring her back to the castle where Jim and Abigail would be married. They would bite Abigail and infect her with their strain so her mind would be like Jim's and completely open to King Sadazars mind control.

The King told Jim of a bridge just a few miles downstream. The King was genius! They would not fall down cliff or get wet!

"Vampires," Jim sent another mental message to the hundreds in his coven, "Don't jump off cliff. Climb down and cross river. We must catch Ab-by–gail and bring her with Eric to the King. They will become one of us!"

He heard the hundreds of other vampires around him snarl, shriek and cry out in a victorious response to him. It was a glorious night! They were an unstoppable force.

If King Sadazar was with them, who could stop them? Not even God could kill them. "The King is God," Jim repeated this to himself as if it was the chorus of a hymn. Glorious was the night indeed. "The King was God." And the God worked through Jim!

***

We plummeted in the darkness. I kept expecting to hit the rock wall of the cliff or river, but we continued a seemingly endless fall through the freezing dark fog.

"Vampire to your right, Eric!" Abigail yelled at me from the dark.

I instinctively slashed to my right as a cold hand grabbed my throat, and I heard an inarticulate curse of a failed vampire as my blade sank into flesh and stuck into bone. Ribcage, I thought.

I say that it cursed me because although the failed vampire's syllables were unrecognizable, they were delivered like an oath when my sword sank into flesh. As I tried to pull my sword out, I felt through the blade, the vampire's body yank away from me as it slammed into the cliff, freeing my sword. I felt branches slap my face and heard the whistle of the granite wall inches away from me, but it happened too fast to be aware of fear. I was about to curse Abigail for leading me into death as it felt like a cold bolt of electricity shot through my body and paralyzed me. I hit the rocky bottom of the rushing river and fought to the icy surface as the current flipped me over and over like I was in a washing machine full of frigid water. My sword was still stubbornly gripped in my right hand. I felt the concussion and heavy splashes as vampires plummeted into the river around me.

"Swim with the current, Eric! We need distance from these things!" Abigail exclaimed through mouthfuls of river water..

I could see nothing. In the dark fog, I only felt the icy penetrating cold that was mercifully numb, but I knew it would soon incapacitate me. The current pummeled me against the rocks. Loaded with a pack, guns, and a sword, I could barely stay afloat. I wanted to ditch everything to swim, but I knew that I would need my sword and the contents of my pack to survive, not just in the next week, but in the next few minutes.

I would need fire. Soon. This wet cold would kill me as quick as a vampire's sword thrust.

"Eric, duck!" Abigail screamed.

I was fighting to keep my head above the river water, coughing up what I had swallowed or inhaled, and struggling to take a breath of air untainted with water, when the butt of a falling vampire grazed my shoulder, pushing me far under the surface. Panic seized me as I struggled to reach the surface. I had just exhaled and my conscious mind fought my instinct's desire to breathe deeply which would have filled my lungs with even more the icy river water.

I lost sense of up and down as the current picked up and thrashed me in its merciless grip like a doll. My face scuffed an underwater boulder, but the river pushed me further in a confused direction, ever downstream. As my arms naturally reached higher, my feet sought something solid below. I found purchase and pushed off the stoney bottom and exploded through the surface following the bubbles. I took a gasp of air mixed with drops of water. Coughing, I was submerged again. I felt like I was swimming for the bottom as I couldn't tell up from down, but I couldn't stop my motion. I was flailing to get from where I was with no concern for where I was going. I had water in my lungs. I even forgot about dumping my pack which was now waterlogged and weighing me down ever more. The sword stayed locked in my right hand with a death grip. I couldn't let go even if I wanted to. I felt myself losing consciousness and even losing concern for my well being. I was about to gratefully breath in the river water, when I felt a strong hand grab my shoulder. I no longer cared if it was one of the degenerate vampires.

I was yanked to the surface. I couldn't cough as my face broke the plane of the water. Each gasp for breath seemed to only fill my throat as my lungs felt filled to the top with water.

"Up here, Eric!" Abigail hissed as she pulled me up the rock face that she was standing on.

I scrambled feeling more like I was slapping the rock face where she was perched. I was unable to grab anything with frozen, numbed hands with the sword still locked in an icy deathlike grip in my right hand. Finally I made it up, sitting at her feet as she slapped my back encouraging me to cough up all the water. I slowly began to realize that I would survive as my panic subsided. Each breath was deeper than the one before, but my breathing sounded like shallow hoarse wheezes.

I had no breath to speak out loud so I swore in my head as I realized that we were sitting on a boulder in midstream.

She turned toward the oncoming current. I could see her eyes lit with combative fury. Her teeth set in determination as her two inch fangs were exposed as she growled at what was floating down the river toward us.

I saw a failed vampire caught in the current reaching for us, not with desire to be saved, but rather with a hunger for my blood as I locked eyes with it. I felt my blood seem to boil despite the cold. I hated those things with every fiber. Even with the threat of death in an icy river, they wished for my life over their own. In the name of humanity, I would have been tempted to save its life if it looked like it wanted rescue from what I had just escaped.

Abigail's sword sliced across the vampire's neck, cleanly decapitating it. I caught sight of the head. Even beheaded, I saw its desire for my blood in its eyes before it disappeared, submerged in the inky black waters.

I finally regained my strength and stood beside her. Abigail and I killed about ten more that floated past us. Then she waited for a minute before saying, "That should be it. Can you make it to shore?" she asked as I heard her teeth chattering in the cold night above the rushing water and above the sound of my own chattering teeth.

I nodded, yes. As my body began shivering, I knew that I had no choice. I needed fire.

"Where's your pack?" I asked as I saw her only with the rifle slung across her back and sword in hand.

"I had to ditch it to make it up this rock," she said.

I said nothing.

She glared at me as she demanded. "Don't look at me like that. If I didn't make it up here, you would have drowned. Besides, I knew that you would be too stubborn to let go of your pack. We have enough essentials for now."

I shrugged my shivering shoulders. She was right and thinking more clearly than me, but I was more than irritable at that moment.

"You ready?" she asked.

I nodded.

I could barely see anything in the foggy gloom and watched as she leapt into the water. I followed her. The biting shock of the icy water froze me even more. Although I was still numb, now I had deep bone pains that throbbed like a swollen tooth especially in areas of past injuries like my knees, elbows, wrists, and especially my left shoulder as well as my freshly twisted ankle. The water sped up in this section but it was shallower. We were in some shoals. I pushed perpendicular to the current and felt as if I was climbing a slight grade as it continued to push us further downstream, but we stayed upright. When I made it to shore, I resisted the urge to collapse on the rocky beach.

"We need fire. Now," I said.

"Yes," she agreed with ragged, steamy breath. She also fought the urge to plop down and rest.

As a vampire, she had a resilience that I didn't have, but cold can freeze even the blood of a vampiress just as fast as a man's. Their immortality wasn't supernatural, and they were bound to the laws of physics but not as much as people. I also knew that it would drive her bloodlust through the roof if she was not warmed soon. Blood fired their internal furnaces as I had witnessed the night before. Although I trusted her to a point, I did not wish to push it by any means, especially since she was under their control just minutes ago.

I scabbarded my sword, sloughed off my pack, and tried rummaging through it, cursing at my numbed, shaky fingers that refused to work. Abigail impatiently looked over my shoulder, adding to my irritation. We both cursed some more. I wasn't sure what she was mad about. I was pissed off at the haste that I packed that afternoon. I didn't bother waterproofing anything and I had no dry clothes, nor did I know where anything was. I angrily pushed everything aside, digging my hands deeper into the frigid wetness of my belongings. She tried to help dig in the tight pack. With her night vision, she would have been better than me at finding a lighter, but I nudged her aside and kept searching until I exclaimed, "Found it!"

I looked at her and noticed that I now had better night vision.

I cursed in a shivering voice as I realized that the misty fog had changed into a light snow. The flakes daintily drifted around us like white rose petals. I could almost feel the temperature plummet. However I felt the warmth of victory merely by holding up a cigarette lighter. With hands that pretty much refused to function, I flicked the soaked mechanism a few times before any sparks issued. It took about ten more strikes until a flame confidently arose like a summoned demon. We smiled at each other with the warmth of relief.

"Gather wood," she said, but I was already moving. She followed.

I picked up the heavier logs and she looked for the smaller wood. She wasn't slacking. She was an expert outdoorswoman and as knowledgeable about fire making as anyone. Far better than me, but in my miserable, driven state, I didn't consider that at the moment.

It was the smaller stuff that was the most important for kindling, not that heavier stuff that I was gathering, but my frozen mind wasn't functioning on all cylinders and I wanted to get the biggest chunks of wood that I could find. She wasn't any better at conscious thought, but her outdoors wisdom and instinct were superior to my own at this skill.

I was dragging a large wet log, grunting from the effort. Everything was soaked from the heavy misting fog that accumulated in the river valley like water in a vessel, and a layer of ice was forming over the wetness. I dropped the wood where we had been piling our firemaking material. It was in a small ravine that gave us the bare minimum of concealment.

I heard her moan, "This won't work."

"What?" I asked.

"Everything is not just damp. It's soaking wet," she said as she angrily threw down some dripping wet birch bark.

"Can you, like, break a branch to get to the dry wood?" I suggested in a freezing and shaky voice.

She glared at me for a moment and demanded with chattering teeth, "Give me the damn lighter."

Her cold, numbed fingers barely worked the mechanism of the lighters' wheel. I stared hopelessly through the falling snow. I shifted my stance and could feel the stiffness from ice forming on the outer layer of my coat. I watched her strike the cigarette lighter a few times without even getting a spark.

Impatiently, I grabbed it from her. Her eyes flared with vampiric fury as she watched my equally ineffective attempts.

"You're a big help," she said, not even trying to hide her sarcasm. I knew that she was right. She had spent far more time surviving in the wilderness than I had. She had years. I had weeks.

The realization that she was right in her sarcasm pissed me off even more than if she had been wrong. I tried a few more times and only achieved a weak flame from the lighter. I shakily held it to a small stick that I had whittled so the smaller flakes could catch. The flame would not catch.

"No! Hold the flame to the birch bark," she commanded. "It has chemicals that light even when wet."

As I moved the lighter, the flame went out. Then it wouldn't light at all despite my numb thumb spastically working at the wheel. I shook it and heard no lighter fluid splashing. The fuel was used up.

"You idiot!" she snapped through chattering teeth. "It's empty."

I swore and threw the lighter down. It popped harshly. As it exploded, tiny shards of plastic peppered my face.

I instantly looked at her letting her know that I screwed up but was in no mood to get scolded. "I have another lighter buried in my pack."

She said nothing but only glared at me with tightly compressed, bluing lips. I knew that Abigail tended to pack her gear meticulously and would have had a lighter and kindling with something extremely flammable like petroleum jelly worked into cotton balls in an easy to reach pocket of her backpack.

"What?" I asked.

"Nothing," she said.

"You should've kept your pack," I snapped.

"You should've drowned," she shot right back.

Her rebuke was so harsh and sharp in its delivery, yet I so deserved it that I couldn't help but snort a laugh.

She followed me as I stormed back to my pack. This time as I tried to dig through the wet contents, I scraped my numbed hands on the contents that were now starting to freeze on the edges. With numb hands I could barely feel anything that I grasped. I knew that I probably touched the lighter a few times without being able to feel it.

I heard her ragged breath behind me as I crouched desperately over my pack.

"I'm sorry, Abigail." I said as I continued my desperate rummage.

"Me too," she said.

"You did nothing wrong," I said.

"We're in this together. Let's calm down and not be so rash." she said back. "Stand up and face me, Eric."

I turned to her. It was slight, but I felt a wave of suspicion hit me because I knew she could be warmed by my fresh blood, but after looking in her clear eyes, I regretted that thought and I immediately hugged Abigail. Her arms reciprocated and pulled me tightly towards her. Somehow through the press of the freezing wet clothes, I could feel her warmth. I never wanted to let go of this woman as I felt my anger fired from my frustration and desperation melt like snowflakes in a campfire.

Still embraced, I pulled my head back to look at her. Her pale face glowed, framed by her frozen hair. In fact, only the deep pools of her eyes seemed liquid, warm, and untouched by frost.

"We're desperate, angry, panicked, near death," she said. "We're moving spastically. Let's slow down just a tad and do things right. Let's rethink."

Although there were vampires prowling the otherside of the river up the cliff, we did need to slow down and get a fire going or hypothermia would kill us quicker than our living enemies, but in my panicked and primal state, I wanted to tell her that her reasoning was stupid. We needed fire now. We had to rush. However she was correct.

I pulled her close and buried my face in her hair. I let my mind relax. I remembered a meditation where you focus on the senses that calmed one's nerves and helped a person's mind to work more fluidly under stress.

The first sense I noticed was the sense of touch. I was frozen to the point of numbness on the outside, and my bones ached horribly. I also felt a radiant heat that was probably more affection than actual warmth from Abigail's body. Her cheek against my cheek felt cold, but I could also feel human warmth under her cold layers of skin. I went to my peripheral sight and saw the vamipiress' hair and left ear and the dark shapes of the mountains over her shoulder as well as falling snow. I heard the river and our desperate breathing. I tasted blood and realized that I had bit the edge of my tongue when I struck the river after leaping from the cliff. Finally, I smelled the sweet scent of Abigail's hair washed fresh with the icy, spring fed river. I felt myself melt into her embrace a little more. There wasn't even a hint of romance as there had been in the past. This embrace went even deeper. It was an almost desperate hug of comfort in companionship and survival. I was ready to systematically try to start a fire with wet kindling and numb fingers. It seemed impossible, but we needed to succeed, and I now had hope, faith, and love on my side.

I tensed as I smelled something beyond the vampiress.

"What?" she asked.

"I smell fire. Smoke," I said through chattering teeth.

"No you don't," she said.

"Yes, I do."

It was very faint in the cold air, but I thought that it was close.

She pulled away and I watched her delicate nostrils flare, her capabilities for scenting human and animal blood far exceeded her ability to smell anything else. She made a face.

"What's wrong?" I asked.

"Humans. I don't want to get kicked out of a human camp again."

"We need to risk it. We're dying. We need heat, shelter within minutes. Besides, they could be vampires."

"No. Vampires don't sit around campfires at night. They-- we hunt at night."

I stepped away from her and said, "Let's find the camp. It can't be far."

She looked at me with worry.

"What?" I asked.

"I don't just smell smoke."

"What, then?"

"I smell blood, fresh, living blood." she admitted. "Your blood. The blood of the campers. After that plunge, I need rejuvenation. Also, those vampires really got in my head."

"Control yourself," I said.

She gave me a sharp look and said, "I will, but I just wanted you to know that there are a number of reasons why I dislike this situation."

"I am aware of that, but we need to survive. We need fire now." I turned and stiffly flung my heavy frozen pack on my shoulder. "Let's go."

"The campers might raise hell with us approaching this late at night," she warned.

I patted the rifle slung on my shoulder and said, "Well, I have a bit of a hellraiser myself."

I didn't mean to talk trash, but we both needed fire and shelter now, and as screwed up as it sounds, I was desperate enough to kill vampires or people to get it if either tried to repel us. We had minutes to get to a fire before hypothermia set in if it hadn't already.

She asked me through chattering teeth, "Would you be comfortable going into a camp of vampires for fire, were the situation reversed?"

"Yes. We have a choice, life or death. Fire or hypothermia."

"You're right," she said, understandably reluctant to encounter people, "Let's recon it first."

"Wise words," I said, having trouble making full sentences. It felt like my brain was freezing and getting more sluggish by the second. The blood in my arteries felt like a slush that was slowly freezing solid.

I turned and walked, following my nose, shivering and going to the smoke downstream with the vampiress reluctantly following me.

About a hundred yards downstream, I heard her say, "Eric, wait," as she ran to the stream.

She stepped through the rapidly forming ice on the calmer surface of the river, and reached down, struggling to pull her nearly waterlogged backpack that was snagged on a fallen tree. I went in the water and helped her drag it onto the shore from the knee deep water. She insisted on stashing it and her black vampire's cloak quickly under some beached driftwood. When it was concealed in a half assed manner, I again led the way to the campfire.

I rounded a bend and I felt hope fire up in my heart as I saw the shimmering red light on the rock cliff face from the flickering flames. It warmed me just to see the dancing red glow. It felt like home. I knew there may be hostile people around the fire, but my desire to warm my bones before hypothermia set in overrode that fear.

I crept around the rock face and saw that the source of the fire light emitted from a small cave. Although Abigail was usually my guide by night, I kept the lead because my eyes were better suited for looking into the brightness of the fire as well as dealing with other humans. I was afraid my chattering teeth would alert a guard.

I started to draw my sword. I looked back at Abigail to ensure that she had her sword in hand, but Abigail shook her head instead and I saw her black rifle held in her two hands, ready for action.

I nodded my head in agreement, quietly sheathing my sword and readying my own rifle. Usually firearms were weapons of last resort because the explosive noise attracted all abominations of modern pathology and could attract a full horde of zombies, not to mention the vampires on the cliff on the other side of the river. There was also an unwritten law to use fists first against fellow human survivors, then knives or any other quiet weapon. You didn't want to attract a horde to your fight. The fate of zombism was not a curse a person wished on even their worst enemy. Even murder was seen as moral in comparison. Also, there were no factories manufacturing new bullets. Bullets were worth more than gold. Although gold and silver were still valuable, a man with a loaded gun could take all he wanted from a defenseless miser. Firearms were already plentiful but useless without ammo. So bullets and long bladed weapons were indeed the most valuable currency in these wild lands, but I could barely feel my finger on the trigger and my feet felt like ice blocks in my boots. Stealth felt impossible.

I looked into the mouth of the cave and could feel the blast of the heat on my face and I gratefully breathed it in as I took in the sight. A total of six people were in the cave. Four adults and two kids. Five of them lay in a circle around the fire in peaceful slumber. A sixth person, a middle aged man, sat cross legged with a sword across his lap at the entrance. A rifle as well rested beside him as his head rested against the cave wall. I let out a breath when I saw that the guard was sound asleep.

Abigail stepped past me and walked quietly on the sandy floor at the mouth of the warm cave. As she reached for the sleeping guard's rifle, his eyes popped open. He grabbed her arm. I cautiously stepped forward. He looked at my rifle barrel pointed at his face. When he made eye contact with me, I shook my head, "No." I had one finger on the trigger and the pointer finger of my other hand over my lips.

He released Abigail's arm and she moved his rifle away from his reach. With the armed guard quietly subdued we looked around at the ones who were still in peaceful slumber while keeping one eye on the unarmed guard. He wanted to scream to warn his fellows, but I kept my firearm aimed at him.

In the cave, the two children, two women, and the other man were still asleep. One of the women and the man had long guns next to them. The other woman had a handgun near her head.

Abigail walked to the recumbent man and took his gun. She gently shook him and said in an equally gentle sing-song voice, "Wake up."

He opened his eyes sleepily and blinked a few times before his eyes popped open wide with panic. Waking up to seeing two armed people standing above you is the worst kind of wake up.

"What the hell?" he demanded.

I placed my foot on the rifle by one of the women as she awoke. She grabbed at it and then looked into my eyes with fear as I aimed my rifle at her face.

I started to reassure her when Abigail spoke up. She had a classy feminine voice. I found her words relieving my own stress as she said, "We mean you no harm but we fell in the river and we need your fire now or we will die. Now stay exactly as you are," she added glaring at the man who was laying down. He had his hands under him and was prepared to spring up.

"You could have just asked politely," said the guard who was now wide awake but showed no sign of resisting.

His calm demeanor did not soothe my nerves. I knew that being passive was either a sign of actual passivity or a complete act by a well trained fighter just before springing into action, and with a scar on his solid face, this man looked like a badass.

"We could've," I said with skepticism, "but as you can see, we're desperate for fire."

"You can go back to sleep," Abigail said sweetly, almost motherly. "As soon as our clothes are dry, we will leave. We want nothing from here other than warmth, and Eric and I apologize for the intrusion."

My lips pressed together when she used my real name rather than my alias, but I kept quiet. Neither of our minds were firing on all pistons.

"Put the guns down, and we'll believe you," said the guard, "and we will welcome you to share the fire."

As we considered his words, the guard said, "Rachael, don't."

I looked and saw Rachael was removing a handgun from her sleeping bag. Terror and confusion lit Rachael's face as she aimed at us. I felt like she didn't really want to kill us, but would if her child was in danger. I couldn't blame her getting startled awake, but I wasn't going to die of a bullet wound either.

Abigail brought the barrel of her firearm to point at Rachael's face. Despite the firearm in Rachael's hand, a child ran into Rachael's arms crying, "Mommy!"

I lowered my rifle and slowly pushed Abigail's gun down, but Abigail raised it back up at the woman. My eyes never left Rachael's as her gun was aimed at my face. She was now intent on killing us, but I couldn't shoot her with the child crouching in front of her. I pushed the barrel of Abigail's rifle down again.

Chapter Eight

"Eric," Abigail said in protest at me lowering my firearm. She was more on edge being around humans.

"They have kids here," I said, ignoring Rachael and her handgun that was pointed at my face as I looked at Abigail who brought her rifle back up to point at Rachael.

"They will be more protective, ready to kill to protect," she said.

I worried that Abigail was correct and that I was a fool. She had better instincts from two years surviving in the Forbidden Zone. I had only been here as a reporter for two weeks, but I slung the rifle over my shoulder and stepped to the fire, facing it to warm myself. I turned away from the armed woman who pointed her handgun at my back.

I said, "Rachael, you may keep your gun, just don't point it at us please. We just need the warmth of the fire and then we'll go. You have my word."

After a reluctant pause, Abigail lowered her rifle that was aimed at Rachael, slung it over her shoulder, and stepped up beside me with her hands over the fire.

From the corner of my eyes, I saw Rachael relax and then her eyes widened as she looked at the guard at the entrance of the cave. I followed her eyes and saw the guard pointing a handgun at us. Abigail glared at me. Her eyes seemed to tell me that we shouldn't have lowered our rifles.

"Please," I said to the group, "If we were bad, we would've killed you as your guard slept."

Despite the situation, I kept my hands over the fire. Through the cold numbness, I began to feel the welcomed pain as my fingers slowly began to warm and I didn't think I was capable of a quick draw anyway. Abigail was right, I shouldn't have slung the rifle over my shoulder, I worried as I tried to appear calm.

"Asleep! Damn it, Jerry," the other man cursed the guard. It seemed like sleeping on guard duty was a common occurrence for Jerry.

"I--" Jerry stammered. "I wasn't asleep, Richard."

"Put your gun down, Jer. Just keep it handy. I think they are OK," Rachael said.

"Why did you sneak up on us, if you mean well?" asked Jerry.

I guessed he was being the hard ass from the embarrassment of getting caught napping.

So I said, "If you're pointing your gun at us after we lowered ours, it tells me that there was nothing we could do to get on your good side and as you can see by our frozen, wet clothes, we needed the fire immediately. We're desperate."

Jerry held his gun aimed at me for another few tense seconds before sighing and lowering it.

I said, "We'll pay for this hospitality. We have food. Heck we'll even stand guard with you."

"How did you end up taking a swim this time of night?" The man, Richard, who had been sleeping by the fire asked. He was standing up now and looked outside the cave and scowled when he saw some snowflakes blow inside and melt over the fire. "I am Richard, by-the-way," he added as he picked up his rifle in a nonthreatening manner.

I looked at Abigail. She had a flash of sadness flash over her eyes. Richard was the name of her vampiric father by the bite. He had given his life trying to save her when we escaped from Craigsville. He had loved her as if she was his daughter. Vampires had that familial love for those they had turned, and Abigail had given her vampiric father nothing but scorn. It wasn't until after he was gone that she realized his true paternal love for her, and I knew she suffered the regret.

Abigail answered Richard, "A horde of those failed--" she caught herself using a term only used in vampiric social circles, "zombie like vampires chased us off the cliff. I, uh, couldn't see in the dark well, but we guessed there were easily a dozen of them. We had nowhere else to go but off the cliff and into the river."

I could tell she was minimizing their numbers so as not to alarm the people.

I finished by saying, "By the sounds of their screams, we guessed how many there were. We were very fortunate to have landed in that deep pool."

Richard whistled, "That cliff's at least seventy feet high. I'd be reluctant to jump off of that during broad daylight in summer. How could you even see the river below in the dark?"

"The Lord was watching us," I said, hoping that I sounded sincere.

I was sincere, but before entering the Forbidden Zone, I saw no reason to rely on a force beyond me. Although I found myself praying more now, I still felt like a hypocrite whenever I expressed such sentiment because I had thought it had sounded foolish and sappy when others would use it in my prior life in the Safe Zone.

"Amen," Rachael answered.

That response prompted me to say a silent prayer of thanks. I also vowed to say the Our Father as a legit prayer from now on rather than an incantation.

We made quick introductions and I learned that the other woman was named Christy. The two little girls were about seven or eight. Melanie belonged to Rachael and Richard. Susan belonged to Jerry and Christy.

We talked a bit over the next half hour. Although they were relaxed, after the silent stand off, the adrenaline was too amped up to immediately go back to sleep. When our relations warmed as much as our bodies, they welcomed us to spend the night. We agreed. After Abigail agreed to share the next watch with Rachael, she went out to grab her backpack and black hooded vampire's cloak. As she left, I prepared an area for the two of us to sleep.

I noticed that Richard gave me an odd look when Abigail went out into the night by herself. There was grim judgment in his eyes at me for staying behind to lay out our bedding. I wanted to say to him, "If you only knew," but I kept my thoughts to myself.

Abigail came back and we began to lay out or hang our soaken belongings to dry. Abigail was careful not to fully unfurl her cloak to give herself away as a vampire. It just looked like a black blanket. Richard looked at her cloak and then looked away. He then looked at me and asked,

"Did you lead the vampires here?"

"No," I replied with fake confidence. "They may have been stupid, but only a few followed us off the bluffs. We killed the few who followed us into the river."

Richard then looked directly at Abigal as he tapped his fingers on his rifle's trigger guard and asked, "And you young lady." Abigail looked at him as he paused before asking, "How long have you been a vampire?"

I paused for a moment as I tried to determine if I could draw my handgun from my appendix holster and shoot before he responded with his rifle that sat in his lap.

***

He was becoming a night owl. That's when all the action happened in the Forbidden Zone.

As Tommy looked at the recent video of Eric's fight and plummet into the river, his cell phone buzzed. He flinched when he saw that it was Don Renton/The Specter on the other end. Tommy instinctively rubbed his nose that he suspected might be broken from the big man's fist.

Tommy answered his phone. He did his best to sound nonchalant, despite the beating that the big man had given him on their last meeting when he said, "How's it going, Mr. Renton?"

"Where are they?" It sounded like a growl from a lion protecting his den and cubs before a savage pounce on an intruder.

Tommy tried to sound innocent, but he feared some glee crept into his voice, "Are you talking about King Sadazar and his brood? Have you figured out how to kill them yet?"

Don screamed at him, "You know who I want! Eric! Abigail! Where are they?"

Tommy had to hold the phone a few feet from his ear, but could hear every syllable of the screamed demand. Over the phone, that was the severity of the lion's pounce. He was grateful the big man was far away at the moment.

"The Southern Appalachian Mountains," Tommy replied, keeping the smile from his face to keep the glee from his voice when he gave the vague location. He knew that Don was still fuming over Eric punching him out for a second time.

"Keep it up and I'll pay you a visit, again, Laurens."

Tommy lied, "I am getting choppy video feeds. I can't find them and there is a heavy winter storm over their area, and I can't locate where the inconsistent video is coming from, but I haven't seen them yet. The drones are not functioning and they can't fly in the wind."

"Liar!"

Tommy blew out a pent up breath and said forcefully with the bravado of being separated from the man monster, "Your job is to seek the destruction of King Sadazar, not to settle your personal score."

There was a pause, a calm before the storm, and Tommy held the phone far from his ear as he anticipated the release.

But it wasn't a scream, more of a grinding explanation to a wayward toddler, "For one, my job is none of your damn business, Laurens, and two, it's to keep a semblance of peace in the Forbidden Zone. I can't get to King Sadazar at present, but I can end the threat that your friend poses. Where is he?"

Tommy replied, "I told you already: In the Southern Appalachia region–"

Don shot right back, "Dammit, Laurens!"

Tommy couldn't help but taunt now. He may regret it later but he let loose as he continued to lie, "I can't locate their position, but currently, Abigail and Eric are squaring off against King Sadazar's brood. If you're patient, they may accomplish what you are too chicken shit to do yourself!" Tommy left out a lot, especially the part of their escape off the cliff.

There was a crashing sound and the line went dead. Tommy would probably pay later, but he didn't care, for the moment, as he gently and spitefully rubbed the bridge of his painful nose.

"Jackass," Tommy muttered as he set the phone down and watched Eric's video feed from his body cams. It looked like there was about to be a shootout in the cave with the people. They knew that Abigail was a vampire. Tommy worried that the people in the cave would accomplish what Don couldn't.

Chapter Nine

Abigail and I stared at Richard for a moment unable to answer. Everyone had their fingers on the triggers and butts of their firearms. I never thought that I would be in a situation where I'd be willing to take a human life in defense of a vampire, but here I was.

The children eyed Abigail with uncertainty, but not the abject terror that I would have expected. Either they didn't think she was really a vampire or they had seen their parents handle vampires rather easily in a deadly manner.

I flicked my pupils in Abigail's direction. I was beginning to be able to tell the difference between people and vampires at a glance. There are subtle differences, but I couldn't see anything about her that would have betrayed her nature to an untrained eye other than her cloak that she had kept half folded so that it only looked like a damp blanket. Both of us were pale from our swim and Abigail's lips weren't overly blueish. Thanks to the fire, they were red again from warming up. However, Richard seemed to know for certain.

Abigail did not try to lie, instead she asked, "Why do you suspect that of me?"

"You avoid looking directly into the fire, which is a good trait of a woodswoman. However, I can tell that you can see into the dark recesses of the cave and out into the night. Also, I know chivalry was dying before it all went down, but Eric was perfectly comfortable sending you into the night alone to get your backpack. Don't get me wrong, I can tell he's courageous, but I can also see that you are far more comfortable out there in the dark than he is. You also are happy to continue staying awake for the next watch while any sane human is ready to sleep, especially after a winter swim."

"You act like the Queen of the Night," Rachael summed it up as she ruefully laughed.

The tension stretched the very seconds that passed. Fingers caressed the triggers of our firearms as our eyes shifted from one person to another and then back to the vampiress. No one wanted to make the first move, but no one wanted to be the last to shoot if a gunfight erupted.

Little Melanie ran into Rachael's arms and asked, "Mommy, is that a good vampire or a bad one?"

Abigail instantly relaxed and asked, "You know of other good vampires?"

Richard relaxed as well and said, "Yes and I can see that you are a good one."

"How so?" Abigail asked.

"You basically referred to yourself as one just now, and I assume only a good one would do that. Besides, your boyfriend is as healthy as anyone I have seen, maybe better. A bad vampire would've drained him of blood, energy, health, anything. Instead, I see you have helped him as he helps you." Richard said.

Before I could instinctively deny that we were boyfriend/girlfriend, Abigail asked with eyes bright with optimism, "You mentioned good ones. Who do you know who is a good vampire?"

It was odd. I felt a twinge of jealousy at her desire to find other vampires. Intellectually, I knew we would eventually have to go our own ways, but damn, I didn't want that day to come.

Richard laughed as if setting up for a lengthy monologue. I could tell that he was long winded and that usually annoyed me. However, I was tired and content to just sit quietly by the fire and listen as he said, "I know you don't know every vampire. I'm not sure how many of you exist. You guys tend to stay out past my bedtime."

"So you know a vampire personally? Who?" I quickly interrupted to get him to the point despite being willing to listen just a few seconds earlier.

He scowled at the interruption and said, "Yes. There is a friend of ours. His name is Brandon, and he is a vampire. We have a good relationship with him. He keeps an eye on our cave at night as he hunts wild game, drinks the blood, and leaves us the carcass to eat. Then he sleeps in the back of the cave while we protect him during the day. It's a great symbiotic relationship. Symbiotic means mutually beneficial such as–

"Yes, I know what that means," I said.

I looked at Abigail and saw that she was tearing up slightly. I immediately felt guilty for that twinge of jealousy. I had no right to feel that way.

"What is it, little lady?" Richard asked.

"Brandon was a good vampire. A great man." Abigail said.

"Was?" Richard prompted.

Abigail nodded sadly, "We found him dead. Killed by other vampires. The same ones that Eric and I faced this evening."

I looked around and saw sadness on the faces of everyone in the cave. The two little girls began to tear up. The men and women swore bitterly. It wasn't just symbiosis but rather an actual friendship. It did bring me hope. I had thought that Abigail was the only decent vampire alive. I was always skeptical about trying to form an alliance with any other one of them but her. I sighed ruefully at the loss of Brandon. I really wished that I had known him before Sadazar's clan defiled him.

"Damn! What happened?" asked Richard with a softer voice.

Abigail was about to respond, but stopped, placing a finger over her full lips as she looked out the mouth of the cave. Her eyes widened with worry.

"What?" Richard asked with a worried hiss.

Abigail clenched her lips and glared at him as she whispered, "We have visitors outside."

I shuddered as I saw a dark form appear at the edge of the light at the mouth of the cave. It peeked around the edge of the opening. The black maw of its hood was turned down in fear of the firelight and its features were completely hidden in darkness. Seeing a faceless hooded maw unnerved me more than seeing its monstrous face. Its appearance reeked of the forbidden unknown.

"Hello friends, fellow human," the form said in a guttural and stupid voice, that was also bright with false cheer.

"Don't invite him inside," Abigail whispered. "It may not stop them from charging, but maintaining a threshold will cut their psychic power over us."

Richard nodded to her and addressed the vampire. "Hello. What do you want?"

"We, I mean, I– I am harmless, simple human, alone, unarmed, harmless traveler wish to share fire with fellow human, friend. May we, I mean, I come in alone?"

Richard laughed. "No, we're crowded and well armed."

The others in the cave chuckled as well. They could take on a lone vampire with their firepower. Everyone already had a firearm in his or her hands. The stupid vampires tended not to know how to use a gun and rarely a blade, but rather, they relied simply on savage bloodlust driven power, and the vampire outside the cave was obviously a very stupid one and although his tone wouldn't win him a welcome, it did give the people a sense of false security. The campers seemed hopeful that he would just wander off and find an easier source of blood. It was nice to see that not all people were prone to wantonly kill vampires.

Abigail however bit her lower lip, keeping her fangs hidden. Only her front even, humanlike incisors showed. Either she could see, smell, or just knew that there were far more than just a few vampires.

The failed vampire persisted. "Put down guns. I harmless, unarmed, and lonely, human, like you. As I say, I am alone– lonely fellow human. Let me in. I will give you all the food you need. Just invite me in, fellow humans."

"No. We already have food," said Richard.

"Beer," the vampire said and added, "all beer all you can drink."

The people laughed but their fingers wrapped tighter around their triggers. "Go away," Richard said with a laugh that was now becoming tinged with annoyance.

"I have all the money you want. Gold. I give it to you for some friendship. I lonely, harmless human, like you. Invite please," the vampire persisted. After a pause, he said, "All the weapons and bullets you want, I give to you, human."

"Weapons? You said you were harmless and unarmed," Jerry said with an edge hardening his voice.

"Dammit!" "Idiot!" a few other vampires hissed outside the cave.

"Shut up! They hear you," the first vampire hissed back at his fellows and then spoke into the cave again. "Please humans, let us– me in. I have food. All the food--" The black hooded form began to say but was cut off by a hissed whisper from another vampire hidden by the rock wall of the cave. There were at least three other vampires outside that we could hear, seeking entry into the cave

"Idiot. You said food already," a fourth vampire scolded.

"Dang it," said the first black form.

"Tell them you have girls. Tell them you have girls," another scolding vampire advised in a hiss. "All men like girls."

"We– I have girls. Sexy, willing girls. I can offer the men," the vampire said.

"The men are married already," Christy retorted.

Christy had been the quietest of the group. She had not laughed at the vampire like the others and could not conceal her annoyance anymore. She was not really scared. She was ready to kill the intruder. She readied her rifle with the butt against her shoulder, and the rest of us followed her lead.

I could hear the vampires argue amongst themselves in harsh hissy whispers about their next ploy.

We, in the cave, were now all on our feet, ready for war. However Richard and Jerry still laughed as if they expected to just shoot a few idiot vamps. They sorely underestimated their foes. I would have joined in their laughter at how stupid our adversaries sounded, but the horror that had slowly spread across Abigail's face told me that she knew something we didn't. I was hoping that we were dealing with a few stragglers. I didn't think the whole horde would scale down the cliff and try to cross the cold, violent, and swollen river. They were legion in number and the one at the door appeared dry. They must have crossed by using a bridge. I felt guilty for leading them to the family, but I had no time to dwell on that.

Abigail suddenly sprang into action pointing towards the mouth of the cave. She ordered in a quiet but urgent voice, "Quick! Move the fire to the narrow opening, and make the fire bigger. It will keep them out, for now. They are about to rush and there are a lot of them."

The people looked at her with confusion. She would have done it herself, but with her vampiric sensitivities to light and fire, she could not get as close to the fire as we could.

She almost growled through her clenched teeth as she said, "I can see literally dozens crawling outside in the darkness. I know there are many more. I can smell them. They are massing for an attack. Build the fire brighter, push it in the narrow opening, and it will keep them out," she said confidently, but added in a softer worried voice, "Until they decide to really attack as daylight nears."

I was already moving the fire towards the opening, gingerly pulling the burning logs by the unburned ends.

The vampires at the opening seemed to pierce my ear with inhuman shrieks as they saw that we were preparing for a fight. It was obvious that they had given up on talking and were preparing to violently attack us for our blood.

"Go ahead and come in, you vampiric bastard. We will warm you up with lead," Richard screamed back at them.

I cocked my rifle with a slide of the charging handle and caught the already chambered bullet and let the bolt slide home with a noisy effect. Bryan had taught me that sometimes the sound of a gun's action said as much as an actual gunshot, but you didn't have to waste a bullet.

I was hoping that working the slide would scare them away, but it had the opposite effect. The vampires screamed hideously and charged in a mass of black of flapping cloaks. There were dozens attempting to breach the narrow opening at once. They wedged into each other making easy targets in the confines of the mouth of the cave. I felt like I was suddenly deaf as gunfire exploded in the tight confines of the cave as the campers opened up. I was blessed not to catch a bullet in the back as I heard the fiery rounds scream past my ear from the blazing guns behind me. With the realization of the vampires' numbers, the campers were nearing panic.

I immediately dropped to the sandy ground of the cave's floor like a moth dodging a bat's radar, and aimed my firearm from the cave's floor and fired, but the vampires retreated leaving their dead and the screaming wounded vampires in their panicked wake. I scored a headshot at a vampire who was running away. Yes, a head or a heart shot kills them. Anything else and they have an uncanny way of healing, although it may take a few days of them holing up and licking their wounds like dogs.

Jerry dispatched a few of the wounded who had made it in the cave with his sword.

"Add more wood like Abigail said," I ordered. "Get a big blaze going to keep them out."

The campers stood there watching me, so I acted on my own orders and tossed more logs on the growing inferno.

Rachael said worriedly, "We don't have enough wood to make it to morning at this rate."

Abigail hissed, "Don't let them hear of our weakness."

I was trying to form a plan and I told her, "Rachael, say it louder."

"What?" she asked.

We had about five hours of night left and probably two hours worth of wood if we burned it bright enough to keep those creeps from charging us.

So I shouted loud enough for the vampires to hear, "Go easy on the wood! We have less than an hour's worth left to fuel a fire this bright!"

Everyone looked at me with surprise. Richard looked at our wood supply and I could tell he was planning on giving me an exact estimate on the exact number of hours, minutes and probably even seconds left of the fire.

I then said loud enough for only those around me to hear, "They will probably hold off from attacking for another hour. In the meantime, we need a plan, either we sharpen punji sticks to stop a full charge or figure an escape route, or something. We won't make it to morning anyway unless we do something drastically different. Now!"

Immediately after I said it, I realized that the stakes would have to come from our already limited firewood.

"I got a working truck hidden in a shed up on this ridge, above us," said Jerry.

"A lot of good that does us here!" Rachael scolded.

I held a finger up to silence her. "Any boats or canoes on the river?"

They looked at me like I was an idiot.

"Faileds don't swim well," I said, not knowing if it was true or not but assuming. I also didn't account for the fact we'd have to fight our way to the crafts and continue to fight as we launched into the rapids at night.

Abigail didn't say anything, but by the look on her face, I knew that it was a very stupid suggestion on my part.

"How far back does this cave go?" I asked when I took their silence for lack of canoes and realized that would not have been a good option anyway, but I was grasping for some means of escape or victory, and trying to trigger them into thinking of a plan as well. "Can we get out through a different passage?"

"This cave dead ends." Abigail said. Her nocturnal eyes could see through the darkness that gathered in the deep corners of the cave that were only impenetrable darkness for me. She stood far from the fire toward the back of the cave. I could tell that the newly stoked, blazing fire was far too bright for her.

The others agreed. As they did, I realized that I felt no breeze from the back of the cave. However there was one going up to the ceiling above the place where the fire originally burned.

I then looked up at the crack in the ceiling that had acted as a natural chimney until we moved the fire closer to the mouth. The natural chimney was about three feet wide in diameter. However with the fire moved to the front, most of the smoke now blew out the mouth of the cave towards the vampires. The chimney looked big enough for me to climb up if given a boost. The opening was less than eight feet above the cave's floor, and I knew that the vampires outside could not see us past the bright blaze of the fire, if we were to climb it..

"Where does this natural chimney go?" I asked.

"Up there," Richard said in a smart assed tone.

I glared at him.

He explained, "Seriously, that's all I know. I also can just look up there and tell you that none of us can climb it."

"I can," I said with more confidence than I actually felt, "And then we can get to Jerry's truck."

I had taken a rock climbing course in college. Although I was out of practice and not in as good rock climbing shape as I had been back in the day, the climb looked doable. However, the exercise regimen of Mountain Warriors gave me some extra confidence that I could still scale it.

"So you get away and save your own ass, but what about us?" Richard demanded.

"Gonna call the cops?" asked Rachael. "I'm telling you, there's no cavalry gonna save us. Rescuers are fables these days and vampires are real."

"Then you are lucky to know me, because I will save your ass, and haul you all up," I said. I pulled a rope from my pack.

Richard sneered, "That's just 550 parachute cord."

"So? It's rope." I asked.

"No. It's not rope. It's cord, and that's not NFPA approved for rescue," he retorted. When I looked at him with irritation, he mistook it for ignorance. Richard added, "The NFPA rates rescue equipment! That's the National Fire Protection--"

"I am sure they would rate it potentially strong enough to use incase of a vampire attack, idiot," I said in a sudden rage. The warming of the fire brought back the intensity that had raged through my blood when I battled the vampires not long ago.

Richard stepped to my face, angered by my insult. That set me off, and I grabbed him by the collar and slammed him against the rock wall. It took the fire out of him.

I quietly growled in his face so the vampires wouldn't hear the plan, "I am going up that chute. A rope, a cord, whatever the hell you wanna call it will be lowered. Anyone who wants to escape with me, can. I entrust you to tie a knot approved by the NPAF--"

"That's NFPA--" he started to correct.

"Shut up and give me a boost when I am ready," I said as I let go of his collar and put on my still damp gloves.

I quickly shoved the drying but still slightly damp clothes into my backpack and as I worked I told them the number of tugs that would work as our code back and forth along the rope. I slung my pack over my shoulder. I probably should have left it behind, but I was just thinking about getting the hell out of there.

Richard's face was grim, still smarting from my insult, but he laced his fingers together so that his hands resembled a hammock. I stepped into them and he lifted me up with Jerry's and Abigail's assistance pushing on my booted feet and buttocks. I grasped the opening of the chute and my wet gloves sizzled very slightly on the hot stone of the natural chimney. I irritably thought of Richard telling us that the cave needed a more efficient insulation for the ceiling than rock, but pulled myself up instead of dwelling on it. My muscles were still stiff from my unplanned swim, but through the pain, it felt good to use them.

I climbed a few feet and the sizzling of the gloves slowed with each foot that I ascended, but now I was starting to feel the burn finally seeping through. The climbing was fast as I had decent hand holds on each side of me, but I worried if I could keep climbing the heated stones of the natural chimney as my hands were pained from the heat that burned through the wet gloves. Even worse the water turned to steam and really stung, but I had no choice. I scrambled upward as quickly as I could and found to my relief that the stone rapidly cooled because of the cold weather so that I could climb without the gloves, but I kept them on my hands with the realization that the rock would quickly freeze my hands the closer I got to the surface at the top. I was hoping it wasn't much higher because I was running out of rope to lower.

I finally reached the upper opening, pulled myself out, and looked around. I was on a knob overlooking the river from fifty feet above. A half inch of snow covered the ground and its white patina brightened the dismal night. More snow continued to sprinkle down upon me. A steep, but noticeable path disappeared into the mountain towering above me. The lay of the land above me was almost as steep as a cliff. It would be dangerous for a fighting retreat on snow slick paths in the dark of night.

As for the vampiric enemies, I saw nothing but shadows in the cloudless night and wished that Abigail was up here with me with her night vision. I gave another quick look and tried to remember the positions of the shadows for future reference to keep tabs whether they moved or not. The black cloaks of the vampires could deceptively appear as boulders that turned into sudden phantoms, but in this snow, I was sure they would stand out. However, I had yet to see a vampire in the blowing blizzard on this dark night. I also thought I would hear them scream if I was spotted, but vampires weren't always predictable, especially the failed.

I then tied off the rope to a sturdy tree with a diameter of four inches and sent it down tied to a rock for added drop weight until I felt the campers tug back to signal that the rope was in their hands. I tugged three times to signal back. I felt three distinct tugs signaling that they were tying someone. I went back to my watch for night creeps.

I kept my hands on the rope until I felt two distinct tugs in reply, and began to pull. I did it slowly to allow the person to climb so as not to put too much tension on the cord. Richard was right. The rope was not designed for this purpose, and yes, I called it rope, not cord, but technically he was right. I also kept the rope away from the rock ledge to try to limit the fraying. I was surprised at the heaviness of the person at the other end, believing that they would send the children up first.

I hoped that it wasn't Richard. I didn't want to stand on the ledge with him critiquing everything that I did as we raised the others. I was afraid that I would probably throw him back down the chimney and that wouldn't set well with my conscience when I finally calmed down, but I was on edge and wanted nothing more than to get to the truck and split the hell out of Dodge.

After a minute, Jerry's bearded face appeared in the opening. I offered my hand, he took it, and I pulled him up.

"Thanks, brother," he said in a volume that was conversational rather than stealthy.

"Shh," I hissed. "I was expecting to see the kids first," I whispered as he untied himself.

It looked like Richard used a rope of his own to act as a harness. He had looped it around Jerry's crotch, waist, and shoulders, and the well tied knots were easy to undo. As annoying as I found Richard to be, I was impressed with the skill that he used to tie it around Jerry. The makeshift harness actually looked comfortable. The ropes didn't dig into Jerry's crotch too harshly.

Jerry replied quieter than his original greeting, "No offense man, but we just met you and you hang out with a vampiress. We wanted a few adults from our group up here first before sending the kids."

I couldn't take offense at his caution, so I just nodded back, and continued our operation.

Christy ascended next and then the two kids. Rachael appeared the fifth time the rope was raised and I was filled with more and more optimism. Each time that I brought someone new up, I instructed them to be quiet and stay down so as not to give our positions away.

I was hoping that Abigail would come up next, but when I felt a dead weight, I knew it was a backpack. I quickly raised the rest of the baggage, getting more and more irritated. Yes, leaving behind belongings full of life saving gear would put us at an inconvenience, but, we really needed to get to the truck before the vampires figured things out. Even if they weren't that bright, some of them were probably roving these hills. With hundreds of them wandering around, regardless of them being faileds, it was a matter of time before they stumbled upon us. Where they lacked in intelligence, they more than made up with sense of smell, night vision, and who knew what other advantages besides sheer numbers.

Finally, I felt the tugs. This was the quickest the harness had been tied. I guessed it was Abigail and she didn't have the patience for Richard's precision. I could also tell it was her by her weight and she climbed like a monkey up the chimney. I could barely keep up with raising the rope.

I was so grateful to see her pretty face peek up at me from the slit in the rock. She wore her black hooded cloak, "Little Black Riding Hood never looked so good," I whispered.

"Thanks," she whispered back as I offered my hand and pulled her up. "It's good to get away from that blowhard."

I noticed that the knot wasn't the professionally tied knot that Richard had used on the others.

"How did you get away with tying it like that?" I asked as I untied her.

"I did it myself," she said.

"How did Richard let you get away with that?" I asked.

She rolled her eyes and said in a calm, ladylike voice, "I bared my fangs and growled at him rather savagely. He shut up."

I smiled as I said, "You do look fierce when you act angry."

"Trust me," she said with an exasperated sigh, "I did not have to act at all."

She looked at me with a sexy half smile as I laughed quietly and lowered the rope.

I felt the tugs and began to pull. I felt a sudden thrashing and heard terrified screaming down the chimney.

I pulled with everything that I had. Richard was barely climbing. It almost felt like he was fighting me. I worried that he was being pulled back down by the vampires.

"Help," I hissed.

Abigail and Jerry helped me pull the rope up. With each thrash that Richard made, I feared that the line would snap. Although the cord was designed to hold 550 lbs, that was for dead weight. Although I didn't know the stats, I knew that the working rating was much much lower than the static 550 lbs, and less than Richard's weight.

I heard Richard's daughter behind me plead, "Daddy! Please God, help my dad. Don't drop him Eric. Please."

That drove my determination to bring him up alive more than any other form of motivation possible. However, I worried about his appearance, whether I should have the child's mother shield her eyes in the case that a vampire was ripping Richard apart when he appeared. I guessed it had to be a brutal attack the way he screamed and thrashed as we pulled him up the chute.

"He needs to shut the hell up," Abigail said through gritted teeth. Her eyes peered away from the chimney, scanning the snowy darkness. "The vampires across the river are taking notice of his screams as he nears the top."

"Can they see us?" I asked, looking in the same direction, but only seeing shadows on the black and snowy white bulk of the cliff.

"No," she said. Then after a pause she swore in a tone that bespoke hopelessness.

Before I could ask her what she saw, I heard the ear splitting howling shriek of a vampire spotting its prey answered by dozens of others. The sound was high above us.

"They found the truck, not us. Somehow they guessed our plans," Abigail said and then let go of the rope and added in a harsh whispered order, "Rachael! Help Eric pull him up, I'll stand guard."

The screams of the vampires communicating echoed all around us. It was eerie, but it also thankfully covered Richard's screaming to a degree.

As soon as Rachael had her hands on the rope, Abigail drew her sword and leapt down the trail. Her sword arced down in a flash. I didn't see what she was swinging at until the blade bit deep into a shadow that seemed to solidify from the very night air. I heard the distinct sounds of a body flopping and a head thunking to the ground.

Abigail attacked two more shadows, their dying screams, louder than Richard's oaths, brought cries from the children.

Another form loomed over Abigail, easily a foot taller than her. It stood just out of her sword reach. It spoke calmly in a resonant masculine voice. "Sister, put down weapon and share cattle with us--"

She leapt like a panther. The leap itself chambered her sword and she cleft the giant vampire's head. She then lowered her sword and scanned the valley below with a warning. "Hurry. This was a small group separated from the main contingent. We can't hold them off forever, and shut Richard up."

Jerry grunted with the strain of the rope. He quietly said in my ear with admiration of Abigail, "Brother, you sure know how to pick 'em. That's a hell of a woman."

"Keep pulling," I said to Rachael and Jerry as I saw Richard's panicked face appear below us. I pulled my hand gun and aimed it slightly behind his head to shoot any of the vampires who would be climbing behind and attacking him. "Quit yelling!" I ordered Richard quietly but harshly through gritted teeth.

His panicked eyes met mine and he commanded me, "Don't point that damned gun at me."

"I'm pointing it at the vampires attacking you," I rasped.

"What vampires?" he asked, looking beneath him with panic.

"What were you screaming and thrashing about?" I asked.

"I am afraid of heights and enclosed spaces. Those phobias are called--"

"Get your ass up here!" I hissed through gritted teeth in a rage brought on by relief that he wasn't being attacked. I grabbed his arm and yanked him out of the hole.

"Careful. My shoulder dislocates easily," Richard warned.

"Shut up!" I growled through clenched teeth and pulled him up by his coat collar behind his neck.

Abigail stood guard with her sword at the ready and said sharply, "Get him untied and we need to move like yesterday. We may be screwed anyway!"

I holstered my handgun and started at a knot. Richard interrupted me and said. "You've been untying the wrong knot on this harness. Next time untie this one." He then started to tie what he thought was the correct knot to educate me.

His eyes widened as I suddenly drew my sword and sliced through his harness. Deep inside I wanted to slice deeper. Instead, I grabbed his collar with one hand and ordered through gritted teeth, "Shut the hell up and arm yourself!"

He pulled a firearm but Abigail said, "No firearms. Use swords or machetes."

"Why, they know we are here. No sense hiding. Besides, we're driving out of here," Jerry said.

"Most of them still think that we are in the cave, for now," Abigail said. "I don't think that anyone else knows we escaped other than the ones I killed. They have been hearing his screams channeled through the cave below."

"How do you know?" I asked her.

"There are no other screams from our enemies on the hillside other than up by the truck," she said. "If they knew we were here, we'd know it."

"They've been screaming all night," said Christy.

Abigail said, "That's normal for them on the hunt. If they knew where we were, we'd hear a cacophony of triumphant shrieks from all around us. The tone would be noticeably different."

We heard a distant shriek high above us. It was answered by a few others and then suddenly the cacophony was deafening. It seemed that the entire lower portion of the mountain was moving like a fluttering black flag against the white of the snow covered hill. I knew that that was the coven charging uphill to find us. The tone wasn't triumphant. It was the frustrated cry of the damned who realized that they had been fooled.

An even more frustrated wailing sound echoed up the chimney and seemed to split my eardrums. Whoever screamed then yelled, "Ab-by-gail!"

"Well they know we're out of the cave," Abigail said as she peered into the dark seeing what we couldn't. "but not exactly where we are, for now. I think that was Jim who screamed my name."

"You're on a first name basis with them?" Richard asked.

Abigail glared at him and said, "Let's go!"

Chapter Ten

Jim had gathered at the mouth of the cave with the hundreds in his coven. The intense fire blinded him and burned the skin of his hands and face even at a distance of twenty five feet. He couldn't imagine how Abigail could sit in the cave with the intense light. Not to mention going insane from scent and the thundering pulse of arterial blood in the humans around her. Jim didn't know what haunted him more, the smell, the taste or the sound of a heart's blood beats.

For Jim, he was almost driven to madness with the scent of humans. He wanted to rush into the deadly fire and barely restrained himself. But even more, he could also smell the sweet vampiress scent of Abigail, which drove him nearly crazy for another reason. She would be a great mate once she was infected with King Sadazar's bloodline virus, which would bring her mind up to his. As she was now, she was inferior, but King Sadazar would change her for the better.

Jim knew that Abigail seemed more intelligent than him, but that was surface and fake. Her overactive mind was only rebellious. Once she was a minion of King Sadazar in his coven, her mind would be linked to the King's and to Jim's, and King Sadazar was the smartest man and vampire in the world. So, like Jim, Abigail too would be one of the smartest in the world strictly because King Sadazar's mind would work through her.

From twenty five feet from the cavern's mouth, Jim forced himself to peer inside with squinted eyes. It still hurt his eyeballs and brain. He wondered what the humans were up to in the cave, but he could see nothing but the inferno at the front of the cave. It was like trying to stare at something on the opposite side of the sun.

"Ab-by-gail," he chanted, but he knew the threshold of the cave slightly protected her from his mind.

He wanted her. He tried to sense if she was in danger surrounded by humans. He sensed no danger, but it could not be good being surrounded by enemy people behind the inferno. Eric must have psychic control over her, he reasoned. There was no other explanation for why she rebuffed Jim's offer to join with her brethren and be his wife. King Sadazar's Coven had everything a vampire could desire. Jim had never experienced true happiness until he was a vampire in the King's coven. At least that is what King Sadazar had told Jim, and Jim always believed what the King told him.

Jim stepped away from the blast of light and studied the hill above the cave. The humans may be up to something. They couldn't have enough wood to sustain a fire that big. They also stopped shooting out of the cave.

He racked his brain, "What could humans be up to?"

Then it dawned on him. He mumbled to himself, "If way in, maybe other way out."

He looked at the hill above him and saw a few of his brethren crawling on the hill. Like cockroaches, he thought. Jim had hated cockroaches before King Sadazar changed him into a vampire. Now he liked his fellow creatures of the dark. He loved his brethren in King

Sadazar's coven. Like cockroaches, vampires were survivors. Hated by humans. Loved by the King of Kings. King Sadazar. He could not even think of the name of his master without applying the title of King first.

Those vampires on the hill above were considered the stupidest by others outside the King's Coven. Most of them couldn't speak or follow orders. They only followed Jim's psychic control and ultimately, King Sadazar. They hunted for blood, but sometimes they were the smartest. They instinctively knew where to go.

Humans must be up there, Jim thought. That's where they went.

But how humans get there? He wondered.

As he looked above, the smell of humans reached him. His vampiric nose sensed that the scent came from higher up the hill and was not wafting through the smoke. The humans must have gone out the back of the cave. Abigail's sweet scent too was up. Up above.

He heard a shriek of a coven member at the top of the hill. It was one of those who couldn't articulate speech, only scream. Instantly Jim received a vision through its eyes. He jumped from vampire mind to mind, seeing nothing but snow covered hills. He went to another vampire's mind and Jim clearly saw the truck that the humans wanted to escape in. That was what the warning cry was about. He needed to get his coven to the truck to ambush the humans. He sent some of the soldier vampires who were capable enough to handle complex weapons like swords and firearms up there, with the orders not to shoot unless necessary. They needed beating hearts. Trying to extract blood from a dead human was hard. No blood flow. The humans had to be alive.

He watched as other vampires around him arrived with discarded bottles and cans that lined the river. Jim realized that they were filled with river water. His coven began to throw the vessels at the fire.

There may be some humans yet inside or he could follow the passage and find their trail.

His coven members were geniuses, he thought proudly as he watched their inspiring and valiant efforts. Most missed the fire because they had trouble getting close enough and it was hard to aim due to the brightness of the conflagration, but enough hit and the fire died down so that a few brave vampires rushed inside the cave. They cried in pain but mostly victorious war cries as they breached the subdued fire.

One vampire who made it inside shrieked incoherently and then others joined in. From the pain and frustration in the wailing voices, Jim knew that the cave was empty. All the humans escaped up the hill, somehow. Worse. Ab-by-gail was gone too. He knew that, but he wanted to find her trail inside the cave.

He let out a shriek and all the vampires echoed it back. They ran up the hill, slipping on the snow, to ambush the humans when they got near the truck. Jim walked inside the cave and screamed, "Ab-by-gail!" at the chimney. He couldn't climb that natural chimney. Immediately he left the cave and began to sprint up the snowy hill.

"Ab-by-gail!" he screamed. "Wait for mate! Wait for me! Wait for husband! Ab-by-gail!"

***

I watched as the roiling mass of vampires moved up the mountain on either side of us, stark black shadows on the snowy canvas of the hill. The natural chimney sat on top of a knob at a steep angle of the hill so the vampires avoided coming straight at us. Abigail was right; they didn't know exactly where we were, but they were quickly surrounding us simply in their numbers and determination to find us.

"We need to shoot our way out," Richard said.

Abigail's eyes grimly looked over the ridge above us. "No. There is a legion moving above us. We're going to need every bullet we have to fight for our lives when we get there. I think that they know where your truck is and they want to ambush us."

"I'm blasting away," Richard said. "We need our guns!"

"Put your guns away and listen to the lady," Jerry said. "We have no choice but to trust her."

Richard looked around and shrugged when he saw everyone else draw swords and machetes. He drew his own as well.

Abigail quickly ordered, "I'll take point! I'm moving fast! Keep up! Eric, you're tail end Charlie to watch our six!" She sprinted past us and began scrambling up the path. "Keep up!" she said one last time.

We all followed her. The vamps were scrambling up the snow slick slopes as fast as they could on either side. All of them were shrieking in their terrifying and monstrously frustrated voices.

There were a few of the shadowy vampires on the trail ahead. I was blown away at Abigail's speed as she killed them and then scrambled over fallen vampires she had slain that she met on the run without breaking stride. Even with her sword attacks, she moved as fast as us as she blazed the trail as if taking on light jungle foliage with a machete. On rare occasions, I had to stop, turn around, and strike down a vampire coming up on our rear. I was grateful that these were failed vampires. Besides not being very bright, they were not the best fighters nor was this lot any good at mind control. Jim and Cindy seemed to be the champions at that. However, after turning around to kill them I had to struggle to keep up with my group, and the steep, snow slick trail was treacherous, but I had to kill them before they could emit a cry of victory that would alert the rest of the coven.

Many times, I slipped on the snow and almost plummeted down the cliff. After the snow replaced the fog and brightened the landscape, I had no trouble seeing the fate that a fall would bring me.

The vampires screamed as I killed them, but their cries seemed to be lost in the cries of all the hunting vampires on the hillside. I wasn't sure if they were warcries to stir motivation, if they were forms of communication, or if they were just driven and insane, baying like bloodhounds on a distant scent. Regardless, the cries all around us masked the screams of those who I killed. It was an extremely unnerving and never ending tirade that continually assaulted my ears and very soul. As I have said, vampires can scream like no human can.

Between fighting and running uphill, I was soon out of breath. My sleeves were wet with vampire blood and remains of the river water. Vampires don't rot like zombies. Their blood smells similar to the metallic taste of human blood, but the difference was enough that I still despised the smell of it. I always worried about a possible vampiric infection from incidental contact with their blood on my hands.

One of the kids fell behind and I scooped her up in one arm and ran uphill with my sword in the other. She gasped slightly, but was otherwise quiet. She was a tough little girl. A young Abigail, I thought.

Fifty feet below the crest, Abigail called a halt. I could see she was tired, but like me she did her best to put on a strong appearance. The others bent over with their hands on their thighs just above their knees. Jerry had his girl in his arms. I gave the girl that I had found to Richard.

"Oh, thanks," he said stupidly.

Rachael watched this and screamed about them losing track of their kid, "Richard! You idiot!"

"I--" he began.

"Quiet," Abigail hissed. Her voice was barely audible over the howls of the vampires who were looking for us.

I nervously looked around in fear the vampires heard the arguing couple, but they were shrieking all around us in their hungered madness that all of our voices blended in with theirs. If they were smart, these vampires should have been in stealthy hunter mode. It's how Abigail's old coven hunted. Where Abigail's coven had brains, these guys had sheer numbers and maddening raw determination.

Abigail said, "They're massed for an ambush at the top, on that ledge, up this easy trail. They probably don't realize that we have a vampire leading us through the night. They think that I'm a prisoner, so they think they're invisible."

I wanted to ask how she knew all that, but instead, I looked up at the crest and could see nothing but a dark snowy mountain that looked like a giant sleeping hunchback beneath the cloudy sky, but the snow seemed to provide its own light. However my vision was still very limited compared to hers. I was grateful beyond words for her guidance at night.

She continued. "Keep your heads down and follow just underneath this line of boulders. It should get you to the top a few hundred yards upstream. It should be closer to where your truck is parked."

I looked at the almost trailess path we would have to forge. It was steep and snowy, ending in a drop of a hundred feet to our left. I usually wasn't that scared of heights, but I was worried now. Especially with having to carry kids on an ice slicked way.

"What about you?" I asked Abigail after I looked over the edge.

Abigail replied, "I'll wait here to make sure you are not followed and then just before you should make your run, I will go straight up here and meet them with guns blazing and make a diversion for you."

"No!" I stated.

She replied with worry on her face, "They probably won't kill me. I can probably talk my way out of it. These faileds aren't very bright and one of them wants me to be his mate."

"No!" I repeated.

Everything about her plan was wrong. I did not want to risk losing her. I didn't think the two families would wait in the truck to rescue a vampire, even if the vampire was Abigail. These failed vampires would probably kill her, or even worse. I felt a surge of protective homicidal jealousy at the mere thought of that failed vampire Jim claiming Abigail as a mate and turning her stupid and psychotic with his degenerative bloodline. It would kill me if they did to her what they did to Brandon.

And even worse to picture Abigail as Jim's bride.

"It's our best option," said Richard. "She'll live. She's one of them."

In a burst of rage, I thrust the point of my sword in his throat. The point puckered his skin, but didn't draw blood. "Yes. She's a vamp, but she is not one of them! She is one of us," I said "them" with the emphasis as if spitting a cockroach from my mouth.

"Everybody calm down," Jerry said. "Maybe Abigail should keep leading us. At least until we get to the top. That trail you pointed out, ma'am, I don't know if we can follow it in the dark without risking falling off the cliff. Especially as slick as the snow is."

"Sorry, Richard," I said as I lowered my sword. "I know she's a vampire, but even if your wife, Rachael, turned into a vampire, would you leave her behind, alone?"

Abigail looked at me with an expression of confusion on her face, but didn't say anything. I was defending her as if she was my wife. Yes, we were partners and friends, but we never discussed how long we'd be together or the deeper nature of the partnership. Such deeply felt admissions were only said when our passions were aroused in life or death situations.

Richard shrugged and said, "I see your point and understand your passion, Eric, but don't ever point your sword at me again. Also, Jerry's right. Lead the way, Abigail."

"I'll cover our rear," I said.

Abigail looked downtrail behind us and said, "Very well. You should be fine. Keep up and keep your heads down."

She led the way. We followed the rocky incline and at a slower pace than we had been running, not just due to the precarious nature of the trail, but also to ensure a degree of silence. I could hear the growling and chopped conversations of the vampires waiting for us above as well as their howls. Abigail said that vampires could hear and feel the pulse of people's beating heart, but it was less physically audible but rather psychic. They mentally connected with the rhythm of the electric pulse of the neurons in the hearts of people.

However, in the distance was the never ending shrieking and howling. Although we moved away from them, I could still hear them. By the tones of their guttural utterings, I knew that they were getting impatient for human blood. I could feel my blood pulse thundering in my head, reverberating my hatred for that line of fallen people. I wished that I could calm my heart for fear that they would sense it, but vampires had their own thundering hearts, I guessed.

We came just below the lip of the crest. Abigail led us off of the path by scaling a boulder and we followed her up and stopped with her on the pinnacle. It was a high point on the ridge and it gave us a 360 vantage point and it was surrounded by thick rhododendron foliage, giving us a degree of camouflage as we ducked beneath the low canopy. I hadn't noticed until now, but the clouds had cleared some and the dim starlight reflecting off the snow gave us a better vision of what we faced. However, the sliver of the moon was still hidden.

Abigail stopped and waited for us at the lip of the ridge behind a larger boulder and in some brush. When we gathered around her, she made a quiet, "Shh," sound. I wasn't sure why until I looked where we would have come up if we had stayed on the original trail. Had she not issued the warning, one of us probably would have sworn. Even with her warning, I almost let loose with a whispered oath. Scurrying over the top, hunched over like cockroaches, were dozens of black cloaked vampires searching and waiting for us.

We watched from a stand of rhododendrons, camouflaged for the moment.

It was night, but the black cloaks of the coven stood out against the starlit snow like it was daylight. I could hear their impatient growls and snarlings. A few followed the trail going just beneath our perch. If they looked down they would have seen our footprints in the snow. If they looked up they might have spotted us.

I grimly half smiled as one of those idiots screamed as he fell off of the ledge and plunged down the mountain.

Keeping hunched over myself, I scanned around us and saw the stupidest of the faileds wandering aimlessly through the forest. Even avoiding the main group, we would have to rely on Abigail's night vision to lead us past the stupidest of the faileds. If one of them spotted us, they would scream incoherently with their victory cries and bring the entire coven upon us. My greatest fear was to hear one of them scream that distinct cry of victory. I had heard it before when Bryan Critter and me were pursued by Abigail's coven, that night that she saved us.

Abigail whispered, "Jerry, where is your truck?"

"A few hundred yards in about that direction, I think," he answered.

"You think?" Richard mocked in a harsh whisper.

"I see it," Abigail confirmed as she peaked over the boulder where we crouched.

"How the hell can you see anything in this darkness, dear," Richard asked.

Abigail ignored him as she looked over the surroundings. I saw her nostril flare delicately. Besides great night vision, vampires also acquired a tremendous sense of smell, especially for blood, even for their own kind.

"OK. They aren't smelling your blood. The wind is blowing in our direction, and the cold lessens the sense of smell," Abigail began.

"Like smoking pot in a restaurant's walk-in fridge," Jerry offered.

"I guess," Abigail said.

"Regardless of the cold, how do you know that they are capable of smelling our blood?" Richard asked.

"Because I have been smelling your blood the whole time I have been with you." she replied tersely, staring him right in the eyes. "Now, keep the firearms holstered, but swords ready. We will walk quietly."

I watched the blood leave her face as she swore, "Oh crap!" Her eyes were downwind from us. I could feel the light draft in my hair blowing toward the vampires.

"What?" asked Rachael.

"Draw your guns! We'll have to fight on the run," Abigail replied.

"Why?"

Downwind a vampire shrieked. The cry was higher in pitch and sounded triumphant compared to the other screams that we had been hearing, and the other ones let loose a horrible victorious wailing as well. Their noses were in the air. I looked and saw that we were sandwiched between two hordes.

Abigail was about to give an order when I saw her face freeze.

"Abigail," I said when I realized something took hold of her mind. I had seen that blank look on her face when she turned on me just before that fight that led to our leap into the river. I could feel something static-like in my mind as if they were intruding in and tugging on my thoughts as well, but the effect on Abigail seemed amplified.

"I say, Ab-by-igail, my mate. I can smell your sweet vampiress scent," Jim's loud voice sounded within a hundred yards of us. "Come out so we may see you and talk."

I hated Jim's phony accent as much as I hated his vampiric nature. It then dawned on me that he reminded me of a time that I was in a college theatrical play. There were two extremely arrogant actors, who thought they were hilariously funny when they told the lamest jokes, but as long as the quips were delivered with a bad Shakespearean accent, they laughed hysterically at their own poor humor.

I watched Abigail's nostrils flare again. The difference this time was that her focus was on us. I could almost see the hunger for human blood begin to overwhelm her mind as her eyes were aflame with desire.

I swore.

"What is it?" Christy asked me. "Is something wrong?"

"Make a run for it!" I hissed as urgently and quietly as I could. "Sprint for the truck!."

I grabbed Abigail by her shoulder and shook her and hissed, "Come on, Abigail!"

Everyone began to run except Abigail who stared at me hungrily. "Abigail! We need to run! Abigail!" I shook her with both force and compassion and yelled, "Abigail!"

She shook her head and looked at me confused and I heard a change in timbre of the vampiric screams in reaction to my yell. They not only smelled us, but they heard me and knew where we were.

I repeated urgently, and inadvertently louder, "Abigail! We need to run. Now!"

She nodded as if she just heard my urgent command for the first time.

Gunfire erupted around us. The pounding of it worried me, but it seemed to get through to her. Indeed the reports of a firearm cut through their mind control better than screaming her name.

"Yes. Let's go," Abigail said, but distantly.

Chapter Eleven

Jerry, Chisty, Rachael, Richard and their two girls ran ahead firing rounds at the vampires blocking the way. I was impressed with their children who kept up without crying from terror. I myself wanted to scream with a warcry to overwhelm my own terror, and I had been trapped in the caverns of the vampires. The two families were definitely warriors, but surviving out here for two years, you had to be.

"Abigail! Come on!" I yelled at Abigail.

I yelled to reach her over the howling vampires and exploding sound of gunfire as well as to reach her through the fog that the other vampires had woven in her mind.

I was trying to yank her with me as I ran, but she slowed me as she tried to stand still. Holding her hand, my sprint turned into a shambling jog as she stumbled behind only so as not to fall over, but she wasn't running to keep up nor to escape to the truck.

I looked over my shoulder to yell at her again and was struck by the look of confusion in her normally clear eyes. She made eye contact with me and they turned lucid, but her voice was distant as she said to me, "You need to leave me. I am about to betray you, betray you all. As I controlled your mind once, so they have me."

The distance in her voice terrified me. I felt like I was losing her.

"Abigail! Stay with me! I love you," I blurted out desperately to get her to move.

Her eyes cleared far more with that statement than my earlier shake of her body, my pleading her name, and even the gunshots.

"Let's go," I said.

She nodded. Her eyes cleared but they were still filled with doubt and worry, but she began to run on her own.

We sprinted together. I had my rifle strapped to my back. In the darkened scrubby forest, I let my handgun lead the way as my other hand gripped hers in a life grip. The ridge top forest was more of a dense, viney chaparral jungle full of thorns and I felt that my rifle would get tangled. Although the rifle held 30 rounds, my Glock held 18 bullets and was great for close quarter combat in the scrubby brush. A rifle would be cumbersome if a boulder turned into a vampire right in front of me and grabbed my rifle.

Abigail kept pace with me, but she did not go for her firearms but still held her sword clenched in a fist. I didn't tell her to draw a firearm because of her state of mind. I had been in her vulnerable mental situation myself a week earlier. If she attacked me, I could see her sword coming down on my head a lot better than the instant death that would fire from her rifle's barrel.

We kept up with the two families pretty easily. I was amazed at their skills in a gunfight. I was able to save my ammo and mostly spent my time leaping over wounded and dead vampires to keep up with them. The wounded reached for us with gnarled hands and ravenous eyes. To them, I occasionally delivered the coup de grace bullet to the head.

Our group reached the destination and we shot the few vampires who were guarding the truck, but I could hear the screams of the other vamps who were rapidly converging on us.

An old shed had collapsed on the truck. The shed was made of rotted wood that had finally given up to decay. When it was erect, I could tell that it was just large enough to encapsulate the truck. I could see the shiny paint of the vehicle beneath the debris, but couldn't distinguish the color due to the dark. What I saw looked as good as any serviceable vehicle this deep into the apocalypse.

Jerry cursed as he looked it over and started to remove the rotted wood. I could tell he loved his truck, obviously more than the shed. The rest of us formed a perimeter around the vehicle and shot at the vanguard of the vampiric attack as they converged on us. I knew the main coven, hundreds of the bastards, was just behind these guys and we needed to leave before they got here.

As Jerry was kicking and throwing rotted wood off to get to the driver's door, a black form lunged from the shadows. I pumped two bullets in the area of its nose and my gun clicked empty. I raised the gun to slam the butt into its head, but the vampire collapsed and stayed down, dead.

As I slid a fresh magazine into the handgun, I heard Richard exclaim, "Dang it, I'm all out of ammo."

I heard Jerry open the driver's side door. He yelled, "Get in the truck bed!"

"I can't," yelled Richard. "It's full of crap."

"Get in!" I yelled at him as I picked up his daughter and put her in the back of the pickup truck on top of the debris. I picked up the other girl and placed her in as well as I heard Christy's gun fire and the plop of a dead vampire lifelessly hit the deck a few feet from me.

Jerry attempted to fire up the truck. It turned roughly and died. He cursed as the rest of us climbed in the truck's bed except Abigail. She stood outside with that confused look on her face.

"Get in, Abigail," I commanded.

Her eyes cleared and she smiled sorrowfully at me, as if suddenly recognizing me and bidding a final farewell to a good friend, but then her face darkened into a shark-like intensity. I saw her blood hunger in her eyes as she stared at me or rather through me.

"Abigail!" I shouted.

Again she looked confused as she came out of the trance. She said, "I can't go with you, Eric. I am a danger to you all."

"What's wrong with her eyes, Mommy," asked one of the girls.

"Nothing!" I snapped at the girl. "Get in Abigail!"

I was near panicking as I could hear Jerry trying to start the engine. It sounded like it would actually catch in one of the next attempts.

Again Abigail's eyes cleared and she grasped my hand and climbed in beside me. I gave her a one armed hug and she sank into me. I had my woman back, I thought as the engine fired to life, but as Jerry put the pickup in gear, black shapes seemed to form from the darkness all around us, but the engine coughed and died. He screamed a string of encouraging oaths at his vehicle.

Three vampires stood in front of the truck and pointed rifles at Jerry through the windshield. The rest of us aimed over the bed of the truck like gunwales on a boat, but we held our fire. We were surrounded and very low on ammo. We would be cut down, but I knew that vampires preferred us with beating hearts. I hoped those smart enough to work with firearms would be smart enough to want to capture us alive with pulsing hearts and flowing blood.

The engine thundered to life again, and Jerry suddenly turned on the bright headlamps, blinding the vampires in front, and he floored it. The vampires in front scattered. The engine caught with a violent start like a rearing calvary horse and almost caused some of us to fall out of the bed. The truck leapt forward and died with a cough. It was eerily silent other than some of us bitterly cursing the truck and the screams of the vampires.

"You humans may go, I say," a horrible faux-British accent declared. "Just let my mate Ab-by-gail be reunited with her kind."

"No," I yelled back

"And you may go free," he added without heeding me.

I felt that Jim was totally attuned with Abigail to the point where nothing else in his periphery was observable including my voice.

If I could have shot him, I felt that Abigail would be free, but I couldn't determine which one was him from the dozens black shadows that surrounded us.

Richard startled me when he said, "I'm sorry but she needs to go, buddy."

Before I could get angry at him, I saw the hungry lioness look in her eyes as she looked upon us as sheep. I was barely aware of Jerry attempting to start the engine. The truck would catch and die.

"Abigail!" I screamed.

She shook herself out of it, and with cold sobriety said, "I must go. I'm about to lose control of my bloodlust."

Before I could argue she climbed out of the pick up and ran toward Jim's voice who stood in the group thirty meters away.

"Let them go," Abigail told the vampires.

"Abigail!" I screamed desperately. I couldn't let them turn her into a failed psycho vampire like they did to Brandon.

"I say, you may join us too Eric, my chap," Jim said with a tone of victorious delight.

I moved to leave the truck and Richard grabbed me and said, "Are you mad?"

I saw the look of hunger in the eyes of the vampires as they stared at us. Abigail stood beside Jim. With distant eyes, she looked through me and said, "Go," in a voice deep with loss of will. Jim had her mind almost completely under his control, but with her at his side, he now focused his power on me, and that gave her the ability to tell us to go. She had willingly sacrificed herself for us.

I aimed my handgun at Jim's chest, but before I could pull the trigger, the engine caught and the truck surged forward again like a rearing calvary horse slamming me into the debris of the bed.

I heard Jim shout, "Get them, I say!"

Splintered wood caught up in the windstorm of sudden acceleration showered me with rotten wood and nails. The truck skidded and slid on the light snow. The vampires surged around us and I opened up with my freshly reloaded Glock until it emptied. I caught one final look at Abigail in the distance. Her eyes were heavy and saddened, and it burned my heart. She knew that she was sacrificing herself for us.

Within seconds we were beyond the reach of the vampires. A few of them fired rifles at us, but the reports barely registered in my mind. I barely felt the jarring bumps of the rutted road, nor the frozen knife-like fingers of the air whistling past the truck, slicing through my clothes still slightly damp from the river and vampire blood. All I could think about is what would happen to Abigail's mind if the faileds bit and turned her. I worried not only of the obvious mind control they had over her, but that the alternate strain of that horrible strain of vampiric virus would turn her sharp mind into mush. I kept remembering the feral dog intensity in Brandon's eyes, as well as Abigail saying that he had been a better vampire than she was. He must have been a great man, I thought, and that only filled me with regret about leaving her behind.

"Abigail," I muttered to the whistling wind in the truck's wake.

After rocketing and sliding over the dirt fire roads for about ten minutes we turned onto a paved road and Jerry opened the throttle. For fifteen minutes or more, we traveled down the mountainous roads that resembled ski slopes more than paved thoroughfares. I was sure we were going to skid off the road and flip at every turn. As we rode, we tossed the rotted wood from the truck bed.

After a few miles more, I pounded on the cab and yelled at Jerry to slow down. We were past the vampires and there was no sense risking a wreck on the snowy road. He slowed down a little but we all still clung to the truck as we kept tossing out the debris. In retrospect, it wasn't smart throwing out the debris. We were leaving behind a trail that the vampires could follow.

Soon we left the path of the snow storm and the roads were mostly clear of ice and snow. After brooding in the cold wind and relaxing with the smoother drive, a raging anger beset me.

I turned to Richard and repeated Bryan's pet peeve verbatim into his face, yelling over the wind and the grind of the engine, "Guns are artillery pieces, Mr. Know-it-all. We call them rifles, firearms, or handguns! Not guns!"

He looked at me with the same confusion Abigail wore under Jim's spell. In my madness, I was yelling at him for something he said much earlier. It was stupid on my part really, but I persisted, "They are firearms, not guns!" I screamed.

"Are you out of your head?" he asked.

"Yes!" I said and banged heavily on the cab with my clenched fist.

Jerry slowed the truck slightly and rolled down the window, "What's up?"

"Stop the truck. I want out," I screamed.

"Are you nuts?" Jerry yelled back at me through the open window.

"Just do what he says, Jerry," Richard said. "Eric's lost his damn mind."

I glared at Richard and he asked, "What? You want out. It's what you want, right?"

The truck pulled over and I grabbed my pack, weaponry, and jumped out. We gave a quick wave of goodbye, and they were gone. I stood alone on an abandoned road on a dark winter night with the goal of finding an army of vampires and somehow defeating them to rescue a hypnotized vampiress from them. I thought through it as bluntly as I could.

In the quiet of the night, I remembered the last words of Richard and Jerry. Know-it-all Richard was correct on one point, I had lost my mind. Whether it was due to my love for her or Jim's psychic meddlings in my own mind, I didn't know, nor did I really care. Alone with the quiet of the night and ragings of my thoughts, I began to realize that I was quite mad in my desire to save Abigail from a fate worse than death, but we had promised each other that we would rather die than succumb to the degenerative bite of Jim's coven. My given word to a friend meant more to me than my rifle.

I got off the road and headed into the woods, back toward Abigail and the horde of vampires who had captured her. It was a suicide mission, but she had sacrificed herself for us. I was driven by my devotion to return that favor.

Chapter Twelve

I had covered my sleeping bag with a tarp and buried this quick sleeping set up in oak leaves for added warmth and camouflage. My sleeping gear was still a bit damp from the impromptu swim, but it wasn't too bad, and besides, I had no choice.

Although I had become somewhat used to night travel, I knew that the vampires would see me walking in the woods long before I would see them. There was no way I could sneak up on a full army of them, especially the failed. Although the stupid vampires were less disciplined, they were more unpredictable. They tended to wander like a loose herd of cats rather than following each other in lines or formations like Abigail's old coven. Without Abigail as my guide, I'd only travel by day. By night I had to be still. They would see me long before I spotted them. I guessed it was an hour or two before sunrise.

Before setting up camp, I had only walked a quarter mile from the road before snuggling into the sleeping bag. I didn't think I would get any sleep with the thoughts weighing on my mind as well as still feeling the cold of the river in my bones and joints. However, I mercifully sank into a dark, abysmally dreamless void within a moment of laying down.

I awoke cold, with the sun in my eyes as it rose just a fist or two distance over the horizon. I hoped to wake up immediately at sunrise, but I guessed that it was about 8:30 to 9 o'clock in the morning. In retrospect, I probably needed the extra rest.

I stretched, surprised at the soreness that quickly reminded me of the climb up the chimney and the running battle not to mention the brutal assault of the river thrashing me against the boulders. My head also hurt where I had hit a rock when I had fallen fighting the vampires, and the pain was spreading like a migraine through my skull. And nevermind the countless injuries I had acquired since entering the Forbidden Zone.

I dug a quick hole in the forest floor and brought a fire to life to make instant coffee. It actually tasted good under the circumstances. It was funny. With all that was going on, I dwelled on how I disliked drinking it out of a metal canteen cup and missed a ceramic coffee cup. The metal provided no insulation and the coffee went from scalding hot to nearly ice way too fast, but regardless, the hot coffee hit the spot, despite everything.

I quickly ate a main entree from an MRE. I then slowly finished the rest of the packages of preserved food without tasting much as I studied a topographical map and sat over the small but warm fire. It wasn't much of a rest, but I was driven. I had a second cup of instant coffee and I continued to study the map long after I settled on a plan. I let my eyes and mind wander the map as if I were hiking the terrain. I studied it, trying to imagine the mysteries hidden in the deep valleys beneath the majestic peaks and ridgelines.

When I gulped down the remains of my rapidly cooling coffee, I quickly folded my map, packed my gear, and set off to find Abigail before the night. I felt like I could take on the army of the vampires by day before darkness brought their total reign.

I had a sense of where the legion was headed and I set course to intercept them. Earlier, Abigail had told me where she suspected their lair to be. I hoped that she was correct.

It had broken my heart when she left us. Despite being under their influence, I saw enough of her sadness in her eyes. She was in control of herself enough to know that she was sacrificing herself for us. It wasn't that she was uncontrollably pulled to them. No. She thought she was giving her life, not just for me, but the uncaring people of those two families. I wished that I had jumped off the truck and fought for her, but it worked out better than me trying to take on the horde single handedly at night, that's if I could find the horde while they slept during the daylight, and that's if they didn't make it back to their home. I didn't relish the thought of trying to find Abigail on the vampire's home turf even in daylight.

The sun was bright and the day warmed just enough that I was comfortable with a fast stride once I began my search, but I didn't drench my coat with sweat. Most of the patches of snow from the night before had melted by the sun's zenith.

It was just after noon when I cut upon their trail. Although I was nowhere near the tracker that Critter or Abigail were, even I could see the sign left from hundreds of vampires. At first, I couldn't pick out any one sign or bootprint, just a mass of ruffled leaves and crushed sticks. I looked hard at any patch of mud, remaining snow, or dusty sand to see the individual footprints. I longed to see any sign that Abigail was with them, that Abigail was alive, but I saw no sign of her boot tread in the mass of them. I was sure that Critter or Abigail could have, and I vowed to acquire his skill one day.

I pushed myself onward to the point of exhaustion as I followed the trail of leaves turned over like turbulence from a jet. The more I taxed my body, the less work my mind could do dwelling on things. Just a few days ago, I vowed to Abigail that I would kill her if I ever saw her again. At the moment when I delivered that threat, I also had an overwhelming desire to kiss her on the lips. It had been a crazy night to say the least and my mind had felt like it had been blasted into a mush of insanity by another vampire's psychic powers.

However as I tracked her I would have traded temporary passion for a lifetime as a vampire just to reunite with her. At other moments, I wondered if it was my own desires or Jim's psionic abilities overriding my rational mind to pursue them. He had said that they wanted both of us in their army. Did that coven drop some psychic bug in my mind that drew me to them?

Currently, I was trying to save her from her own kind. If I dwelled on it, I realized it was a fool's errand. She had been subjected to crucifixion from one group of humans and then banishment from the Mountain Warriors who she had rescued in the past. Maybe, despite how hideous this group of vampires were, it might be the best for her. At least they would not come at her literally with torches and pitchforks like my former tribe had done to us, or was that my own cowardice trying to talk me out of a nearly suicidal mission?.

Whatever was driving me, it came back to my own desires. Yes I wanted what was best for her, but was I blindly following my passions rather than reason and logic? Was I risking my life to stifle her wishes only to fulfill my own madness? She voluntarily stayed behind with her kind. We really had no agreement how long we would stay together. It was more out of convenience. We were both outcasts, but we were different. With vampirism, we may have even been two different species. As much as it rendered my heart asunder, eventually we would have to separate and no one would blame me for running from a coven of hundreds of vampires. No one that is, but me.

No! I had plainly seen her despair as she stood with Jim. I couldn't live with that image as my last memory of her. It was less bravery on my part, but rather, I couldn't live with that. I would rather meet my death by the sword than that heartbreak.

As my mind dwelled on these thoughts, I broke into a sprint up a steep incline until exhaustion and shortness of breath drove those thoughts from my mind, and I continued to push myself onward. By mid afternoon, I was left with a reptilian, single minded urge to fulfill my mad desire to save her.

What drove the urge? I allowed myself to answer that question because it was easy: Of everyone in the world, she, a vampire woman, was the only person who I trusted with my life, and she would do the same fool's errand for me. She had done just that in the past, and even last night. I owed it to her. I could live my life without her, I couldn't live it if I abandoned her to a fate worse than death. We had both vowed to each other to end our lives before becoming what they turned Brandon into, but I would rescue her. I had to. I took my promises seriously.

I pressed on. I went quicker as mid afternoon wore on. I needed to find her before night, but as the shadows lengthened, a terror threatened to slow my stride. I either had to overtake them and find their daytime repose site soon, while the sun was up, or wait for tomorrow. By then she could be changed into one of them if not already.

Occasionally I came across a few small zombie hordes.

It's funny; zombies had been my biggest fear when I first entered the Forbidden Zone. Vampires were only a dark myth at the time. Now, I would slash down a gaggle of them and not think twice to note the feat in my mind or recording device any more than I would keep count of the times I urinate each day. Now, zombies were simply a smelly annoyance rather than a terror unless they charged at me in an overwhelming horde, of course.

I still pushed on, and lost the trail as a stiff breeze picked up further disturbing their leafy trail. The sun was enveloped by a cloud that resembled a slab of gray sheet rock and the wind began to howl and blow. The strong gusts of wind blew the leaves wildly. I could no longer see consistent traces of their trail, but I continued to follow their general direction because so far they had not altered their path at all except to detour insurmountable obstacles.

I was about to stop for the evening. Sunset was within a half hour. I paused when I saw an old graveyard before me the size of a few football fields placed side by side. It was situated in a small valley. My morbid curiosity propelled me forward.

If the vampires stopped traveling before daylight, this would be their place to go to repose unmolested. Vamps were aware that people tended to avoid graveyards and they used them as safe places. Also, some of them acquired a morbid taste in their undead life. I stepped into the graveyard in the gathering gloom of premature twilight under the dismal clouds.

Although the wind was beginning to die down, the sudden gusts still ruffled the leaves slightly to give me a startle. With my nerves drawn taught, the sound of rustling leaves made a stirring sound that resembled being stalked by a creeping corpse.

I walked amid the ancient tombstones and noted the dates were from the 1900s, 1800s and even a few from the 1700s. The idea of antiquity always fascinated me, even in this morbid place. Touching a place, such as a tombstone, occupied by those who lived in the distant past gave me a sense of immortality for the human race as a whole, and I needed that sense of continuation in an era that many people called the end of times.

On an instinctive level, the graveyard unsettled me and it took a moment for me to realize why. Deep inside, I was expecting it to have been maintained by a caretaker. Such an expectation was absurd, of course, in a post apocalypse world. The living could barely care for themselves in a land that claimed the lives of 90% of the population in only two years, but to see the cemetery overgrown by trampled grass and covered by a thick sheet of leaves blown down from the mountain forest above did not sit well with something in my soul.

I also noticed hundreds of mounds under the leaves. I took them for burial mounds at first. I continued on until I stood in the center of the grave yard.

Ahead of me I saw a large marble mausoleum. It was stately and elegant. Although I found it distasteful to picture Abigail sleeping in a coffin, the mausoleum seemed like the classiest way to do it. Above all, I had an uncanny sense that she was near. We had that connection.

I hesitantly called out for her. It was a weak call where a person tries to be loud enough to be heard, but the throat reflexively tightens paradoxically to be silent.

"Abigail!" I croaked.

Nothing responded. I called her name a little more harshly where it sounded more like a hoarse, whispered yell. "Abigail!"

I thought I heard the wind crackle the leaves slightly, but no gust of wind had blown. I looked around and saw nothing. It was a little foolish to call her if I suspected other vampires were in the vicinity, but I could sense that she was near, very near, and she was far more tolerant of the sunlight than most of her kind. I was confident that she would wake up before the others did. Plus that, she knew the sound of my voice.

I finally called her name, letting a yell clearly leave my throat without restriction. I heard the rustle of leaves around me, and saw the hundreds of leafy mounds throughout the graveyard shift under the leaves. I also heard the snarls, grunts, and growls of failed vampires grumpily awakening from their daytime slumber.

Terror struck me as I realized the mounds were not burial mounds, but vampires sleeping beneath the hastily piled leaves, similar to what I did to camouflage my sleeping bag. A vampire could use their cloaks as emergency shelters from the sun as well. The leaves just added protection and camouflage.

The slate gray clouds and the nearness to sunset made the hour dangerous. I had less than fifteen minutes before they arose enmasse. Something inside screamed at me to run but I stood in horror as I watched the leaves fall away from one pile as a black figure slowly rose and stood before me.

The vampiric hooded figure had its back to me and slowly turned around. I steeled my nerves for the horror of seeing its hunger for my blood in its eyes. As it faced me, it removed its hood slightly from its face but I only saw dire concern on the features as Abigail said in a distant voice laced with the hypnotic effect of her captors, "Eric, you must leave, now!"

I was horrified at first that she had seemed to revert to the likes of the savage bloodsuckers, laying as if in a grave, but I was overwhelmed at the happiness to see her alive and somewhat lucid.

I ran up and hugged her. She embraced me back, tighter. She then released the embrace but held onto my shoulders. She looked at me from under her hood so that I could see her worry.

"Let's go, Abigail," I said, grabbing her wrist to pull her with me.

"No," she whispered with her lips near my ear to prevent the other sleeping vampires from hearing. Although many were snarling and shifting beneath their leafy mounds, none of them arose, yet. It was still daylight, but barely.

She said, "This is a fight that I can not run from. I have to stay. You have to bring back an army: The Mountain Warriors, Craigsville, or anyone to defeat this pack. These idiots are building an army of failed vampires. The strain of virus that they carry is horrible. If they continue, they will get you even if you put miles between us. I must stop them. I would rather turn you with my bloodline than you be infected with these--" she couldn't finish. Then she said, "But I don't want you infected at all! So you must leave now."

"Not without you," I said.

"Why do you want me to go with you?" she asked, confused.

I was surprised by her question and immediately asked her, "Do you prefer the company of faileds to me?"

"Of course not!" she said with pure disgust, "But humans wish to kill or banish me, and vampires, for the most part, wish to consume or turn you. I must accept that I must stay with vampires and find a decent group. It will keep us both safe."

At this moment, I realized that my true feelings for her were about to manifest. I could not hide them. As I looked into her eyes, I couldn't deny my love for her, no matter how impossible such a union would be, but neither could I truly say them out loud at that moment with the shuffling of the mounds around us. You never let an enemy know your weakness. I didn't want any of them to hear me profess my love for her. They would use that against us. Use it against her.

"Come with me, Abigail," I said. "We need each other. We work well together."

She shook her head no, "Why do you want me to go with you? These guys are desperate for me. They will pursue us relentlessly. After what Cindy did to me, I am marked. They will always know my movements, and if I'm with you, they will know yours as well. I have to stay and end it."

I blew out a pent up breath and said, "This is no hyperbole, but you're the only person in the world who I trust, and who I care for. You are my truest friend." I struggled with the next sentence to find the correct words. "I-- I have a-- I have a love for you," I whispered.

I had blurted out that I loved her last night as I was trying to get her to run, but looking her in the eyes, I didn't feel comfortable saying my feeling that promised a future that I couldn't deliver, nor did I want the vampires around us to hear me make such an admission that they could use against us.

She looked at me with uncertainty for a moment before saying in a patronizing tone that irritated me, "As flattered as I am, I must find a way to destroy this army of failures from the inside before it not only devours all the humans in this region, including you, but also destroys all the decent vampires like Brandon."

I think that I succeeded when I tried to keep the distaste from my face when she mentioned decent vampires. Abigail was the only one who I could ever see myself trusting.

I did say, "You're just one woman. What can you do against this army?"

She replied, "As stupid as they are, they come from a different blood line. They are idiot savants at psionics, especially against other vampires. They will always have a degree of control over me and you are in danger. They draw power from The Mind in Asheville, but more importantly from King Sadazar himself. If I can get near him, I can kill him and end this, but in the meantime, they can control me as easily as I could control you when The Mind from Shining Rock gave us power, maybe better. It's scary. I can not even move my feet to follow you. They have me. Don't let them get you. Please. Honor my request. Go!"

I then repeated, "How do you think you'll destroy this army, alone?"

"I may need your help," she said.

She told me of a theme park-like castle that was the headquarters of the vampire King Sadazar five miles away at the end of a cove. It was made of local granite by a local eccentric before the apocalypse, and it was impregnable. She told me of an arsenal in its dungeon, that if I could take control of the castle, I could pick the vampires off one after another as they attempted to storm the castle, but better yet, she suggested that I bring an army of men. Her plan sounded crazy, but she said that she had no choice. I could see some power had her locked in place, and I wasn't sure how she could kill the King while under that control.

I agreed to keep an eye open for an opportunity. Possibly lead the Mountain Warriors or some other group of people to attack. Such an attack would be a few days away, but I couldn't abandon Abigail for so long. They would turn her into an idiot, psychopathic vampire by then, unless she succeeded in assassinating their king.

She had seen the valley and the castle when Jim used his psionic power to show her a mental vision of the area. His goal was to impress her with the power of King Sadazar's fortress and realm. Abigail had seen a rock formation that might be tipped over to destroy the castle, but she couldn't be sure. She wasn't sure what to believe from Jim's questionable mental processes whether from lack of moral trustworthiness or faulty mental integrity as a near imbecile.

Abigail and I didn't have time to solidify any plan, but I saw her face take on a strength under the hood. It was the power a vampire has at night after the sun sets. With a start, I suddenly realized it was minutes before sunset and her nature was prepared to rule the night. She noticed her returning strength as well.

"They'll smell your blood and will awaken earlier. You need to leave, now and without me. Even if I could move, they will find you if I'm with you. If we're together, you will never be safe, even if I could move my feet to run with you. Go." she commanded as she looked over the stirring mounds and then stared almost threateningly at me.

I needed more information about the castle but I knew I needed to go. With the stark clouds and setting sun, they could awake and attack at any moment. I could see some of the mounds begin to stir even more and hear their grumblings. I couldn't be caught in the center of hundreds of vampires after sunset.

I pulled on her hand to lead her, but she sat down on the ground and angrily stared at me as blood hunger took over her face. She bared her fangs at me to emphasize my need to leave and said, "Go! Now!"

I pulled on her arm one more time, but she wouldn't budge.

"Go!" she commanded again with a fanged snarl.

From the strength of her insistence, inability to move her feet, as well as the nearness to night, I had no choice as the other vampires were now sitting up from the graves like the undead they were. A few were standing and looking in my direction. The sleep was leaving their faces and their eyes turned hungry, almost fiery with bloodlust.

I turned from her and started to walk fast on my way out of the graveyard. I tried to walk casually but quickly to avoid triggering their predatory instinct to chase a running target, but when a few mounds in front and around me surged upward, I was out of options.

Many failed vampires suddenly stood before me, blocking my way as the leaves tumbled off their cloaks. Their nostrils flared and throbbed as they smelled my blood. Three blocked my way standing a few feet from me. I launched into them as I drew my sword and sliced at the first one in a single motion. He fell headlessly to the ground.

The setting sun was in front of me but its light was stifled behind the slate gray cloud bank. The sky appeared almost as if it were night. I ignored the other two vampires as I sprinted out of the graveyard. The remaining ones howled at the sky and the other vampires in their mounds stood, dropping their leaves, and began to shriek for my blood as well. All of them were on their feet and coming after me in a wild sprint. Hundreds of them.

I thought I was doomed. Even if I fought through them, night was minutes away. They had boundless energy to pursue once it was dark. However I was blessed as the red sun suddenly burst through the clouds, looking like it was resting lazily on a distant mountain like a giant gold coin. It even blinded me temporarily as I raced toward it.

The vampires behind me shrieked and collapsed back down using their hooded cloaks to shield them from the remaining rays. The hooded cloaks not only protected them when walking, but they were like portable, wearable tents. Bent over, they looked like a flock of black sheep at that moment. As the others fell to the ground, only Abigail stood straight, watching me. I only had a few minutes to get some distance before the sun was completely gone behind the horizon.

I sprinted, heedless of direction, taking the path of least resistance into a valley once I left the cemetery rushing through the surrounding woods and putting as much space between myself and them.

It wasn't until it was actually fifteen minutes after full dark that I realized that I was headed in the same direction that the vampires had been heading all day. I swore, but with no choice, I continued to run, scrambling off trail and up a steep hill trying to get off their likely path through a steep ravine.

Once I was fifty yards above the trail at the bottom of the ravine. I paused and hunkered down at my vantage point. I was too close to their castle to continue running blindly in the dark woods. Over the pounding of my blood pulse in my ears and my own heavy breathing, I could hear them crunching the leaves with their steps and snarling in their desire for human blood as they followed the trail beneath me.

I had quickly piled up some leaves behind a small natural rock wall that was barely a foot high and buried myself in an attempt not to just conceal myself from their sight, but also to limit my scent. I didn't know if my hasty camouflage would work, but sometimes, the best camouflage was staying still. Running through the woods at this time of night, this close to their headquarters was out of the question. They would see me long before I saw them.

I waited, and soon I saw the parade of distorted, hunched over, hooded figures marching round the bend at the bottom of the ravine and continued past me in the valley below. I felt relatively safe with ten inches of leaves piled over my head and body as I watched them from beneath my cover. They were following a trail along a small creek. It was a small fire road wide enough for a four wheel drive fire truck.

Although I was following Abigail's advice on how to focus on my sense of smell to mentally block them scenting me, I was expecting at any minute for one of them to lift its head, sniffing the air in my direction and howling in bloodlust, before sprinting at me followed by the terrible horde.

By the way, I know groups of vampires have more respectable names than horde, but this group, besides Abigail, was little better than a horde of zombies.

As I thought of her, I saw one vampire in the group with a straight, almost aristocratic stature, head held high with grace rather than arrogance. That vampire turned and looked straight at me for a moment. I caught my breath as I realized that Abigail had indeed seen me. It took a lot of energy for Jim and his crew to keep mental domination over Abigail, especially with her seemingly indomitable spirit. Her glance did inspire me. She was still Abigail and she did not betray me.

I lowered my head and heard the crunching of leaves within a few dozen meters of me as well as the inarticulate grumbling of extremely stupid failed vampires that walked on the hill where I was hidden above the mob below. A few of them passed by too close. One even stepped on the heel of my boot without the vampire noticing, but whether it was due to great discipline on my part or that I was in a scared, frozen state, I can't honestly say, but I moved not a muscle until they were long gone, and focused on calming the neurons of their brains that sensed smell as Abigail had taught me to do.

It was probably thirty minutes after I heard the last foot step and inarticulate grumble before I came to a squat and surveyed the area. I saw nothing but was well aware that if there was a vampire within a quarter mile, he probably was watching me. It was not a good feeling, but I wanted to find the headquarters. I had to.

I stood still when I heard the rumble of an engine and watched the fire road. Soon after, I saw Jerry's truck headed into the direction of King Sadazar's castle. I was about to shout a warning and flag it down, when I saw that it was driven by a vampire. All six of the family members were tied up in the back and eight vampires armed with rifles sitting over them. To be armed with rifles and operating a truck, I reasoned that these were fairly intelligent vampires by the standards of the faileds. I guess that they captured the two families and were taking the people to the castle as tribute to their king rather than devouring them, or I hoped that was the case. Now I had the desire to not just rescue Abigail but save the families. Deep inside, I knew it was my fault that they were caught. I had inadvertently led the vampiric horde to their cave.

I set off in darkness stalking an army of the creatures of the night. Occasionally, I saw the downed ruins of a helicopter. Another time, I saw an undetonated rocket laying in the forest. I gave the device a wide berth, but I wondered if I could possibly use the explosive material in it to attack the castle, but I dismissed that idea. I had absolutely no idea how to dismantle a missile without detonating it, nor how to make it into a bomb for that matter. That was something else I wanted to learn for later, that's if I survived this night.

However, passing the destruction of this advanced weaponry chilled me to my spine. I had seen vampires with powers to mentally scroll through a computer and influence other electrical devices as they could with human and animal neurons, but to cause helicopters to fail electronically and to override radio controlled rockets and cause them to crash... I really wanted to run from such power, but I couldn't.

"Abigail," I murmured.

It was then that I realized that a coven with this power probably was the reason that Jerry couldn't start his truck. It was only when Abigail stood with him, that the truck was able to leave. I can't tell you how I knew, but I knew that she sacrificed herself so that she could have enough of her mind to override Jim and let the truck start, and let us run without her.

"Abigail," I said again with even more determination.

I took my time, limiting quick movement. For instance, if I had to scratch my face, I didn't jerk my hand up, but rather, I reached slowly. I knew that adversaries see sudden, quick movements. I also stayed well off of the well worn trail as I followed the path of least resistance that they most assuredly took. Off the trail, I would probably run into the most idiotic of the failed vampires who I could defeat easier. It was a slow deliberate hike. My usual thoughts and worries stayed away as my sole focus was keeping an eye out for vampires.

The moon was out and bright even if it was but a sliver, so I figured if I moved slowly there was a good chance that I would see a failed vampire carelessly walking through the woods long before he would see me. I had my doubts, but my hopes were that I could achieve this. That hope was all that I had.

Around midnight after a few hours of traveling at a quarter or less of the speed of the horde, I came to a point where the small creek flow was almost nonexistent. Mountains and ridges surrounded me so I guessed I was nearing the end of the valley where the castle was situated. I slowed my pace even more, and soon saw the castle towering against the hilly backdrop where the ravine opened into a spoon shaped cove. I had been forced to walk on the gravelly road due to the sheer steepness of the valley. I didn't like walking in the open, but it was a necessity at this point. Thankfully it was clear of vampires.

As I looked at the castle, I stepped off of the gravel road and dropped to the ground behind the shell of a burned out helicopter in the brush near the road. I tried to avoid looking at the desiccated remains of the helicopter crew. I knew that the fate they suffered may well be my own or worse this very night.

I blinked when I saw what looked like a roiling black river headed straight at me on the road from the castle. I stared at it trying to figure out what it was at first. With horror, I realized that it was a sea of failed humanity. The pack of vampires was leaving their home and going back into the woods. Hundreds of them. For what reason, I could only guess. If I had to bet, I would probably guess that bloodlust drove them onward. They had to be starving for blood at this time. I knew that they were too busy attacking Abigail, me, as well as the two families to get a chance to sate their bloodlust. They had to be starving and near crazy. This wouldn't be a good night to be found by them, to put it mildly. I guessed that they dropped off their prize, Abigail, and then set off for their nightly hunt.

I stayed ducked down behind the wreckage of the helicopter as they neared me.

I heard the inarticulate grumbling as I saw the mass of hooded bodies flow past me. Again, I focused on their minds to block their sense of smell. I was surprised again when I saw the straight, black shrouded figure of Abigail. She had the aristocratic posture that Richard's coven inherited from his bloodline. I worried that they had already turned her into one of them. I worried that she would now seek me for blood. I wondered what had happened in the castle when she was in there for over an hour or so before I arrived.

I froze as again as she alone turned and made eye contact with me. Of course I could not see her features in the dark under her hood in the night, but I knew with her night vision she could see me literally plain as day, maybe better, but she turned away and pretended that I wasn't there. That gave me hope that they hadn't turned her, yet. Again, I wondered what had happened to her in that castle, and what caused them to lead her away into the night with her mind intact.

I felt uncomfortable for her when I noticed that her hands seemed to be restrained in front of her and that creepy (creepy even for an undead) vamp, Jim, walked possessively close to her. On impulse, I was tempted to try to rescue Abigail, but that was foolish. I couldn't stalk vampires or attack a vampire army single handedly at night. Besides, at this time of night, Abigail was more likely to rescue me even with her hands bound in this situation, but it infuriated me to see Jim walking so close to her. Yes, some of it was jealousy. I did love her.

As they passed me by, I looked into the direction that they came from and saw a massive drawbridge fifty yards long and thirty wide in the process of rising up from a deep moat. Two idiot vampires operated it, pulling a rope with spastic, uncoordinated efforts. They had rifles strapped to their shoulders.

I watched the rest of the vampires march by me and lay quietly until I was sure the last one had passed. That last vampire was a chubby, moon-faced fellow with a waddle, who would stop occasionally and stare happily, smiling into space before starting to walk again. I actually envied his contentment in this mad world.

I saw a rock formation above the castle as Abigail told me in the cemetery, but it was a little far in front of the castle. Causing the boulders to fall might take out the drawbridge, but that would be the extent. However, I didn't think it could do much damage to the castle other than maybe psychologically to the vampires if a lone man destroyed part of their home.

With the ramparts and a moat before it, the castle itself looked impenetrable from an attack. If I could get in and kill the remaining inhabitants, especially the king, while the others hunted, I could probably hold off the failed vampires throughout the night and pick them off one by one until the sun came up. That is if I could even get inside and hold it.

The hills around the castle looked steep and I doubted that I could get inside through a back way before sunrise. By then, the horde would return and the two families would be dead if they were still alive. The vampires would be back before dawn. Time was on the vampires' side. Time stood directly against Abigail, me, and the families. I had to get in right away. Each second that the families spent in a vampire's lair could lead to an exponential amount of PTSD even if they weren't bitten. I had known many people who claimed disability for PTSD in the Safe Zone, and although I am not minimizing what they went through, however, anything most of them had experienced would pale to what those children could face inside that castle. I could smell the stench of rotting human corpses even from this distance. The failed vampires were notorious for bad hygiene. Richard's coven hated the vampiric failures, and Abigail despised it when I brought the faileds up in comparison to her more intelligent kindred.

I also knew that both the men and the women in those families were decent people and good fighters to have at one's side once I got in there. Although I wasn't sure how many vampires or other monstrosities were in the castle, I was hopeful that I could quickly liberate the family and then hold off the army of vampires when they returned. My goal was that the vampire horde would perish from the sunlight if I could hold them until dawn. That's if I could figure a way inside and survive against whoever was still inside.

I had to somehow enter through the front because I didn't have time to circle and find a way over the cliffs in the rear. I needed them to lower the drawbridge, but how?

I suddenly came up with a plan. It was a crazy ass plan, but I felt like I had no choice. I blew out a breath and got to work. I started by slicing my pinky finger on my left hand. I watch my blood bleed blackly in the night. I wiped the drops across the front of my coat.

There was no way that I could hide my blood scent from the vampires at this point. The die had been cast.

Chapter Thirteen

As Abigail stood in the graveyard in the fading sunlight, she watched Eric run away as the vampires rose around her and pursued him. She wanted to escape with him. She had lied when she said that her feet were frozen. She could move, but she had other plans.

During the long hike the night before, she had time to talk to the more intelligent ones, especially Jim. They weren't much for stimulating conversation, but she realized they all had a cunning and that they could not be allowed to roam free over the Forbidden Zone. They were a danger to both people and other vampires. The only reason she had survived with her mind intact was because Jim was infatuated with her and was obsessed with making her his mate. She also discovered that King Sadazar wanted her to appear before him with her intelligence to pump her for information before turning her into a failed vampire.

Although she knew she needed to get out of that situation quickly, she wanted to gain all the knowledge she could so that this perverted brood could be exterminated.

The one thing worrying her the most was King Sadazar. Jim had told her that he was a brilliant vampire and a military genius. King Sadazar's virus was the one that this army was infected with and Jim told her that if she was lucky, the king would infect her himself so that she could be like the rest of them and be an appropriate mate for him.

Abigail's desire was to run, however besides being somewhat under their control and would always be able to be tracked after what Cindy did to her, she felt a duty driving her. Deep inside she felt a responsibility for the plague of vampires. She, of course, was not responsible, but the reason why people hated and distrusted her in both Craigsville and in the Mountain Warrior's tribe was due to the atrocities committed by other vampires, especially ones like this pack. Abigail wanted to live a normal life one day, and that never could occur while other vampires hunted people.

She could have left with Eric in the graveyard, but she knew it was useless. They would find her and him as well. So she pretended to be unable to move her feet so that he could run without her. If she was with him, his life would always be in danger until Sadazar was dead.

During the day, she had had more power over her mind, but she was afraid that when night fell, even if she was far away, that they could influence her to attack Eric or track the two of them. That was one thing she would rather die than do.

So after Eric had run off, the sun had set, and the vampires around her rose, she continued to follow them hoping her feigned submission was believable. It was an easy ruse with the faileds, especially Jim, the leader of this detachment, who was blinded by his infatuation for her. However, if Sadazar was as brilliant as Jim believed, Abigail could be walking into not just the den, but the very mouth of a lion. However she was hoping if she had a chance, she could assassinate the Vampire King, and with him dead, his horde would fall apart.

Shortly after entering the ravine on the march from the graveyard, she smelled Eric's blood in the woods above her. She used a bit of her own mind control to hide Eric's scent from the other vampires, but even beyond smell, she could sense her friend. She could feel his heart beating with her own and that connection strengthened her own resolve.

His scent no longer stirred intense feelings of hunger in her as long as her guard was up. However the real feeling it stirred was a desire for his romantic companionship. But she knew that was a pipe dream. She could see his passion for her in the way he looked at her, but also sensed his equally strong repulsion to everything vampiric. As much as she loved Eric and wanted him, she equally desired to never see him again. Such a companionship could only lead to doom for the both of them, more so for Eric. The situation was too ambiguous, the conflicting feelings too extreme, but deep inside, beyond all the misgivings, she loved him with all her heart, and she knew he felt the same.

When she made eye contact with him as they passed his hide the first time, she suddenly desired to be eternally together with him although she knew that was a foolish thought. She loved him as a human. He did not wish to become a vampire, and she wasn't even sure if a mere kiss on the lips was enough to infect him through saliva. She gritted her teeth in futile anger at the situation.

As they approached the castle, the drawbridge lowered. Abigail caught the scent of death, rotting humans. These horrid vampires neglected to bury their victims, she immediately knew. She wasn't sure if it was due to poor hygiene or to use the stench as a repellent against human invaders. She also knew that some vampire covens reveled in the stench of death especially the ancient decrepit lines. Hers had been one of the more civilized covens who didn't dwell in such degenerate conditions, and her sensibilities found the place offensive for a number of reasons.

She crossed the bridge and looked down into the moat. The water had long dried, but it was a steep seventy foot high fall onto jagged rocks below. It looked like it could be deadly or at least debilitating even for a vampire to suffer such a plummet.

She was curious about how stupid her fellow travelers were. Jim had ordered a drooling idiot to carry her backpack for her, but they never tried to disarm her. Jim had wanted another failed to carry her M-16 as a gentlemanly favor to assist a lady, but Abigail insisted she carried it as if doing them a favor. When Jim persisted even more to have someone else carry the burden of her rifle, Abigail persisted more to the point that Jim finally relented. She was amazed how quickly they assumed that she became one of them even though she had yet to acquire their virus. She wondered if they were that stupid or if they were that confident of their mind control over her, or maybe they were so under the Sadazar's power that they believed all other vampires wanted to be like them. They were indeed blissful in their stupidity.

A shudder shot up her spine. If King Sadazar was indeed an antediluvian vampire, he might very well already have that power over her without her knowledge.

Now as Abigail entered the castle and the heavy drawbridge closed behind her with the thudding finality of a giant coffin lid, she realized the futility of being armed and surrounded by her enemies. There were well over thirty vampires armed with semi automatic rifles and hundreds more vampires not smart enough to operate a firearm. These vampires carried slightly less effective weapons like swords and staffs. Although none were very bright, they moved with a confident sense that she could tell they would be formidable enemies in a fire fight with either firearms or sticks and swords. By their demeanor, she guessed a few had prior military service before turning into vamps.

She scowled as she noticed millions of large cockroaches leisurely pacing the hall in front of her, packed tightly like the floor of a standing area concert for a popular band. The roaches acted as if they owned the place. The insects didn't even bother to scurry away as the vampires marched through the halls. She cringed as the hard exoskeletons crunched under her boots. From the hundreds of vampires around her, it was louder than walking through a leafy forest. The roaches who escaped the stomping then rushed in to eat their smashed brethren.

Despite the disgusting inhabitants, failed vampires and roaches alike as well as the stench of death, the decor of the castle was breathtaking. Tapestries, curtains, and carpets of medieval decadence covered everything. An occasional torch, although unneeded for a vampire to see in the castle, gave a magical ambiance to her sensitive eyes as well as all the other vampires around her.

Although she appreciated the woven artwork that she could see through the cockroaches that seemed to cover everything including the roof and walls, she considered that a torch or flaming arrow shot through a window would set the whole place on fire, that is if Eric was able to scrounge up an army to lay siege to this castle.

If things got really bad, she figured that she could start the fire herself as a distraction so that she may escape or to end it all, but she pushed the thought of self immolation from her mind. She would survive, she determined quietly, but she preferred to have her mind intact above living or dying.

She looked over the dense coverings of curtains and tapestries a little more and shuddered again at the thought of getting trapped in such an inferno. The only way to escape a living cremation would be dashing oneself on the stones at the bottom of the moat or trying to scale the cliff behind the castle, if it came down to it.

Eric had been right, it was foolish to have taken this burden on her shoulders to enter the castle alone and as their prisoner, but she was still armed, untied, and her mind was sound despite them having a degree of control over her.

Other decorations far more ghastly than the tapestries caught her attention and made her catch her breath. Dead and rotting human victims covered with cockroaches hung from gibbets throughout the halls. In medieval times people hung the executed in gibbets in the open air to serve as warnings. However these monsters hung them as trophies in the enclosed confines of the accursed castle. The stench caused her to dry heave and she guessed that these degenerates not only enjoyed and reveled in the smell of death, but probably used it as a human repellent and repellent against sane vampires such as herself.

As they progressed, she cast her glance down the side passages off the main hallway. She was tempted to slip out of the formation and disappear. Those assigned to guard her had a distant look as if the King had a hold of their minds, and she knew she could probably just casually walk away, but as escape crossed her mind, it felt like a giant hand savagely grabbed the back of her neck. The unseen fingers with sharp nails dug into her neck muscles almost causing her to sink to her knees in pain. She brought her hands up to her neck and realized that nothing physical had grabbed her. It was a psychic pull of a master vampire. More powerful than any that she had encountered in the past or was even aware existed in the world of vampires. Whatever the power was seemed to physically propel her into a great throne room. The other vampires around her seemed OK, however she could sense an awe and reverence about them as they entered the great hall.

Although Abigail had been a vampire for over a year and had seen many monstrous science experiments to the point that she was quite jaded in the horror department, a terror gripped her mind as the hold on her neck propelled her forward to a giant vampire, King Sadazar, who sat on the throne: a throne made of human skulls. Sadazar could have easily placed her in a trance and just had her walk in a daze, but she could tell that he reveled in the brute force of his psionic power and domination over her. She could read him. He wanted her lucid to have full awareness of his power and he enjoyed shocking her civilized sensibilities. She could tell he despised civilized vampires as much as civilized vampires despised him.

The Vampire King smiled hideously at her when they made eye contact. His fangs were bared. In fact, she could tell they were permanently barred. While most vampires had two to three inch fangs that they could keep hidden behind their lips, King Sadazar's fangs reached eight inches from his mouth and extended down past his pointed chin. His face was ancient and monstrous, no longer human if it ever was. He was a gargoyle-like creature, even in his mannerisms. As she got a better look, she could see that he didn't sit on his butt on the throne. Instead he perched in a squat like a bird of prey, as he hungrily eyed her from upon his throne.

The King stood up and stepped down from the throne onto the raised dias and beckoned her with a wave of his inhumanly long fingers. Immediately the force on her neck propelled her faster, she was powerless and ran to catch her feet up with her propelled body so she didn't fall on her face on the roach covered floor. She realized that the force and sensations of claws in her neck were all in her mind, but before she could rebel, she was standing before the giant vampire king.

Although horribly stooped over, he towered well over two feet above her. She guessed that if he stood fully erect, he would be well over nine feet tall. He stared at her with large eyes, eyes designed to see in the night, intense with intelligence and malicious intent. In his massive head his eyes were the size of two saucer plates.

She had heard that he had undergone a lot of DNA therapy. His oversized face and head were devoid of hair including eyebrows. His arms hung past his knees almost to the roach covered floor, and his spider-like fingers were each at least a foot long. She could also see the tips of leathery wings sticking up over his broad shoulders.

She wasn't sure how much of these changes were purposeful or a natural progress of being a vampire. She had always worried how much she would continue to change with her infection. Would she evolve to look like him? All the vampires she knew had only been vampires for a few years at the most. This guy had thousands of years to change if what Jim had told her was true.

However he seemed to revel in his frightening appearance. She guessed that from his facial tattoos and heavy facial piercings that added to his almost reptilian features.

She bowed her head in a show of submission so that he would not see the hatred burning in her eyes. The vampires around her however fell to their knees and prostrated themselves and hummed a deep tone that she took as a sign of worship.

"Ah. Ab-by-gail... You have come to me at last," Sadazar said in a sickly warm and deep grating voice that didn't sound as if it was issued from a human throat. He held his hands together as if praying and tapped the tips of his foot long fingers together. He had a strange and ancient accent that she couldn't place. She guessed that it was from a long dead language.

With her head only tilted down a little, Abigail stood tall amongst the prone worshippers. She felt as if she figured out the psionic effect that Sadazar used against her, and she believed that she could beat it.

She still had the rifle on her back and her handgun on her hip as well as her sheathed sword and knives. She reasoned that taking him out might shut down the minds of his coven. King Sadazar would have to look for a different way to defeat her, she thought.

Abigail lifted her head and looked calmly in his eyes as she said, "I apologize, King Sadazar, I don't know the customs and etiquette of your coven."

He smiled slightly, and quit tapping his fingers. He cocked his head slightly. A studied look shaded his eyes as if reading her soul.

"You will learn," he cooed in an ancient and gravelly voice. It was a threat that caused her to tremble suddenly.

Abigail felt as if an electric bolt suddenly shot down from her head into her limbs. The excruciating pain sent her down to her knees with her forehead crashing to the stone floor, killing a gushy cockroach in the process, but it happened so painfully and brutally quick that It took a moment for her to realize that she was kneeling prone on the ground with the other vampires.

King Sadazar's loud grating baritone but nasal voice resounded through the great hall, "You are legend, Ab-by-gail. A rebel. As are we. I am surprised that my minions brought you here instead of devouring you. I can see that they are starving for blood. Arise Jim."

"Yes, my lord," Jim said as he stood up with his head yet bowed. He had dropped his fake British accent. His voice trembled before his master.

The king asked, "Why bring this outsider to our coven before turning her with our strain?"

"Great King, my mate, Misty, was killed," Jim whined like a slightly nervous schoolboy.

"And?" Sadazar asked with a knowing smile.

"I wish Ab-by-gail to be my new mine," he said with possessiveness, strengthening his tone and confidence. "My new mate. My wife. My mine. I beg you please, Great King!"

Abigail shuddered as she felt a cold, slightly damp snake slither under her neck. The vampire king lifted her head up by the chin. She looked up into Sadazar's eyes and realized that what she felt slither over her was his elongated index finger wrapped around her throat, not a snake, but she would rather be touched by a cobra. He studied her face and delicately turned it side to side by her chin. He nodded appraisingly.

"You've great taste in women, my son. She's very pretty," Sadazar said. From the corner of her eyes, Abigail could see the praise caused Jim to smile proudly. The king continued, "Maybe too good. I may just prefer her for myself."

Abigail did not see Jim's reaction because she unconsciously attempted to recoil in horror, but Sadazar's long hands enveloped her head and held her like a bully would hold a baby sparrow.

"No. No," Sadazar laughed. "I have been blessed enough. I will let you have her, Jim, but we must do something to calm her overactive mind so that she would be more like you and your brethren, but let me study her mind for a moment first. She is strong."

He then looked into her horror filled eyes. Her weapons were useless and she was unable to move. She totally was under his mental domination.

He cooed in a rumbling voice. "You think my sons and daughters are stupid. 'Faileds,' is what your arrogant father Richard called them. No, loyal, obedient, assimilated. Those're better words for my children."

Abigail's mind rebelled. She forced herself to regain control of her hand and reached for her sword that was closest to her reach, but his large hands wrapped around her shoulders pinning her arms as

Sadazar's guards simultaneously grabbed her. He could have stopped her with his mind but she realized that he wanted to touch her with his cold, clammy reptilian-like fingers. He enjoyed physical domination as much as mental. He gently wiped the gore of the cockroach from her forehead that still remained after she was forced to prostrate.

King Sadazar proclaimed, "Yes. We must reinfect you with our virus. I heard that you had great power over humans before your coven was shut down in disgrace. We will give you that power over vampires. Ruling humans does not matter because they are like ruling cattle. We, the vampires, are the future, and we, my coven, are the future of vampirism. The goal of our coven is to rule over the other vampires and unite us all under my world wide rule."

King Sadazar looked to Jim and asked, "Have you consummated with your new mate, Jim?"

"No master. Wanted King's permission first," Jim said in a bashful tone that turned Abigail's stomach even more.

"There's no better way to reinfect her than to mate." Sadazar motioned to courtly vampires and ordered, "Prepare the matrimonial chamber for Jim and his new bride."

With grunts and no words, a few vampires dressed as French maids ran off to do his bidding.

Three guards held Abigail in place as Sadazar lightly drummed his fingers on the top of Abigail's head. "You find us repulsive, yet you'll be one of us. Indeed you will eventually acquire my appearance. All vampires eventually look like me. You feared that transformation, and it is true. You'll obey like the rest of your brothers and sisters. They had dreams and rebellious natures like you, but our virus will cure that. Your mind will find peace." He laughed and then looked deep in her eyes, stooping even lower so his face was inches from hers and above the gore in the castle, she almost vomited from the stench of his rotted breath. "The funny thing is," the king continued, "is that you will have your current awareness intact, forever restrained, buried somewhere in your soul where it can't escape, but will always torment you as your body and will follow my domination. Indeed, your will will be my will as I work through you."

Abigail stayed silent. King Sadazar needed no psionic abilities to read the thoughts of horror swimming in the pools of Abigail's eyes. He lingered, gazing at her living terror, as if her eyes were precious jewels.

"Sire!" a female voice called from the back.

Without moving his body, Sadazar flicked the vision of his oversized eyes toward the back of his hall, "Speak, my daughter."

"She loves humans over her kindred, Great King." the female voice reported.

Abigail answered in her own defense. "Not true. I am a vampire. I love vampires."

"Why do you side with humans, dear Abigail?" asked the king.

"I owed one of them my life for saving me from a mob in a human village. They meant to crucify me." Abigail couldn't move, but she flicked her eyes to the scar on her wrist from the crucifixion attempt.

He appraised the scar.

"Eric," he purred with a rumble like a tiger. "He will be one of us too."

King Sadazar looked thoughtfully over his people as if counting his flock.

"How many of us did she and the humans kill?" asked Sadazar.

"Number too high to count, Great King. More than three," a failed vampire answered.

A small part of Abigail quietly laughed at the stupid answer. The answer was closer to "more than seventy," but something inside of her screamed with the knowledge that such stupidity would be her future if she did not find a way to fight back, and fast!.

"Is this true?" Sadazar asked her.

Abigail replied reasonably while knowing that reason and logic wouldn't work with this king, "I had to defend myself. Your offspring attacked other vampires as well as humans."

Sadazar interrupted her, "True, but Jim's given you the chance to join us, and because of your defense of the human, my offspring still hunger for human blood. They didn't feast last night. You can hear them stir. You withheld the blood of those humans. You should've shared. It's not just our coven's rule. All vampires must follow that directive. Even your former, disgraced coven were compelled to share its human cattle with all vampires."

Abigail started to answer but heard a commotion in the back of the hall. A flash of both hunger and worry crossed King Sadazar's face. Abigail looked with horror as she saw the families of Richard, Racheal, Jerry, and Christy and their girls as they were led into the dark hall. The mass of vampires shifted and she heard the groaning and snarling of them in their bloodlust.

King Sadazar raised his voice in a loud stern command, "Guards! Quickly! Take my cattle to my feeding chamber." He clapped his long hands together and boomed, "Now!"

It seemed to Abigail, that despite the King expecting her to share her "human cattle" with other vampires, he didn't follow his own rules. The families were for the King alone.

Sadazar looked down at Abigail. He knew her thoughts and said in a confidential tone, "They are going to my private reserve. They aren't enough to feed all my vampires. My offspring still needs to hunt yet tonight."

The vampires guarding the two families savagely struck at some of the more bold and feral failed vampires, whose bloodlust overrode their obedient natures. The bold ones tried to get at the humans snarling with drool dripping off of their bared fangs. Only the strokes of the flats of the guards' blades, batons, and rifle butts kept the failed vampires at bay. A few times the guards drew blood, slashing in areas that were not deadly or permanently debilitating for a vampire. Abigail wondered how the King kept control over the faileds. Even with psychic power, the bloodlust of failed vampires was legendary when they smelled humans. It had been a while since she had last fed and her own blood thirst was nearly uncontrollable. Even she was stirred by the blood scent of the two families that she could smell over the rotting corpses around her. On top of that, the howls of the others drove even at her own vampiric impulses.

The human families recoiled as dozens of vampires advanced with snarling howling roars and bared fangs. The families didn't seem to see her as she blended in with the hundreds of other black cloaked vampires in the darkened hall.

The guards continued to respond with savagely barked commands and strikes with the dull aspect of their swords, but the failed vampires continued to crowd the humans, and pressed on the guards tightly encircling them. Full bedlam was about to break loose.

The guards led the people off to a side room and the heavy door slammed shut. A bolt crashed with a thud, locking the families in relative safety, and a mass of vampires clawed at the door. Abigail could see claw marks on the solid wooden door from countless past attempts to breach it in the past.

King Sadazar commanded the three holding Abigail. "Guards! Handcuff her. Shackle both her arms and legs. Then take her to the matrimonial chamber so that Jim can have his reward and turn her into one of us."

Panic surged through Abigail. Once handcuffed, she would be defenseless. This was her last chance at escape. She had to shoot the king between the eyes now or it would be over for her and possibly the civilized world if the King's insane plan was unleashed.

She slipped an arm free from one guard's hold as they were distracted by the two human families. She got to a kneeling position, and jabbed her fingers in the throat of another guard. She gouged at the eyes of the third. Just as she was free from their grasp and reaching for her handgun, she suddenly felt an electric shock explode from the back of her head causing her to see a flash of lights. Pain streaked down her limbs and then blackness enveloped her.

She found herself on the floor looking up. She pulled at her arms that were secured behind her back and realized that they were cuffed as were her ankles. A chain connected her legs so that she could walk but not use her full stride to run. Her weapons were gone. She had been unconscious for at least a minute, she reasoned. With one hand, King Sadazar lifted her by her hair so that she stood upright. His strength was beyond superhuman. It was diabolical.

The king smiled at her looking her in the eyes with a possessiveness that ripped at her sanity, and then he instructed three of his minions, "Escort her to the matrimonial suite with Jim. Keep watch until her mind is like ours."

"Thank you, Great King of Kings," Jim said in a giddy voice.

The King smiled at her and said, "And to answer your unasked question, even if you weren't changed by my strain, you will still end up looking like me. All vampires achieve this greatness."

Abigail let out an involuntary scream of terror as she was led away. Jim spoke to her in a soothing, reassuring tone.

"You will enjoy this, my mate. So will I," he promised.

That made Abigail scream louder.

Chapter Fourteen

The fighting of the blood-crazed failed vampires against the guards raged around Abigail. As the horde tried to get into the room where the family was locked, Abigail was half led, half carried to a room just off from the main hall. The matrimonial chamber was enshrined in pink and valentine crimson tapestries. Mirrors ringed the room and ceiling, and everything, including the frilly bed was covered with the disgustingly large cockroaches and their fecal matter. She reasoned that these degenerates probably enjoyed the feel of roaches crawling on them during the act of sexual union. To these sickos, it added to the caress of intercourse. She fought her stomach as it threatened to heave in disgust.

The bed was heart shaped and occupied the center of the room. A horrid flood of ideas of what might happen to her threatened to wreck her perception of sanity, even without the infected bite from Jim. Images from sexually perverse to brutally violent tore at her mind.

She was alone with Jim and three large male vampiric guards who watched with grins of expectation and guns at the ready. Even with chains on her wrists and ankles and smug grins on their faces, they didn't relax their holds on their weapons around her.

She looked at Jim whose eyes blazed with desire. She was not sure if it was arousal or bloodlust. She wanted to scream curses at him.

Instead she pleaded, "Jim, please. Escape with me. We will have freedom. Just you and me. We can do anything. Go anywhere. You won't be bossed around by him anymore."

He shook his head and smiled patronizingly as if she had the mentality of a small child. He said, "I like being bossed around. King Sadazar great vampire. He shares his greatness with our minds."

Despite her real feelings, Abigail managed a seductive smile and said suggestively, "I'll boss you around and be submissive to you at the same time."

As she said that she unconsciously strained against her restraints. It was hopeless. The shackles were made strong enough to withstand the brutal strength of an enraged bull vampire.

Jim nodded and said, "I make sure of it."

He closed the heavy oaken door with a thud of finality. The fighting of the bloodmad vampires could still be heard, but muted. Jim stepped up to her and ran the back of his finger down her face.

"We have romantic consummation. Now. Then I must bite you while we-- while we– you know," his voice trailed off with an oddly adolescent-like shyness..

"Jim--" she said, desperately pulling at her hand cuffs wanting to beg for freedom from the bonds.

"Ab-by-gail!" he replied back passionately as he mistook her desperate plea for arousal.

She almost rolled her eyes.

"No!" she said, but didn't get to say anything else.

Abigail then heard ferocious snarls and screams outside in the great hall and the ringing of sword on sword. The intensity of the fighting grew progressively worse. Despite the raucous fighting outside their room, Jim advanced on her, eyes brightened with a single minded sense of fulfillment and ears seemingly turned off. The three guards watched with equal anticipation. One, who was a mouth breather, had drool dripping off of his exposed fangs. The drool was thick and connected his fangs with his cloak like a slimy string on a monocle.

"Jim, unshackle me and send the guards away, so we can be alone," she said seductively.

He replied, "The guard enjoy, maybe join, and you stay chained."

Neither Jim nor the guards reacted when the reverberating sound of gunfire now joined the clanging of sword on sword. It echoed through the castle. The fighting in the hall was a constant din behind her. She wondered if she could use it for a distraction, but first she had to get free of the cuffs that bound her limbs.

Jim lovingly ran the back of a finger over her face. She hid her disgust only to keep him in her confidence. She forced a seductive smile and then forced it away as she pretended to be concerned.

Abigail said in clipped failed English, "Jim. They fighting. You must stop them. They kill our King Saddazar."

"They just hungered. Want blood of humans. So do we, but later." Jim said. "Great King, stop fighting. Eventually."

"Jim, you must listen to me. I know where hundreds of humans sleep. Enough for every vampire to drink tonight. Not far. Humans easy prey at night. Eric told me of human plot against King."

"Consummate first," he said as he roughly groped her with possessiveness.

With her hands cuffed behind her back, she slammed her shoulder into his chest hard enough to stop him, knocking him so that he fell back and sat on the frilly bed that was also covered with giant cockroaches and their shells crackled under his weight. This got Jim's full attention, firing his passions even more.

"Ab-by-gail!" he said breathlessly.

Abigail insisted firmly, "Get Great King Sadazar. I can save his kingdom."

Jim jumped to his feet and said with passion, "After consummate marriage. Now!"

She heard the King's voice shouting orders in an ancient language outside the door. It boomed above the fighting. Even the King was concerned about the fighting now.

With the full force of her lungs she screamed in a loud voice that only vampires can attain, "Great King Sadazar! I will submit fully to you and save your kingdom with the blood of mankind. Great King Sadazar! Blood of mankind!"

Jim slapped her face and yelled at her, "Quiet. Consume sex union! Now!"

She was about to give up when she gave one last effort, "King Sadazar! King Sadazar!" she screamed repeatedly. "Blood of mankind! Human blood! Blood! Blood feast!"

Jim placed his dirty and odorous hand over her mouth, silencing her. She cringed and bit his fingers, causing him to scream. He let go rubbing his hand. A crazy smile sliced his face in reaction to the pain before passion.

Abigail spat the taste of Jim's fingers from her mouth and screamed again, "King Sadazar! King Sadazar! Blood! Human blood, Great King of Kings!"

The door was flung open and the monstrous king loomed in the doorway, ducking to bring his head inside under the door frame. The fighting outside was almost deafening now with the door opened. He glared at her with eyes full of ancient wisdom, on guard for deceit.

Then the king addressed Jim, "She still has on clothes. Do you need lessons on what to do with a woman? Has your cock failed you?" He growled in sick humor. After making the joke, his eyes grew grim as he looked at her. "Young lady, why did you summon me?

"I can save your kingdom, Great King," she said.

"How will you save my kingdom?"

She looked into his skeptical and probing eyes. She said, "I know you smelled the scent of Eric on me."

"Yes," Sadazar said. "You were both physically close and emotionally as well today in the graveyard. I know that already. I can even smell your emotions, what you call love for each other, on you. I can even read that he dare not even write of his true passions for you in his notes. He lies to himself about his feelings for you, as you do for him," he added mockingly.

Abigail said, "He's leading an army of men, an hour's march away to attack us tomorrow in daylight when they are strong. They sleep now in tents. We can have all the blood we want while they are weak at night. It'll stop the fighting of your minions before anymore are killed and keep your human cattle safe for you. But we must move tonight! Now!"

She forced herself to imagine an army encampment of tents. She wasn't sure if she could fool him with the image that she imagined for him to read in her brain, but she was running out of schemes.

Sadazar glared at her. She could feel his foreign psychic caress in her head as if he was sensing the row of tents that she imagined for him. She saw in his eyes that either he didn't believe her or maybe he didn't really care if there was an army of men.

Abigail persisted. "I can lead the way so your vampires can feed. Let me show my loyalty and keep my mind and I will rule at your side as your submissive queen."

She knew that he would never let her "rule" with him, but she believed that she had to act like she was after power through him. He would not believe her if she acted purely with altruism for him and his coven. His mind was too deviant to think someone would truly love and care for others, but someone who was after power, that was believable.

"Please. I can save," she almost begged.

"No!" he barked.

She insisted, "They'll attack the castle by day if we don't get them now when they're weakened at night."

"No! The castle's impregnable, unlike you when Jim gets done." he said with finality and a wink at Jim. "If they come tomorrow, it'll be like a blood delivery service, and we'll feast then."

He turned, leaving the room and started to close the door behind himself. "Have fun, Jim," the vampire king added with another wink of his monstrous sized eye.

Abigail saw that she lost the battle with the King. Her hope was dying as the King started to close the door, but she had one last desperate chance.

Before the door fully closed, Abigail shouted loud enough for all in the hall to hear above the din of combat that raged for King Sadazar's personal human blood stock. "Bloodfeast! Bloodfeast! Bloodfeast!" she cried. She strengthened it with a mental pulse of the image and scent of human blood. Just like she could hide a human scent, she could also stimulate human scent in their minds.

The din of battle died suddenly as Abigail had their attention.

Abigail continued with the call as well as psychic blasts, "Bloodfeast! There's all the human blood you can drink! A true bloodfeast! Tonight! Bloodfeast! Bloodfeast! Bloodfeast!"

All of the struggle in the hall stopped, replaced by silence other than the clomp of feet running for the door to the matrimonial chamber. The vampires crowded in the doorway around King Sadazar. The door was forced back open from their bustling excitement. They crowded around the king to stare at her. They were driven bloodmad by the news as she imposed the vision of rows of tents full of beating human hearts.

Even King Sadazar couldn't stop them now that she had spilled the beans of a bloodfeast.

"Bloodfeast! Bloodfeast! Bloodfeast!" she shouted a few more times causing them to shout, "Bloodfeast! Bloodfeast! Bloodfeast!" as a reply.

Abigail knew the one word that could get the attention of even the dumbest vampire, and she had fired them up to deadly intensity that couldn't be stilled without an actual bloodfeast. It was the vampiric version of screaming fire in a crowded movie theater.

"Bloodfeast! Bloodfeast! Bloodfeast," they continually screamed back and they began to chant it together, seeming to shake the walls of the castle.

She shouted again, "Bloodfeast! An army, but sleep in tents. Easy pickings!" she said in the clipped English of a failed. "People even more stupider at night. Blood feast!"

"Blood feast! Blood feast! Blood feast!" they shouted back.

King Sadazar actually looked relieved as the fighting turned to cheers. "Quiet!" he bellowed far louder than all the vampires in the castle together.

He said to her with narrow and suspicious eyes, "Tell us where this army is, so the others may hunt, and then you and Jim can continue."

"Yes! We continue, Great King," Jim said as he held desperately to Abigail's shoulder..

Abigail said, "I will lead them, Great King. I need blood too as you can see. I gain trust, by killing people. I wish to be accepted by you, and rule as your queen with my mind intact. Let me show my loyalty."

He glared at her with less suspicion and more with simmering anger as he realized that the young vampiress was far smarter, more cunning than he had anticipated. His vampires milled and pushed excitedly around him chanting, "Bloodfeast! Bloodfeast Bloodfeast!"

Sadizar couldn't tell them no at this point. For all his psychic dominance over them, the bloodmadness was beyond even his control.

"Guards!" Sadazar commanded. "Watch her! Unshackle her feet. Cuff the hands in front of her. She leads you to blood. Any trick, bite her, drink her blood, and bring her back in a compliant state, infected with our strain."

"I can infect her with consummate now, Great King!" Jim stated.

The King ignored him. If Abigail was reinfected she would be unable to lead the bloodmad vampires. The change laid a vampire up for a while and his clan was at the end of their patience. The King gestured to the three guards who looked as disappointed as Jim, but they obeyed his psychic command.

Her hands were uncuffed from behind and then re-cuffed in front. Her legs seemed to stretch gratefully on their own accord once freed. She wasn't completely happy, but she was getting a chance to fight back, escape, or at least delay the rape that had been about to occur on the roach infested heart shaped bed. A delay meant a fighting chance and that's all she wanted.

"Go!" King Sadazar solemnly ordered her.

Abigail led the way through the door crunching through the cockroaches under her boots. Jim walked beside her with a disappointed scowl etched deeply on his face, but the rest of the vampiric horde was bubbling over with excited snarls and howls. The fighting had ceased, and the horde followed Abigail out of the castle.

***

Five vampires were left behind in the castle to act as the rear guard after the others had left to follow Abigail. With jealous rage, they watched their brethren march away as they looked over the moat. It took all their discipline to not follow, especially after hearing the new vampiress scream, "Bloodfeast!" That chant still echoed through their heads.

The five were as high functioning as failed vampires could get. They didn't have great psionic abilities, but they could shoot firearms with accuracy, strategize a little, but most importantly, they could follow basic yet somewhat complex orders especially with King Sadazar's psychic influence.

The castle was so well fortified that anyone of these rear guards could defend the castle from a hundred men if armed with a semi automatic rifle and a good supply of ammo. Of which they were all well armed and more importantly well trained in the defense of the castle. No armed attack could get past them in this fortress, especially at night.

However, they were miserable. They had not had human blood in three days because that new vampiress, Abigail, ruined their hunt the night before. They angrily lowered the drawbridge and watched her lead the hundreds of vampires over the moat. Then reluctantly, they raised the drawbridge as ordered.

"I want to hunt!" A tall thin vampire who always looked short of blood even after just feeding. His hollow cheeks were always pale and sweaty. He quit pulling on the rope when the drawbridge was only halfway up. He let out a final whimper like a hungry wolf. The other vampire who was helping him raise the drawbridge stopped as well in solemn, unspoken agreement

"Quit whining. Raise bridge now. We feast when they get back with prisoners," ordered the stout middle aged vampire who stood watching the others work with his thick arms crossed over his barrel chest. He was the boss in the castle, after the King of course, and did his best to try to look and act the part of what he thought the vampiric captain of the guard should.

He had been kicked out of the Army after ten years service for a series of alcohol related incidents. Being "The Captain" wasn't different from when he was a Staff Sergeant, and it had a lot more perks.

However the thin whiny one still looked into the distance without obeying his order.

The Captain barked, "Get back to work. Put back into it! Quit whining like little bitch dog! Now! Move!"

"I know I eat when they get back, but I like hunt, fight, slay!" whined the slender guard as he went back to work pulling on the rope.

The other vampires grunted and agreed. Even the Captain of the guard nodded. He wanted to hunt too, but maintaining discipline was more important.

The Captain said agreeably, "Some vampires drink hospital blood to avoid killing or drink animals. Disgusting. I like pulse of hot human blood shooting in my mouth, like drinking hot blood drinking fountain."

There was a round of laughing and grunting in agreement. There was nothing like fresh hot pulsing blood. Unlike animal blood or hospital blood, fresh warm human blood was as intoxicating as whiskey for a vampire especially after an adrenalized hunt.

The thought of fresh blood stirred the Captain.

The Captain had forgotten his name from his previous life once he had been turned into one of King Sadizar's vampires. Now he simply knew himself as Captain. He loved his new appellation and his job. This was all he wanted in life besides a chance to hunt.

Right now he was fantasizing about the King feeding on his six humans in the cage. He dreamed about who King Sadazar would sink his fangs into first, the strong, vital men and women? The soft, innocent, and sweet tasting kids. Oh, if he could at least hear their helpless screams as he tortured them. They all looked and smelled delicious.

The drawbridge finally closed with a resounding thud.

The captain then muttered, "I want hunt too."

"You say not say that," one of the other vampires complained with a rough laugh.

The captain grunted and said, "I sayed that, but I Captain and can sayed that if want. You can't if I order. I want hunt! I want feed now."

They all laughed as the two vampires finished raising the drawbridge, tying off the rope to the drawbridge. The night began to pass slowly for the watch..

"What? Who called for blood delivery service?" asked the skinny vamp who had run up to the watchtower after raising the drawbridge. From above he laughed as if he joked.

"What talk about, you?" demanded the Captain in a slightly grouchy tone.

The skinny vamp explained. "Like pizza delivery, but human. Human come this way, Cap'n!"

"What?" demanded the Captain.

"One human approaching," the skinny vamp called down again.

"Human? Not vamp?" asked the Captain.

"Yes sir!" the skinny one yelled back with excitement. "Human!"

The captain sprinted to an open window in the stonewall and looked out. He saw that it was definitely a human and not a vampire who was approaching. The person had a weak headlamp lit on his forehead and was stumbling on the road, obviously not used to running at night. Terror marked this human's face that went far beyond just fear of the dark. All the vampiric guards caught the scent of fresh blood, not blood confined in the veins and arteries, but free flowing blood from a fresh wound. He either had the blood of another person on him or someone had freshly cut, shot, or bit him. The scent nearly drove them all insane.

As his headlamp flashed upon the castle, they heard the human exclaim, "Oh thank God. Please open up! Vampires attacked our camp. They killed and drank all the blood except mine. I am the last one! There is no more blood for them!"

"Dammit," the captain swore. That meant no blood would be coming back for them and with guard duty, that meant no hunting until the next night, and it was hard to sleep during the day when blood starved.

"Please! Open up!" The man called to the guard tower, "I am wounded and dying. I am unarmed but will help defend against the vampires if I can borrow a firearm or knife, but open quickly. I'm dying and vampires are on my trail."

The captain was about to excitedly lower the drawbridge himself, but then he stopped as he worried about a trap. His thick eyebrows compressed against each other over his crooked nose as he thought. He scanned the immediate flat land on the other side of the moat that was devoid of any hiding places for the human's potential backup to hide if indeed it was some kind of trap. The human seemed to be lying about vampires trailing him. He heard none of the vampires screaming the cry of the hunt. Maybe the human was just terrified. The Captain pondered the situation for a moment as the desperate man waited for the drawbridge to lower.

"Please!" The human called as he desperately kept shooting terrified glances behind himself. "Get me in before the vampires come back! I'm the last human! I'll have to run away from here if you don't hurry."

The skinny vampire said, "Captain, if he chased, we need let him in. I go nuts if I watch another vamp feed on him in front of us, across moat."

"Shh, human might hear you," the Captain growled.

The man called out with a cracking, desperate voice, constantly looking behind himself, "Please. They are on my trail, and I have no weapons! Please let me in!" He cried in a plea with emotional strain.

Something seemed fishy to the captain.

The human coiled his legs to run away from the castle and said, "I have to leave now!"

The Captain caught another whiff of the blood from the wounded human.

"Wait, human!" The Captain called.

"Lower bridge! Quick!" ordered the Captain in a harsh whisper, "but raise as soon as he can jump on the drawbridge. We no want other humans getting in or other vampires stealing prey."

"Yes sir!" The vampiric guards responded excitedly.

"Yes, fellow human! We protect you from evil vampires," laughed the skinny vampire as he yelled at the man.

"Thank you so much," the human called back.

"We take care of you, human," laughed another vampire. "Good care!"

"Shh!" the captain warned. He did not want to tip the human that they weren't there to rescue him, but he was chuckling as well at their good fortune. Even an armed human was no match for them, and this one was unarmed and wounded.

The other vampires worked, turning the wheels to lower the drawbridge. The desperate man shifted nervously until it was low enough and then he leapt and scrambled on the bridge as it began to raise back up. The human ran down the fifty meter long bridge.

The captain was pleased. Here was their bloodfeast delivered and no human invaders could get in, nor thieving vampires to rob them of the spoils. The Captain was actually worried more about other vampires stealing his prey than he was afraid of humans. It was night. The vampires ruled. He actually wished there were more people to feed on, but no other humans rushed the castle as the drawbridge was raised.

The man made it down the length of the drawbridge as it was raised and he watched as they finished cranking the wheel. When it was up and locked into place with the thud of a coffin lid, the human asked, "Is that secured? We don't want any vampires getting in here."

The five vampires surrounded him laughing.

"Yes, human," said the captain. "No one else can get in here... or out."

The vampires laughed hungrily at the Captain's words.

"Now we feast," said the skinny vampire. He drew a long thin dagger that was used in vampiric circles to precisely pierce the carotid artery without the horrible rendering of flesh that teeth and fang tended to wreak. It also made sure not to turn a person into a vampire. Stories had been told of vampires biting a person to drink the blood and leaving them to die but didn't drink enough blood to fully kill them. The person, now a new vampire, sought and killed the vampire who turned him as revenge. It was a common tale of human lore in vampiric circles. In this case, the controlled bloodletting would ensure that the human wasn't ravaged too much so that he could be turned and join Sadazar's ever growing army.

Two other vampire guards removed two huge chalices from their cloaks to catch the blood for communal imbibement.

The vampires began to crowd the human with drooling, exposed fangs as they scented his blood from a cut. However the Captain followed his sense of smell and noticed that the "wound" was only a slight cut on the human's pinkie finger, a paper cut at worst. It wasn't a wound at all. He had suspected that something was fishy.

The skinny vampire laughed and lunged with the dagger. The captain screamed as the human's hand dropped to a hilt at his slim waist that had been hidden by his coat and drew a small concealed sword and swung it. The two foot long blade sliced the skinny vamp's head off as the man's headlamp pointed in their eyes. The batteries were weak, but too much for their sensitive eyes and they were temporarily blinded.

The captain stepped back and realized that he had recognized the man from a wanted poster. "It's Eric! Get him!"

"Eric!" the others cried with excitement and surprise.

The vampires drew their swords and rushed the lone man. They outnumbered him. It should be easy, thought the Captain. The human, Eric, was stupider than the Great King thought he was, the Captain thought to himself.

Chapter Fifteen

I had watched the vampires march by from the castle and lay quietly until I was sure the last one had passed. The last was that obese fellow with a waddle, who would stop occasionally and stare happily into space before starting to walk again.

I studied their castle. If I could take out the vampiric king while he was alone, I was hoping this terrible horde would disperse to the winds without the king's influence.

I was stumped without a solution until it dawned on me that there was only one thing that could cause the vampires to head out with Abigail in the lead. I had seen no evidence on the trail that they had fed on blood. Although Abigail was more in control of her impulses than most vampires, even she got a wild look when starved for blood.

This was crazy, I thought as I drew a small pocket knife and lightly sliced the tip of the pinkie on my left hand. In the moonlight, I watched the black drops of blood bead on the tip. I rubbed it across the front of my coat. I had cast the die. Even as small as the cut was, spilled blood would be smelled by any vampire within a quarter mile of me, maybe more. I had to attack now. With the fresh cut, not even Abigail could psychically hide my scent from them.

I felt stupid as I left my rifle and long sword on the ground in a hidden spot, but I couldn't conceal the longer weapons on my person. Besides, I thought my handgun and short sword would be better suited for taking over the castle in close combat. Once I had control, I would use their rifles that I saw bristling with the guards to defend the castle from a breach and hopefully free the two families.

I shook my head at my audacity. I knew my plan was insane and overly optimistic, but that's how I had been living life lately.

I ran at the castle crying for my life. I probably could have won an academy award. A light breeze was at my back wafting the scent of my slightly bloody finger toward the defenders. I purposely cracked my voice to sound desperate. Besides the genuine fear that I had, it was pretty easy to let my voice break. Back in highschool, my adopted father had wanted me to be in the school's choir. I didn't want that, but I had to obey. There were also a few other classmates of the same opinion, and in the same situation. We used to sing horribly on purpose. Looking back I feel sorry for those who took singing seriously, because the rehearsals went much longer than they should have. The purposeful cracking of my voice finally got me kicked out of the choir. Would it fool the vampires?

When the drawbridge lowered, I felt both a sense of relief and dread. Relief because my plan worked and dread because I was a lone human entering the castle of vampires at night.

I heard the vampires laughing and addressing me as "human," as I negotiated with them into letting me inside. It irked me that even the stupidest of vampires thought that they were far superior to people. Abigail had told me that. When I asked her if she thought she was smarter than most people, she gave me that sweet smile of hers and she joked, saying, "I always knew that I was smarter than everyone else even before. Doesn't everyone, no matter their intelligence, including you?"

I had just smiled back at her. Even without psionic abilities, Abigail could read the human experience perfectly. Everyone thinks they are smart. Vampirism just emphasized it.

Again I thought that I couldn't let this horde ruin her mind. I loved her sense of humor among many other traits.

Once the drawbridge had closed behind me, the true terror hit me as five vampires circled me and came at me with that slim dagger. The hungry look in their eyes always hit a nerve when I saw it directed at me. No one other than a psychopath stares at another person like that and there were five of these freaks gazing hungrily at me.

The castle reeked of deathly decay. Something kept crunching beneath my boots, but I didn't have time to see what was the source of the sound as I was about to launch headlong into a deadly fight.

I didn't have to fake apprehension at this point when I saw the sharp knife and communal chalice in their hands as they approached. I had seen Abigail use the slim dagger expertly on a deer to drink its blood, but my apprehension quickly turned to disgust, anger, and raging hatred. I looked at them so that my headlamp would blind them.

They shouted in surprise when, instead of retreating, I flew at them, drawing my blade and sliced the nearest one with a thin hungry look etched into the permanent lines on his face. His head bounced and then rolled across the floor.

"It's Eric! Get him!" An older, heavyset vampire screamed as he stepped back and drew his sword. "Get him!" he ordered again.

They shouted my name in a snarling chorus, driven by madness and hunger.

I had a flashback in my mind of another vampire who imprinted a chanted order to, "Kill! Kill! Kill!" in my head from another battle. I had thought that Abigail had exorcised that chant from my mind, but it flooded back along with an almost insane desire to kill. It hurled me into the pit of maddened fury as I attacked.

The four remaining vampires stepped back to draw their swords which were in easier reach than the rifles strapped across their backs as they realized the bloodletting dagger wasn't enough to stop my fury. They also may have gone for their swords because bullets would kill me and stop the arterial pulse. I think they still saw me as food, rather than a threat.

Regardless, I pounced on one before his sword cleared his hilt. My blade sank deep into the place where the base of his neck met his shoulder. I swore as I tried to yank my sword free after it wedged in the bones.

The captain and the remaining two vampires attacked with the full ferociousness of their flashing blades. I let go of my sword that was still embedded in the neck and retreated until my back was against the drawbridge. I removed my Glock from my appendix holster and unleashed a salvo of three or four bullets into the nearest. My trigger finger worked too spastically to count the rounds.

The wounded vampire screamed as his heart was torn to shreds until his voice turned to gurgles as his lungs and trachea filled with his own blood. I pumped another into his brain through the center of his forehead. His eyes crossed, and he groaned and fell into gurgling silence. His fangs scuffed my right boot as his shattered head hit the floor.

One swung at my head with a sword and I had nowhere to go, so I dropped to a squatting position and fired upward into his chest and face, blowing away his nose. His sword crashed into the wood and steel of the drawbridge inches above me. He collapsed on top of me as I tried to roll to the side away from him. I cursed his blood as it sprayed on me, praying that I did not get infected.

As I threw the dying vampire off of me, my handgun probed the darkness seeking the older stocky vampire who seemed to be incharge. I had heard one of them address him as Captain, but I was alone. He must have run away or was hiding in a dark corner safe from the probing of my human eyes.

I scrambled to my feet, breathing hard, and looked around. I grabbed a few M-16s and swords from the dead vampires for the families, and kept my handgun in my grip.

It was definitely a vampire's castle, so very little attention was paid to good lighting. There were electric chandeliers on the ceiling in the large passage ahead, but they were turned off if they even worked. An occasional torch lit my way. I knew that vampires didn't need the torches, but to their sensitive eyes, sparse fire light gave their homes a magical ambiance. It was similar to the way people use sun lamps in their homes during the dead of winter. I could only imagine how the flickering flames of a small torch looked to their nocturnal vision.

I had a headlamp on my head whose weak batteries made the lamp worthless for my sight beyond a few meters, but I kept it on to blind an attacking vampire.

After quickly eyeing my surroundings, I put a fresh magazine in my handgun and holstered it. I removed my sword from the neck of the vampire with a violent wrench. I had damaged his spinal cord. He was paralyzed but alive. I dispatched him with a crushing slice to his skull and wiped the blood on the dead, twitching vampire's cloak. I walked away from the drawbridge, toward what I thought would be the center of the castle. I was hunting for a king's head.

The stone passageway was probably about 45 degrees Fahrenheit, but I felt an occasional bead of sweat roll down my face and tickle my chest as it ran down to my belly. The sweat was strictly from nerves and fire from the earlier mortal combat.

A torch blazed very distantly. Instinctively, I desired to look toward the primal safety of the firelight, but I knew from Bryan, Critter, and Abigail that not only would that ruin my night vision, but night creatures, such as vampires, would hide far from the light source for an ambush. I purposely focused on the darkest recesses, hallways, and corners that I passed by as I walked.

At times like this, I really wished for her at my side. We had been through a lot together, and I trusted her fully, especially when it hit the fan. I had to rely on her night vision and her knowledge of the ways of the enemy. However, although it was lessening over time, deep in my heart, I still felt a superstitious fear of her as much as I desired her help. Nothing personal. I loved her, but the whole vampire thing seemed insurmountable to pass. Although I told myself that we would eventually have to go our separate ways, now was not the time to part.

I followed a great hallway and passed some smaller halls that branched off. I looked down the side hallways but saw only impenetrable gloomy darkness unlit by torch. This only worried me more because a vampire in his black hooded cloak could stand in the middle of the hall with an assault rifle aimed at me and I would have no clue until the bullets ripped through my body. Since bullets travel faster than the sounds of the reports, I wouldn't even hear them as they shredded me. I didn't believe that would happen because Abigail told me that vampires preferred their victims to have beating hearts for easier feeding. Trying to suck stagnant blood out of a dead animal or human through a cut or fanged bite was very hard. It was unlikely that they would turn my heart to hamburger if they thought that I was still salvageable as food, but that depended on whether they thought I could be easily defeated. I figured they had the home field advantage and the darkness in their favor. As morning began to dawn, I figured they would seek more drastic measures to defeat me. That all said, I still worried about what lurked in every dark corner. Failed vampires didn't follow logic and were unpredictable enemies.

I continued to stick to the main hallway, but stepped to the wall on my right and continued my walk almost sideways so that my back was against the stone. This way I could see in front as well as behind me with nervous back glances. I continued until I made it to the great throne room, and to my utter disgust, occasionally, I would knock a fat cockroach off the wall with my shoulder..

I stopped under a torch and cringed. At first I thought that I was hallucinating when I noticed the floor moving and shimmering. Cockroaches covered everything and made the floor appear to move in dark ripples like the vampires scurrying in their black cloaks up the snow covered hills. I could hear the rattling of their exoskeletons and realized that that was the cause of the crunching sound as I walked. My boots were covered with their muck and their pointy, crushed shells were glued to the sides of my soles with their guts. I almost gagged.

All through the castle, I noticed that rich tapestries, curtains, and rugs decorated the place and that despite it mostly being constructed of granite, great tree trunks acted as support for the stony framework. If things went south, I could torch the place. A part of me regretted that, because whoever built and designed this, definitely had an eye for beauty and art that would be irreplaceable. I also worried about the vampires torching this place to dislodge me, but I didn't think they would consider that as an option, at least they probably wouldn't as long as it was night.

My nostrils flared and I could smell the bad hygiene of the failed vampires above the smell of rotted and drained human corpses. It had a lived in smell. The vamps would not want to leave this place. They would fight to get it back in one piece, not torched. That was my guess and hope.

I cautiously stepped into the great throne room. It was easily the size of a highschool gymnasium and in the dark, I couldn't see its full expanse. I looked around. There were only two torches burning and not bright flames. They were just slightly brighter than candles. There were too many dark corners that were mysteries to an unturned human eye.

I couldn't take the silence only broken by the crunch of roaches under my boots anymore. I was nearing a nervous breakdown. My Glock shook lightly in my hands and I didn't remember exchanging my sword for it. I dared not trek past any more dark corners where I may be attacked from behind. I would rather call down the inhabitants, even if there were thousands of vampires hiding in the dark corners. I desired greatly to face and attack a legion head on rather than wait for the slim dagger in my neck delivered in ambush from behind by a single vampire.

"Hello," I called, "I am a human here on a rescue mission. Any humans? If not, are there any vampires here? Do you hide in terror as a man tramples through your home at night?"

"We're humans! We're in a cage! Help!" I heard a man call from a room with a closed door to my left. I recognized the voice.

I heard someone else, a woman, shush the man in a quieter voice. "It could be a trap, a vampire calling us.

"Jerry, Racheal, is that you?"

"Eric?"

"Yeah."

"What the hell? How'd you find us, man?"

"I'm on my way!" I called back.

Excitement at releasing fellow people and having someone watching my back propelled me toward the door. Although I only knew them for one night, they had proven themselves to be solid people in a fight, and I trusted them enough to put releasing them at the very top of my list. With my handgun probing the darkness around me, I sprinted through the crunchy cockroaches in a combat crouch toward the door where their voices emitted from.

I breathed a sigh of relief when I made it. I turned the handle. It was locked. There was a skeleton key in the lock as if someone had been about to enter, but was scared off suddenly. I guessed that my firing the handgun had changed the plans of whoever was about to enter and feed on them.

I opened the solid wooden door, and leaned a chair against it to keep it opened so I wouldn't get locked inside. I saw the families crammed and locked in a small cage. They stood, stooped over in a five foot high steel cage that was designed as a kennel.

As I smiled at them, grateful to see them all alive, I saw them return my smile with hopeful eyes, and then my smile turned to a sudden look of horror as I saw the conditions they were in.

It had taken a moment for my eyes to adjust to the poor light. When I could focus I saw that scattered around their cage, cockroaches covered the bodies of dead people, numerous dead. There were so many tangled together, I couldn't even begin to count. The corpses littered the floor, left to rot. Whoever ruled the castle seemed to enjoy the charnel smell of rank death.

Decorating the walls of the room on pikes were the heads of prior victims. Some were fresh, some mid-decay with strips of flesh hanging in rancid decor, and others were clean skulls made pearl white by the cockroaches. I almost retched as I saw the skulls of children and even one of a recently killed little girl, no older than six years old. The clean skulls and the ones still covered with rotted flesh were bad enough, but the small girl was so fresh that she had the appearance that she could be brought back to life, and a morbid part of me expected the eyes to open and stare at me any moment like a possessed doll.

A large table next to the cage held a pile of torture devices from ancient technology whose cruelty I could only shudder a guess, to more modern devices like electric prods. These vampires not only fed on blood, but fear, pain, and probably death itself as well. Abigail had told me that some of the more advanced vamps fed almost solely on psychic emotions.

I was still standing in the doorway when It felt like a truck slammed into both my back and chest. After feeling the blow, I was picked up off of my feet and sailed about five meters before slamming to a stone wall and then to the ground of the small room. I first focused on trying to inhale, but I completely had the wind knock out of me. I then realized that my firearm was gone, that I had dropped it in the sudden violence of the attack. I drew my sword as I scrambled to my feet, gasping for breath, and looked around the room but it was empty other than the bodies of the dead and the caged living. I looked into the great hall, but only saw dark shadows. I suspected that whatever hit and threw me was psychic in nature. I think what actually propelled me across the room were the muscles of my own legs commanded by whatever sinister force delivered it.

I then saw my handgun a few feet away on the floor, already covered with a few cockroaches. I resheathed my sword and picked up the firearm. It had crushed a roach when it fell and had its guts on the handle. I scowled and wiped it off, but kept it in my hand. I wasn't playing around. This wasn't a knife fight.

It barely registered that the people in the cage were screaming at me to let them out.

However, what had my full attention was sardonic laughter in the throne room. I peeked out the door and peered around the great hall but could not pinpoint where mocking laughter came from. The laughter continued and grew louder at my confusion. It echoed, bouncing off the walls so that the source couldn't be located. I angrily cursed it, knowing that it was the King himself.

"Eric! Get us out of here!" I heard Richard call me.

But I was too unnerved by what had thrown me. It would have been smarter to have back up, but I had to face this mysterious King Sadazar first. Looking back, I was probably already under his control.

"Come out, coward!" I challenged the King as I stepped into the throne room..

The light of my headlamp popped and went out. I suspected that it was from the vampire's psychic power.

The mocking laughter increased in volume at my frustration.

I was initially scared, but now as the laughter wore on and my breathing came back, I was getting thoroughly pissed off. I walked into the great hall and to one of the torches.

"You'll not find me with that puny light, human," it laughed some more. Although the voice was articulate with an ancient accent, it didn't sound like it came from a human throat, which sent a chill down my spinal cord.

I waited until the torch was in my hand and I lifted high above me before laughing back, "It needn't light my way, when there is so much fuel around. I'll burn you out, blood sucker!" I threatened as I brought the flame to the base of one of the tapestries on the wall. I held it close enough to make my threat believable without being in danger of trapping myself and the families in a conflagration by accidentally lighting it.

The laughter of my mysterious enemy immediately ceased. I forced myself to laugh louder as I held the torch higher and closer to the tapestry. It was a beautifully designed artwork, from what I could see of it that wasn't covered with roaches and their excrement. The picture displayed three knights and a fire breathing dragon in a deadly duel. My other hand held my pistol at chest level, roving, seeking a target.

"Let's discuss things, Eric. I hold you in high regard. You've shaken the world in your short time in the Forbidden Zone. I've always been a rebel myself, and I appreciate a brother in mayhem. I enjoy the show you put on. I have watched you raid the cave of Richard's coven and then rescue your Abigail from Craigsville over the computer feed. It was all entertaining. Even watching you take on my coven was great. I am awed at meeting such a movie star, a true celebrity of the Forbidden Zone." The disembodied voice had oddly sounded sincere with his praise.

I was a bit shocked that he was able to see the video from my camera vest. I had thought that Robert had turned off the transmitter days before I entered the Cavern of the Vampires. Obviously, Tommy still had access to my cameras as well as others.

I replied, "OK, come out so that I may see you and discuss things. I promise not to shoot."

"Then lower your gun, human."

Vampires had a way of saying human as we would say cockroach.

I kept my back to the wall, torch in hand, but holstered my handgun. I waved my empty hand for emphasis, but I still kept the torch near the tapestry "Let's talk, vampire," I said with the same disdain when I emphasized the word, "vampire," that he had used when he had said human.

From the shadows by a throne made of human skulls, a hideously tall and yet stooped "man" stepped forward. A black cloak flowed royally over the cockroach covered floor behind him. I put "man" in quotations because his face was so distorted that it was more gargoyle than human. Even worse was the sardonic evil that gleamed in his oversized eyes. I looked over his facial tattoos and piercings and guessed that he liked whatever gave him his shocking appearance. My hunch was proved correct when I saw him smile maliciously when he spotted the horror on my face.

He smiled even more hideously as he said, "My appearance scares you. All vampires eventually look like me. It's part of our evolution. You will one day look like this after I turn you and so will your beloved Abigail, even without my bite. Even Richard's disgraced coven will be blessed to look like this one day if any survived."

"What do you want?" I demanded before I dwelled on the horror of Abigail eventually looking like that thing.

"No," he said as if we were both involved in the funniest joke ever. "I should ask that question of you. You came to my humble abode seeking something."

"I think we want the same thing. The defeat of the other."

"No, no, no," he purred. "As I said, I like your spirit. I love Abigail's spirit. I would love to acquire them. Both of you. I would love to control you and make you one of my servants."

I was about to laugh mockingly at his threat, but I felt my body lock up and realized that he had taken some kind of psychic control over me. I stood paralyzed but my mind was active, overdriven with panic at the sudden loss of autonomy over my muscles. He walked up to me smiling. As psionic abilities went, he was powerful beyond imagination. It was no surprise why there were so many wrecked helicopters and rockets strewn around the castle like expensive trash. I tried to figure out how to defeat this power, but it felt hopeless. I could sense that he didn't hit me with everything yet. I was just a toy for him and he wanted to play first.

I could only stand there unmoving, with the torch held above me like the macabre Statue of Liberty. I guessed he let me keep it so that the light would show his true monstrous nature. He enjoyed the terror it invoked in me. He kept walking toward my paralyzed form and stopped for a moment when he was within a foot of me. He circled me a few times, looking me over with a combination of hunger and lust, ducking under the torch. I could feel the thick folds of his flowing cloak almost coiling like a snake around my feet, but I was unable to move. It was then that I realized that I had stepped away from the tapestry. I must have been under his spell earlier than I had thought because I didn't remember taking those steps.

He stooped lower so that we were looking at each other, inches away, eye to eye. His breath that assaulted me was horrible beyond words. It blasted me with the rot of a thousand year old grave, like an eternal evil that couldn't die or be restrained.

The only muscles that I could use were to cringe as he touched my head with his elongated fingers that held no human warmth. He was a monster among vampires. I felt little electric twinges in my facial muscles from his touch on my skull as if he plugged into me and connected like a computer. He looked over the top of my skull and his yellow, eight inch dagger-like, encrusted fangs were inches from my eyes.

"Oh my. I should've seen it," he said. "What you want, you can not have without changing into one of us."

I found my mouth was able to move but barely. It was like a dentist injected me with double novocaine, but without the numbness. I asked, "What's that that you think that I want?"

He studied my skull like a clairvoyant studying a crystal ball, constantly breathing harshly in my face as he ran his fingers over my head. "Mmm hmm," he said as if confirming his suspicion.

I blew out some pent up air, trying to discover what autonomy I had over my body under his control.

He brought his bug eyes back to mine and said, "You love her. I saw the same love for you in her head too."

I said nothing. I wanted to savagely deny it just to spite him, but I knew that he would immediately mock the doubt in my voice.

He then laughed reading my mind, "You are too scared to even write down the depths of your true feelings for her. You think that you can't have her because you also despise her superior vampiric nature. You are afraid you'll change from just a romantic kiss, but worry not. I will change you, for both you and for her. You will become my servant. You'll retain your mind as you retain it now, but it'll be useless as it is now, frozen in place. But as a vampire, you will never get to experience your love for Abigail. You will watch her get passed around from Jim, to me, to others, and she will be as helpless as you." The monster laughed and added, "We will even pass you around. Yes, you will be the ultimate of what you call failed vampires. Your mind won't work but you will have the awareness that you are forever doomed as my slave, unable to save yourself and even worse, you'll be worthless to save your beloved, Abigail."

I tried to swing the torch down upon his head, but all it did was cause my arm to tense even more. My muscles spasmed painfully. I felt them writhe like serpents beneath my skin. I cried out in pain involuntarily that it eerily sounded to me like someone else across the throne room had screamed. I tried to draw my gun with my right arm, but my muscles would just bunch to the point of an excruciating contraction. Any movement of resistance that I tried, caused more tension, spasms, and agony, but I was so repulsed by this "king," that fighting him was all I could attempt to do on an atavistic, instinctive level, but that just added to my pain.

He laughed at those futile attempts and his breath increased with his excitement. Although, it repulsed me, his horrid breath gave me hope. If it breathed, it could die, but with his powers, finding his mortality would be the ultimate puzzle, and I had nothing else to do but to de-riddle it, but my time was running dry.

Then his eyes studied mine and I could see the cruel pleasure he took from my helplessness.

I almost cried out from the pain in my right arm as every muscle tissue in it contracted when I instinctively tried to push him away, but instead my arm stayed coiled at my chest. I willed my muscles in my right arm to relax and discovered that although any attempted movements resulted in spasm, I could get my muscles to relax if I focused. Indeed the relaxation of my muscles was the only autonomy that I had while under his control, but relaxation seemed impossible because he was so repulsive. Every instinct I had was either to assault him, run, or compact myself into the fetal position in a primal desire to curl up and hide from the world.

He brushed my cheek with a cold reptilian-like finger in a patronizing manner. "Won't your Abigail be thrilled to come back and see you changed into a vampire like her? Like us?"

He brought his head down and scraped my throat with his fangs. I could feel and smell his rancid breath wafting up from my neck. His eyes studied the horror in my eyes. He was literally fueled by my fear of him. Of everything under his control, I could tell that I could still vomit as I dry heaved. I was tempted to vomit on him as my only act of rebellion, but I had a feeling that he would get off on that.

He reared back for a bite to both drain and to turn me with drool covered fangs. I tried to fight, but instead, I stood there, tensed and went even more painfully rigid with spasms. The muscles in my left arm that held the torch held above my head burned so badly as with an unreleased charlie horse. It was so bad that I thought that my muscles would crack like old plaster struck with a sledgehammer.

He stopped his strike at my neck enjoying the mental and physical torment that he inflicted or rather, that I self inflicted with my resistance.

I willed my muscles to unwind. I felt some relief. I had the control to either torture myself with tensed, spasmed muscles when I resisted or to relax and let go, but relaxing seemed impossible in this situation of horror overload. I tried to recapture my control to relax my muscles, remembering Critter and Bryan forcing me to sit in frigid water and telling me to relax and breathe. Those two would torment me in other ways such as making me hold a pushup position for a half hour and then telling me to relax my muscles that reflexively spasmed to the painful stimuli. I hated those drills but it did give me a degree of control over my body despite the pain that I never knew was possible.

"Relax," I told myself to little avail.

He studied me for another moment and a blast of his fetid breath washed over my face as he laughed again. The humor left his face and a seriousness that was half deadly, half sexual in intensity took over and I knew this was it.

I had one plan left.

As his open mouth with bared 8 inch fangs that came deliberately slowly at my throat, his eyes locked on mine. I focused on the fingers of the hand holding the torch above my head. They were painfully spasmed, clenched around the torch's handle in a deathgrip. It took every ounce of mental effort to relax the painful muscles of my hand and forearm, but I could feel them loosen both painful and sluggish. I couldn't force my hand to open. I could only relax each individual finger with every ounce of effort.

King Sadazar let the tips of his fangs painfully probed my throat and paused, prolonging my mental agony. I didn't think he broke my skin yet, at least I hoped. But the scraping feeling against my neck was agonizing both from the pain and disgust.

I took my mind from my neck and focused solely on relaxing my left hand that held aloft the torch. Slowly, one by one, my fingers unwound. First the pointer finger unfurled, then the middle finger unwound. His fangs were scraping my neck as my ring finger slowly unpeeled from the torch. Only my spasmed pinkie finger held the flame aloft.

He went in for the bite. There was no stopping him now. I could see in his eyes he was not after my torment, but rather, he was solely after my blood.

I laughed weakly through spasming vocal cords and Sadazar backed his head away from my neck to look at me unsure if I had lost my mind. He gave me a queer look and then went back to bite my neck. I felt the torch slowly tip and catch on the final finger as he went in to bite and infect me.

As his fang painfully touched my throat, from the corner of my eyes, I watched the torch precariously balance, tilt, and then fall from my open hand. It flipped over, end over end twice and crashed into the thick rug and also his cloak with a small explosion of sparks. It wasn't much, but it was the only hope that I had.

Chapter Sixteen

I laughed even louder. It was a genuine laugh, more out of madness than humor, as the sparks landed on his royal robe and began to burn. I felt on the edge of the abyss of insanity at this point from pain and the psychic intrusion of this monster. My brain had trouble distinguishing my own thoughts from his psychic commands.

His fang puckered the skin on my throat, but stopped. He stared at me confused for a moment as his focus had been solely on my exposed throat. Then he looked me in the eyes, and I felt a brief victory as I saw confusion and maybe fear in his ancient, arrogant eyes. I laughed louder as he then screamed and stomped on the rug, crushing cockroaches to prevent the spread of the fire. Then he smacked at his royal robes.

I was still rigid and forced my entire body to relax. I collapsed to the ground as my muscles felt nerveless and my face smashed into cockroaches. I sat up in a dazed heap for a second as control returned to my body. The cockroaches began to crawl on my sprawled form.

Sadazar's spell was temporarily broken in his panic to put out the flames. My right hand seemed to work on its own as it snaked to the holster and pulled the Glock.

Sadazar screamed incoherently as he watched me level my handgun with fingers still trembling from the mind control and inflamed muscles. He had lost control of me and continued to scream as I spastically emptied all eighteen rounds into his general direction as he disappeared into a shadow. My aim was off from the darkness, flickering light of the torchfire, and general confusion from his prior mind control, but he was close enough that I got him with a good number of rounds. I felt dark pleasure as I heard the monster's howls of anger turn into a wailing shriek of pain just before my Glock clicked empty.

Hearing him scream, I knew he was wounded, but I had no idea how badly. Knowing the vampires well enough, I had to assume it wasn't fatal, and he would be back, powered by a vengeful spirit and would return just as deadly, maybe more so. However, his mind control was suddenly completely absent and I wondered if the wound that I inflicted on him damaged his mental powers in some way.

I reloaded my Glock and stamped out the remaining sparks on the rug, crunching bugs into it. The wet guts served as a fire extinguisher. Although a cleansing infernal would be the best thing for this death house, I could not torch it now. While it was night, it was my only refuge from the vampiric horde that Abigail had led away from the castle. I did not want to be on the run in the dark forest with a horde of vampires on my trail at night. I wiped the remains of the cockroaches from my face.

As I determined my next move, I almost covered my ears as Sadazar let out the piercing screech of the vampire that people can not achieve. His cry was far worse and far louder than any vampire that I had ever encountered in the past. I felt an involuntary tremble of terror rack my body. I looked around for him but he was hidden in the darkness.

The vampiric shriek was how they signaled other vampires of distress or when finding the scented trail of human blood and the King had the most horrible call of them all. From far away, I heard hundreds in the horde echo his cry. It gave me a small feeling of hope that he now felt the need to call reinforcements.

With the lack of his psychic intrusion on my mind, I believed that I might have disabled him to a degree with my gunshots. However, I was sure that I had less than fifteen minutes before the horde laid siege to their castle, and it was still too many hours until sunrise.

***

"Hey Specs," Tommy said when Don Renton/The Specter answered the phone with an angrier voice than normal.

"What!" Don demanded.

"I found Eric," Tommy said gleefully.

There was a pause as Tommy could almost hear Don's gears angrily turning in his brain, wondering why Tommy sounded so excited to announce what he had been hiding from him.

Don finally asked in a voice dripping with suspicion, "Where?"

"He's in the castle of that so-called King Sadazar. You know, the creep who you can't kill. The one who scares the crap out of you in your worst nightmares."

Tommy could hear The Specter/Don Renton banging his fingers on a keyboard to verify. Tommy held back a laugh, but the delight in his voice brilliantly lit anger in Don's own.

"As a prisoner?" Don asked.

"Nope. He fought his way in."

"Bullshit."

"No. He's in there kicking ass where you have never dared to go."

"Watch it Laurens!"

"He kicked your ass twice from what I saw," Tommy taunted.

Tommy waited for an emotional explosion, but it was silent. Instead he heard King Sadazar's shrieks on the audio from Don's computer as he watched the live feed from Eric's body cam on his own screen. Tommy smiled showing his teeth as he heard Eric's excited voice screaming a warcry and commanding others. Tommy admired his formerly mild mannered friend. Eric's voice didn't break as gunfire ripped around him. It was deep and full of authority. He was a totally different man than he had been a mere two weeks ago when he first entered the Forbidden Zone. Even with the distance, Tommy cringed as he heard an explosive detonation over his computer. He couldn't imagine how it affected Eric.

Tommy laughed as The Specter's booming voice swore heavily. The Specter/Renton had been trying to take out Sadazar's brood for months and couldn't get close, even with warbirds and missiles.

Tommy knew that he was pushing it, but he couldn't resist. "Specs, while you're sitting on your ass, Eric is doing your job. Maybe we should get him a cloak and a skull mask so that he can neutralize the vampires that scare you. Just imagine, Eric, as The Specter!"

He waited for The Specter to rise to his bait after Tommy dished out the ultimate insult, but silence reigned, and then the connection was broken. Don Renton had hung up.

Despite the smile, a chill rattled Tommy's spine and then shot into his arms as his whole body convulsed with fear. He had to physically avoid Don Renton for the next few days. At least until the bruises on Don's face that Eric had made with his fist had fully faded. Don was a very dangerous person to piss off, but man! did it feel great to rub it in just this once.

***

I immediately raced to the room to free the two families as I heard the piercing cries of the vampires echoing back up the valley. Occasionally, I would hear Sadazar shriek in reply from the other room. So loud were his piercing cries that it always sounded like he was right on top of me and I wanted to cover my ears with my hands.

I entered the room where the humans were kept.

"Hurry," Richard pleaded.

"They didn't turn you?" I asked. It was a stupid question, but in the Forbidden Zone it was best not to assume anything.

"Would we be in a cage if we were vampires, idiot?" Richard snarled in panic.

"Watch it," I growled as I flicked a warning stare at him as I studied the lock on their cage. I couldn't blame him for being upset between the setting of the vampire castle and our past encounter. I had reacted similarly when Adam wanted to check me for vampire bites after they abandoned me in the Caverns of the vampires. Also, they were caged with roach covered bodies around them. Roaches, fattened on human remains, covered their cage waiting to dine on their bodies if they weren't turned. Their boots were covered in bug guts as were my own. I then realized my pants were covered in roach guts when I had collapsed on the floor after dropping the torch. In fact I could feel the faint dampness on my butt. I wanted to vomit, so I forced my mind back to freeing the captives.

Richard then asked, "You're free. I should ask you, if the vampires turned you."

I glared at him briefly and looked over the padlock trying to figure out how to open the 5 x 5 x 5 bared cage. I could pick locks, but it would be much quicker to just smash it. The six people were crammed together with the adults stooped over. They didn't want to sit on the roach covered floor. The cage looked like it was made out of cattle panels for a large dog. The confined space had to add to Richard's agitated state. Needless to say, I was a bit agitated too.

"Hurry," Richard said again which triggered something in me as his voice interrupted my concentration.

I snapped back at him, "Gee, I would've thought that you would've know-it-alled your way out, Richard."

"What's with your anger, man?" Richard asked.

I was about to shoot back with a fury of angry words, when I realized the irony. He was correct again which pissed me off more than if he had not been so accurate with his observation of me.

Instead, I replied with compassion, "You're right. I apologize. We're all a bit on edge. Let's just get you all out."

"Thank you," he replied in a calmer voice.

I considered trying to shoot the lock, but I wasn't sure if a ricochet would kill me or those I was trying to rescue. Richard would definitely freak out.

I looked at the table with the torture devices and saw a large ancient hammer that I assumed was to bust the limb bones of the victims, for torture or to suck out the marrow. The tool was like a short handled sledge hammer. I grabbed it with my right hand after I put my Glock into my left. I swung hard with the right hand, but the lock just bounced around. I swung a few more times with the same results. The cattle panel had enough spring that it absorbed the brunt of my attack.

"You need two hands," said Richard.

I glared at him as I swung again with one hand.

He reiterated, "You need to swing with two hands for full strength. That's a Master Lock 930. It's one of the best padlocks and made with hardened steel."

I rolled my eyes. "Who remembers numbers like that? Are you a locksmith or something?" I asked.

"Yes I am," he said.

I glared at him thinking that he was being a smart ass, but he was serious. He knew what he was talking about which, in the stress of the situation, pissed me off more.

"Well, I'm a lock picker," I retorted.

"Then you know that you need two hands for that lock," Richard shouted back.

I resisted saying, two hands around your throat. My butt was wet from roach guts and I was furious at the world and I directed my fury at just smashing the lock a few more times with no good results other than fruitlessly bending the bars on the cage..

I calmed myself and replied as I continually whacked at the lock with one hand. My words were punctuated with grunts, "I am not putting down my Glock with that thing running around out there," I cursed savagely as I swung again.

I caught a side glimpse of King Sadazar fifteen feet from the door. There was both anger and fear on his face. His mind control seemed to have diminished with the pain of his gunshot wounds. I also noticed that I wounded him in the head just above his eyes. I didn't know if it had been a glancing blow or if his skull was thick enough to withstand a bullet. Although it was obviously not fatal, it did seem to render his supernatural psychic powers almost useless. I could only feel something like static hitting my brain from his attempts, but that was the extent of his powers.

As I brought the gun up to shoot at Sadazar, I felt an arm snake around my neck. I cursed as I realized that I forgot about the captain of the guard. He had me in a headlock from behind.

"Behind you, Eric," Richard screamed too late.

"Surrender human," the vampiric Captain screamed in my ear.

I answered with my Glock.

Without seeing him, I instinctively brought up the handgun and pointed it behind my head where I heard his voice. When I felt his chin against the barrel, I instinctively pulled the trigger, blowing his brains out of the top of his head. The sound of the proximal shot sent my ears ringing.

The vampire Captain of the Guard collapsed in a heap behind me. I felt my muscles tense as Sadazar tried to take control. I turned and saw his hideous silhouette and fired out the door toward him. I heard him scream in pain again, and his control released me. Unseen in the darkness, he let loose another wild shriek to call his minions, a little more desperate this time and I heard the horde of hundreds answer in their shrill growling screams. They were much closer. I guessed that we would face a full siege in under five minutes.

I swore in fury as I struck at the lock. I holstered my Glock for a two handed swing.

"Eric?" Richard said hesitantly.

"What?" I snapped.

"I know you don't like suggestions especially when you're wrong, but–."

"Just tell me," I yelled as I swung the hammer ineffectively but with two hands now.

"Why don't you try the keys on his belt?" Richard offered in meekness.

ABIGAIL, VAMPIRE OUTCAST 243

The vampire Captain did indeed have a ring of keys. I saw a short one in the jangle of about a dozen keys that looked like it would fit a padlock. I grabbed the key ring and saw it was attached to his belt by a thin rope. I yanked and the rope snapped off with one try.

"You won't mind?" I asked the dying vampire who stared at the heavens above with rapidly glazing eyes, fangs bared. He was breathing, but he would never rise again. It's eerie how resilient vampires are.

The key worked and the families poured out. I pocketed the key ring. They may come in handy later, I reasoned, whether to unlock something else or to simply throw something heavy at an enemy.

The families surprised me when they ran toward the door at the back of the room instead of out the opened one to the throne room..

Rachael pointed at that door as she yelled with an adrenalized rush, "This seems to be his treasure room. He has an arsenal behind that door in that back room."

I scowled again at the dead bodies that Sadazar left laying around and thought that he must have kept the rotting corpses as souvenirs or trophies, either that or it was the lazy house keeping of an ancient degenerate. Again I wondered if they actually enjoyed the scent of rotting death. What a wicked strain of vampiric virus that infected this coven! I found my mind dwelling on that depravity of this group. I actually yearned to fight against the civilized vampires of Abigail's coven. They would never tolerate such disgusting living conditions. I had hated Abigail's old coven, but I could at least respect them. Not this group. I respected their psychic powers but otherwise held them in total contempt.

We leapt over the dead and used up bodies, crunching through the roaches, and opened the door behind the cage. I was expecting a small closet but we entered a larger room whose walls were lined with rifles, handguns, and of course the much sought after vampiric swords. I saw Abigail's sword and her shortened M-16 carbine as well as her pack. I put her sword and handgun in my belt and slung her M-16 over my shoulder. I smelled her faint feminine scent on the shoulder strap over the stench of the decay of the bodies, and I prayed that she would be alive and sane for me to return the weapons.

I pocketed lots of 5.56mm rounds and loaded magazines for my M-16 and 9mm ones for my handgun and simply discarded my empty magazines.

I looked over and my eyes widened in desire as I saw a bunch of grenades. I ran to a box of them.

"Whoa, grenades!" I said.

Jerry asked, "Have you ever thrown one of them?"

I shook my head no.

"I was in the Marines overseas," Jerry said. "I hated those things."

I could see his dislike cloud his face even in the darkened room, but his eyes were alight with grim desire for a fight.

"Why do you hate grenades? Don't they work?" I asked.

"Oh they work, alright," he said. "Maybe too well, but people's minds don't work when they're nervous. They throw them in rooms with no outlet for the concussion and get wounded or killed themselves, or they don't throw them far enough, or they'll mess up a throw and hit a rock or tree in front of them so that it bounces back and kills them and their buddies. I had one enemy throw one at me, but in his panic, he didn't pull the pin."

"What'd you do?" I asked.

"Pulled the pin and killed the bastard when I threw it back, of course," he said nonchalantly. He concluded with, "I liked to use them, but I always got nervous when those around me, especially newbies, used them."

I said, "Tell me how to use them and I promise not to throw them when I'm around you."

He smiled and gave me a quick rundown on how to use them as he quickly pocketed a few for himself. We smiled and nodded to each other.

I liked Jerry. He was a rebel at heart but treated me with respect. The highest form of respect that a man could receive was from a rebel. Someone who is inclined to show respect only for authority does so out of fear. When that fear is removed, the show of respect disappears. Rebels on the other hand reserved their respect only for those that they saw deserving of it. It wasn't given out of fear but rather what was earned. That smile of grim determination that he gave me was genuine. Abigail's smile was similar.

Sadazar's shriek ripped through the castle again and I found the urge to cover my ears as the pitch and tone seemed to rupture my eardrums. Even more terrifying were the replies from his returning coven. It now sounded like the pack was upon us.

"Let's man the ramparts!" I yelled.

Loaded down with weapons, we ran back into the great hall. I looked over the dark expanse for the King. At first I didn't see him, but then I felt terror seize my spine before my brain registered what I saw. He was about forty feet above the ground in a dimly lit corner of the ceiling. His eyes gleamed brightly as he stared over us like a giant spider waiting to ambush a fly or cockroach.

I immediately opened up with my M-16 as did my companions. The barrage was deafening. The King instantly dropped. Bat wings seemed to sprout from nowhere and he glided into a corner and into darkness.

I don't believe that any of us hit him as he moved breathtakingly fast and without a cry of pain.

Jerry yelled, "Run down the hall! To the drawbridge!"

Before I could ask why, I saw him pull the pin on a grenade and loose the safety. Rachael, Richard, and Christy grabbed the kids and all of us sprinted down the hall. I quickly obeyed as well, remembering his prior warning.

Jerry tossed the mini bomb into the dark corner where the monster had disappeared. Jerry immediately sprinted after us. It detonated.

I felt the genade's concussion chase us down the hall, followed by a soul rendering, vampiric scream of pain and abject horror from the King. There was actual terror in that sound as well, but we didn't have time to dwell on the wounded king. The castle was under attack.

But damn, the deafening explosion had scared the hell out of me. I could feel it hit my ribcage like a fist, driving the air from my lungs and almost knocking me down to the roach covered floor. I hoped it had a far greater effect on King Sadazar, but now he screamed repeatedly for his cursed brood. The horde almost sounded like they were inside the castle's walls, but we arrived right on time.

We scrambled up into the guard towers of the ramparts on either side of the drawbridge. I ran up one side of the drawbridge with Richard and Rachael. Christy and Jerry took the other side. We barely arrived in time and I was horrified to see the vampires already climbing over the walls mere feet from me. I opened fire point blank as the vampiric faces appeared over the lip of the wall. I almost touched them with the barrel of my rifle as I fired. I quickly blasted five as one appeared right after the other, and I heard some of them scream as they plummeted back down into the moat. I shot a few more until nothing else crawled over.

I scanned our wall and my companions were killing them off efficiently as well.

But I had no time to savor any victory. With the ramparts cleared, I raced to the precipice and leaned over the protective walls. I swore at what I saw. The vamps that we had shot were merely the fittest or craziest. Dozens more followed and were scaling the wall beneath me.

Hundreds more stood on the other side of the moat, hesitating to make the leap or scale down. They looked like they were waiting for the drawbridge to lower for them to cross, whether out of habit or stupidity, I didn't know.

However there was still a mass of vampires climbing down the other side of the moat and scaling the walls like cockroaches. From the ramparts we opened up, shooting some more vampires point blank in the faces as they were just reaching the top of the wall. We then began to fire into the moat. I had a hard time hitting them in the dark with iron sites, but we killed or maimed enough of them that the main force stayed on the other side of the moat. We had a moment of reprieve as both sides reassessed the situation and reloaded.

I griped, "With all the amount of weaponry and technology, you'd think that they would have some night vision scopes."

Richard replied, "Actually vampires have great night vision and it would be pointless for them to have night vision scopes. Maybe even blinding to them."

I felt a flash of anger and remembered how Tommy would always say, "The truth only hurts the guilty." I kept my mouth shut. I traveled with a vampiress. I shouldn't have made such a stupid statement. I thought about how weird it was to have such self doubts burning in the very darkest recesses of the back of my mind as I faced a horde of hundreds of vampires.

The desire to be right all the time would kill me, I thought. I had been feeling this way ever since I grew tired of being treated like an idiot with the Mountain Warriors. It went into full force when I stood up for myself against Adam a few days ago. I saw myself as weak prior to that, now this irritation at being corrected seemed to be my new internal demon that I needed to defeat.

After a moment, I let it go and joked, "I guess they would've been wiser to have welders masks for daytime combat."

"Yes, you should know. You travel with one, Abigail." Richard said.

I thought I heard a hint of disgust directed at Abigail in his tone. He confirmed it when he shook his head sadly, "Man if Brandon and your Abigail are into that sick crap we saw in there..." He couldn't finish. "After what I saw, I'll never think of vampires the same."

"Abigail is not," I paused and disgustedly said the rest, "'into that.' She sticks with eating animals," I said.

"Do you know for sure?" asked Richard.

"Yes!" I said firmly. "She told me that we needed to kill these vampires."

"Where is she?" Rachael asked.

"I saw her leave with that horde. She's their prisoner, but she gave us the opportunity to take the castle," I insisted.

"Are you sure she's a prisoner and not one of them now?" Richard asked.

Before, I could answer, King Sadazar's piercing shriek cut the night and sliced into my brain. Although he still lurked in the castle, it felt like he screamed inside my brain. A part of me felt the pointlessness of the fight. If that creature survived thousands of years, as well as gunshots, and a grenade blast, could we ever truly defeat him? I was sure that he faced many human foes in the past and came out victorious. Why would

I be the one fortunate or clever enough to finally end his evilness? My only hope in this fight was that he had not been able to reestablish his mental control over me. I was hoping that that was a sign that we had indeed weakened him, but I worried that my internal doubt may have been planted from his psychic influences. There was so much afoot that went beyond the flesh and blood fight.

But I had no time to dwell on that. A few dozen vampires on the other side were shooting at us in response to Sadazar's cry. They had both firearms and bows and arrows. Even a few rocks sailed past my head and clashed against the walls

Between gunshots, I heard some growling and inarticulate grumbling across the chasm. About thirty vampires responded to their master's call and climbed down into the moat, with some even jumping down onto the jagged rocks to rush us in an attempt to save him. We opened fire and Jerry threw a grenade down below at them.

I caught my breath as I saw the silhouettes of vampires across the moat. There were still hundreds of them, but one that I saw on the other side of the moat stood out. It was definitely the statuesque figure of Abigail. She stood straight, almost aristocratically as the other vampires from Richard's bloodline. The failed vampires around her were stooped and shambled like their king and his kingdom of cockroaches. There was something horrifying about seeing her dark shape on the other side of the gulf of the moat and night with those failed monstrosities. It was metaphorical of her vampire world and my human one, I thought glumly. While at the same time, I acknowledged to myself that the King was correct, I did love her. I pushed that from my mind. We had a fight to worry about first.

I heard Jim's voice call to us, "I say Eric, my ol' boy! We have Abigail. Let Great King go. Even better, join us and you can have her. Or we kill her now."

Richard raised his rifle and fired four or five shots. I saw sparks fly from the rocks in front of the shadowy form that was Abigail. She immediately dropped out of sight behind the rocks, whether wounded or simply seeking cover, I didn't know.

I knocked his barrel down and hissed, "That was Abigail."

He looked at me grimly but said nothing. I couldn't really blame him after having his family imprisoned with the used bodies of other people strewn like garbage. I would have reacted the same way a week ago, but he was wrong about Abigail, and I would defend her with my life.

"Don't shoot at her again," I warned.

"Why?" he asked. "Bullets don't usually kill them."

"Bullets do kill them and even when they recover they still feel the pain. It hurts her when she's shot!" I replied bordering on fury and exasperation.

"After the horror that we have seen in the castle-- You're girl is into that sick shit."

I started to say, "She's not my--" but I couldn't. I couldn't lie so emphatically. No we weren't dating, but... Instead I finished by saying, "She's not 'into that!'"

I scanned the area across the moat but saw no further sign of Abigail. I wondered if she was keeping her head down or if a headshot had indeed killed her.

Jerry cursed at us from the otherside of the ramparts to keep our attention on our enemies as Richard and I stood facing off against each other.

Richard said in a painfully reasonable tone, "Listen, I am sure she is a good person, vampire, whatever, but we can't let them know that we value her. I'm not bartering my wife or daughter for a vampire no matter who it is."

I pinched the bridge of my nose. My emotion aside, Richard's reasoning was brutally logical. To bargain with Jim over Abigail's release would result in the death of not just us but Abigail as well. If Jim thought that we saw her as one of his coven, an enemy in other words, Jim would probably treat her like a fellow vampire rather than a hostage. It would be better for not just us, but for Abigail if Jim believed that we didn't value her, but rather that we saw her as an enemy as much as Jim's coven. I also saw it as wise not to negotiate with this enemy because I did not trust any of them in the slightest, but still it just about killed me.

I only worried that Abigail may have felt that we attempted to kill her, and that we had given up on her with Richard's gunshots. I did not want her as an enemy. Despite all that we had been through, we had only been travel companions for a few days. I worried if she doubted my loyalty to her after she had been coerced to attack me under their psychic control. Afterall, she was disillusioned by the company of people who continuously tried to kill her, and Richard was just another in the string of brutal betrayal by humanity. I was her only human friend and I didn't know how strong that bond was, especially under Jim's, Cindy's, and Sadazar's mind control.

I told Richard firmly, "That's fine that you refuse to bargain with vampires, but don't shoot at Abigail again."

"I aimed beneath her. Besides, vampires can take a bullet," he retorted again.

I resisted the urge to punch him. "Just don't do that again. A head or heart shot kills them and you know it," the icy tone of my voice ended the discussion, and I slapped my rifle to let him know that I would back up my words to defend Abigail with bullets.

We glared at each other until he grimly nodded his head once in agreement. Our eyes shifted back to the enemies on the other side of the gulf.

We fired a few more salvos at some of the more adventurous vampires who climbed down into the moat, but most of them took cover on the other side. Only the crazies were going into the moat.

Something struck my mind.

"I have an idea. Two can play the hostage game," I said to Richard and Rachael after a pause. Jerry and Christy were on the wall on the opposite wall of the drawbridge and out of earshot. The kids had stayed down beneath the rampart.

I yelled across the moat at the vampires, "We have your king hostage. Leave and we will let him live."

The vampires instantly howled with deafening fury. Those failed vampires smart enough to be able to operate rifles and bows sent a barrage of bullets and arrows at us. We ducked. Stoney fragments from the rock wall showered us with shards. That wasn't the reaction that I had in mind.

Richard eyed me and said, "Next time you have a brilliant plan, why don't you run it by the rest of us first?"

"Sure," I snapped at him between the gunshots that we fired back at the horde.

I didn't aim as I mostly blindly fired over the wall as bullets whistled too closely over my head. I usually wouldn't waste bullets like that, but

I was almost weighed down by bullets that we looted from the King's armory.

A handful of more vampires had jumped down into the moat in their fury. They didn't bother to climb down. They were so fueled with rage at my threat to their godlike king. A jump like that would have been suicidal for a person, but most of the vamps immediately stood up and charged. Some crawled toward us despite favoring broken legs from hitting the rock bottom. Their persistent resolve was soul crushing for us, but we easily cut them down now that we were getting used to night firing and the range.

I scanned the other side and still saw no sign of Abigail. I was seriously starting to worry that she had been shot. Even if it wasn't fatal, they still suffered pain like anyone else. Also, if Abigail and I had to make a run for it, if a bullet had shattered Abigail's leg bone, I would be stuck caring for her. Even with vampires, a shattered bone took a few days to recover enough to run. We'd be sitting ducks because once I got to her, and there was no way in hell that I would just leave her to that group. As I was worrying, I caught sight of a black shape slip out from the horde and head to the hills. I wasn't sure if it was her. It was a quick glimpse of a shadow in the night, but it gave me hope, or worry that it was an enemy vampire seeking a back entry into the castle. However the shadow moved fluidly like Abigail, and I knew she would try to join our force in the castle if she could.

"I think we can keep this up until morning when the vamps disburse," Richard said confidently. "It's well past midnight."

I agreed, "They'll probably make one last attempt as dawn nears and then they'll probably scatter to seek shelter somewhere shortly before sunrise. I also think that it will take them a few hours to scale the cliffs to get in the back way."

I felt a confidence surge through me, but then I heard the King screech deafeningly loud from deep in the castle's bowels. The shriek was returned by the King's followers, but they didn't attempt to cross the moat this time. There was a mind jarring calm as I could tell that the shriek from the King was an order to try something different. What that was, I could only guess.

Then, I saw a few sparks of flames among the vampires on the other side of the moat. I was instantly suspicious. They didn't need the fire for light. I then saw the fire blaze at the tip of a few straight sticks.

"Dammit," Jerry swore to my right across the drawbridge. "These crazy bastards really want us dead."

I saw the slender sticks raised by archers at a forty five degree angle, drawn back by a bow.

"Flaming arrows!" I cursed.

A few more arrows were lit by the vampires.

I swore savagely.

"What?" asked Richard.

"Those idiots are shooting flaming arrows into the castle," I exclaimed.

Twenty vampires unleashed the arrows, one right after the other. There were some great shots, but most bounced harmlessly off the castle's stone walls. However I watched with dismay as one flew far over our heads and entered a dark window in the great throne room. The interior immediately lit up like day.

The moat was now clear as the vampires awaited for the flames to take their effect. The fact they were willing to burn down their home to kill us was mind numbingly terrifying.

"We're screwed," Richard said.

If we were flushed out of the castle into the night, Richard would be right as usual. A castle aflame was not a refuge but a death trap.

Chapter Seventeen

"I got a crazy idea," I said.

"You wanna discuss it?" Richard asked.

"No. I'm just going to do it," I said sarcastically. Then I calmly told him, "First let's kill King Sadazar and then this horde."

Richard squinted at me and said, "Tell us your whole plan. We'll help if it's any good."

I explained and to my surprise, the know-it-all liked it.

"We got nothing else going, might as well try that. Let's go!" Richard said.

We left the ramparts. The vampires were patiently waiting for the flames to do their damage.

We stormed the throne room. The tapestries and the rugs were ablaze and lit up the room like daylight. We saw the king curled up in a formerly dark corner, now illuminated up by flickering flames. He was by a door to the rear by the courtyard. Jerry's grenade had done its damage. The king was missing an arm, and it looked like he was missing an eye but I couldn't tell because his face was a bloody mess.

Upon seeing us, as best he could, he stood up immediately on wobbly legs. He hefted a great sword in one hand. The broadsword was about as long as me. I guessed that his pride forced him to stay in the castle until we were forced out or until the flames were too much. Either that or he couldn't escape, but I felt it was more pride on his part. I'm sure he couldn't mentally handle letting humans make this ancient vampire run.

"Help me," he pleaded. From his shaky tone and slurred words, I suspected he may have had a bit of brain damage from the grenade blast or gunshots as he continued to speak. His psionic power was minimal if at all. It was only like mild static in my head. He continued "Please help me, and I'll reward you richly. Weapons, gold, immortality..." He tried to sound sincere, but a demoniac glow blazed in his remaining eye.

I snarled my answer at him full of curses. He screamed fearfully as I and the others lifted our M-16s and opened fire. The pain on his face was the utter terror that I assume that only one who considers himself immortal makes as he faces his end. Mortals fear death of course but we expect it. This was the ultimate assault on his arrogance that he was powerless not just against death, but against mortal humans.

Yes, vampires are resilient, especially the antediluvian types, but the combined fusillade of five semi automatic rifles ripped the vampire king apart. When our magazines emptied, Sadazar was missing both legs. His chest cavity that held the heart and lungs had utterly collapsed in a gory mash of splintered bones and organs that still pulsed with what remained of his resilient heart and his face and head was gruesome, leaking mashed brains and blood. The body moved spastically in its deathroes, but I still decapitated it with my sword to be sure. I never wanted that evil thing to rise again.

My hope was that actually killing the king would shut down his minions' desire to fight, especially with the psychic control that he had over them gone, but the screams of the horde outside was equally ferocious as when I threatened to kill the king. They knew that we had killed their god-King through their mental connection. It didn't calm them but sent them into a pain filled rage. They would charge the walls at any cost even with the castle aflame. My despair was similar when I realized that killing The Mind at Shining Rock didn't kill the vampires of Richard's coven. However, we humans weren't done yet.

I turned to the two families and said, "Get everyone out of this inferno. There's a small yard in the back at the base of the cliff. You should all be safe until the fire burns out."

"But what about the vampires?" asked the child Melanie.

"I'll take care of them," I said more confidently than I felt.

"How so?" asked Richard.

I explained my final plan.

Richard scowled and then looked thoughtful and finally said, "Well, I guess we ain't got much of a choice. This castle will collapse around us in a matter of minutes."

That was true as the flames were already licking up the stout wooden pillars.

"Let's go and finish this," I said, and we sprinted back to the drawbridge.

I had the head of the king in one hand and my rifle in the other.

Rachael went the other way, leading the kids to the temporary safety of the courtyard in the rear, and I thought of the vampire that had run to the hills, but I was confident that Rachael could hold off a rear attack until we were done at the wall.

I had trouble breathing as the smoke began to fill the whole castle as well as my chest. Most of the air that I exhaled was in hacking coughs. I wasn't sure how well a vampire's lungs could handle smoke inhalation. I worried that they would storm the castle and run along the ramparts to get to the kids in the back. I was guessing between the blood desire of the vampires trying to get us or the smoke and fire killing us, I had less than ten minutes to work my plan before the castle fell down upon us.

Jerry, Richard, and Christy reached the ramparts first and were firing at anything scaling the walls.

I stayed down as Jerry tied a rope to the top of the drawbridge and I tied the other end to the opposite wall inside the castle so that it was held upright. I then piled up some fiery tapestries beneath that rope so that the fire would slowly burn through the rope and cause the drawbridge to suddenly crash open. Finally I sliced through the rope on the wheel that raised the bridge and lowered it, but more importantly, held it in place.

My plan was that when the rope that held the drawbridge in place burned through from the tapestry fire, the bridge would collapse, letting our foes inside, but the drawbridge was simply the bait. I was hoping that I could kill them all on the bridge in one rocky swoop by releasing the boulders above us. It was risky. The rate at which the rope burned wasn't timed exactly. I prayed for luck, not sure if God dealt in things such as chance. The fire was already singing the loose fibers of the rope.

"We're ready down here," I yelled, "Keep firing at those things!"

I grabbed the king's head and ran to the top of the ramparts as the others fired into the horde as a good portion tried to cross the moat. Jerry helped me with the king's head. A final gift to his minions.

"Awesome! Be ready for all hell to break loose," I yelled with a laugh fueled by adrenaline. I'm sure that my laugh sounded both jovial and insane.

I then called to the vampires across the moat. "Hey, bloodsuckers! Behold your king!"

I held the King's severed massive head aloft for the vampires across the moat to see.

The vampires greeted the gorey sight with the blood-thirsty shrieks. The roar from hundreds of throats almost deafened me more than their gunfire that slammed into our ramparts.

From behind the wall, I then loaded the King's head in a large sling that I had quickly made from King Sadazar's royal cloak. Jerry stuffed some goodies in its head. I slung the gory remains around my head with the makeshift sling and lobbed it over the rampart and across the moat. It landed with a bounce and was picked up by a vampire who let loose a horrifyingly blood curdling shriek and then he screamed Sadazar's name as he held it up for his horde to witness. Although ruined with gunshots, it was obviously King Sadazar's oversized head of an antediluvian nephilim vampire.

A cacophony of shrieks erupted. It was deafening as the hundreds of vampires screamed at once. They crowded around the king's head as if it was a sacred relic.

"The King is dead," they began to chant. "We need vengeance! We need blood."

Jerry, Christy, and I laughed again to mock them, and then an explosion detonated in the midst of the blood mad mourners as the two grenades that Jerry and I had stuffed up the king's trachea into his mouth and shattered nasal cavity blew. It cleared a diameter of ten meters in the horde. Those vampires lay on the ground, hopefully dead. Beyond the immediate kill zone, a good number crawled or staggered with severe injuries even for a vampire. Many were alive but missing arms and legs.

Jerry emptied a magazine into the group and ran back to join us as we gathered at the base of the drawbridge. We sprinted through the castle as the walls began to fall among us. I took up rear guard and leapt over a pillar that fell just in front of me. A few vampires had scaled the ramparts and were just behind me in full chase. I could hear their wild shrieks on my heels.

The section of roof that the collapsed pillar had held up crashed to the floor just behind us. The large masonry that fell from the roof felt as concussive as the grenades to me, smashing some of the pursuing vampires..

As I was about to exit the castle into the yard, I remembered King Sadazar telling me about watching my camera vest footage. I paused in the smoky building and removed the camera vest and the ballcap with another hidden body camera. I angled the lenses so that the cameras would catch the fiery collapse of the castle. As much as I wanted to strangle Tommy, I thought that I would give him one last show. I didn't like how they had access to my footage to edit and use for propaganda and perverse entertainment. From now on, my reporting would strictly be limited to what I wrote in my notebooks.

After setting up my cameras, I shot a few vampires that ran blindly through the inferno, and I then grabbed Abigail's back pack and weaponry and fled as the ceiling collapsed behind me.

After exiting the castle, we then ran to a small yard in the back at the base of the cliff. The families would be safe from the fire. Once the fire was out then they would be at the mercy of the vampires unless my plan worked.

"Don't screw this up!" Richard said. "My family and I are counting on you."

"Don't worry. It'll be an easier climb than that chimney back at the cave," I lied.

I then sprinted to the cliff with my backpack full of grenades, and began to climb upward. It took longer to climb than I anticipated and I feared that the bridge would open from the burning rope before I had a chance to do my deed. I finally arrived at the height I wanted on the cliff's face. I sprinted along a narrow path that was more of a narrow ledge a foot wide along the sheer rock wall to the rock formation that towered over the moat.

The path had widened as I arrived at the rocky tower that stood thirty feet above me, and I heard the drawbridge's rope snap with a whining ping. It was according to plan, but I was behind schedule. The drawbridge wobbled for a moment and then slammed down into place, bridging the moat. The fifty meters high, thirty meters wide bridge crashed to the other side of the moat crushing some overly eager vampires. The extremely large solid oak and steel door shook the ground beneath my feet like the impact like an explosion.

I opened my backpack and removed my grenades as the vampires charged toward the bridge. I had to work fast.

There was a pit beneath me under the rock formation that I planned to unleash. I planned to throw my grenades and set the rock in motion to fall onto the bridge. Jerry and I guessed that two or three grenades tossed at the base of the rocks would easily cause it to collapse onto the drawbridge, and I had five mini bombs to work with. The rock slide would kill all the vampires on and around the bridge as well as the front of the castle if it hadn't burned down yet. I was preparing to toss down all five grenades. I wasn't playing.

As I prepared to pull the pins, I felt a sharp jab at my back and a shouted command.

"Stop human! Turn around."

I felt a sinking feeling of having let everyone down. I slowly turned, and I saw three shadowy hooded forms pointing their swords at me. They surrounded me in a semicircle. The ledge had widened considerably at the base of the rock formation.

A fourth hooded form appeared from the dark and stood behind them and had an M-16 aimed at my chest.

I looked down and saw the crammed mob of vampires race across the drawbridge. Just as the first one entered the castle, the grenades that Jerry boobytrapped the entrance with, blew, clearing that end of the drawbridge and halting the charge. Those at the vanguard who survived the blast stood on wobbly legs as they came back to their senses, and dozens of dead and mutilated vampiric bodies lay in front of them.

"Drop grenades." The vampire with the rifle ordered in a harsh military commanding voice but atrocious English. "And not in rocks. I see what up to, you!"

I tried to figure a way to fight my way out, but when I saw a fifth hooded vampire appear behind the group, I knew it was the end. More would probably arrive, but I couldn't surrender. I would not let them turn me into a vampire and certainly not a vampire of this polluted line, nor did I desire to feed them with my blood. I was about to turn to jump in the pit and let the grenades detonate in my hands. My sacrifice would set the rock loose and save the families. The castle may have been in flames, but the vampires could easily circumvent it by running along the ramparts to get to the courtyard where the families sought refuge. Such a self-inflicted death would be far more preferable to this vampiric life. I was inspired by Abigail giving herself to Jim's crew for us.

However, just as I was about to pull the pin, and readied my legs to leap in the pit, I saw the fifth shadowy figure appear behind the one with the rifle. I held off on letting go of the safety as the fifth vampire raised a large stone above its head.

I thought that it had to be the most idiotic of the failed vampires, but then that hooded figure smashed the stone against the head of the vampire with the rifle. The vampire with the rifle collapsed and the rifle fell to the ground. The vampire with the rock then took a sword from the fallen vamp's sheath and began attacking the remaining vampires. I then recognized the erect stature and saw that her hands were still cuffed in front.

"Abigail!" I shouted excitedly as my left fist smashed into the nose of the nearest vampire. I drew my handgun with my left hand as I held the grenade in my right and we quickly cut the rest of them down with her sword and my handgun work. It clicked empty as the last vampire fell at my feet.

I wanted to hug her. I was so relieved that she not only survived but had her fighting spirit and wits. They hadn't turned her into their version of a failed vampire.

"Throw those grenades!" she demanded. "Quickly! We gotta get the hell out of here."

I instantly obeyed and watched as the remaining horde began to race across the bridge. After tossing the grenades in the pit, Abigail and I dove away behind some boulders, covering our ears and opening our mouths to avoid the concussion's impact when we hit the deck.

The detonation and the rumbling of the falling stone was deafening even with our hands smashed over our ears. The falling boulders flowed like a river's waterfall down the cliff and wiped out the vampires on the drawbridge as they raced across and those who were crossing beneath in the moat itself below the bridge. When the rocky flow had ceased, the drawbridge was gone as well as the front section of the castle. There were probably thirty vampires left standing looking over the moat from the otherside. All the others were smashed.

"Abigail, I have something for you," I said, pulling out my keys, unlocking her handcuffs, and then, I offered her her weaponry that I still had slung over my back and kept in my belt.

"Thanks," she said as she took her carbine as well as her handgun and sword that I offered, "So romantic. You know how to win a girl's heart," she said with the humor that I loved.

Abigail and I then opened fire from our vantage point. With the blaze of the fire from the castle lighting the scene like a red hell colored day, I had very little issue with cleanly killing each vampire that I aimed at. Abigail was equally kicking butt. Actually with her nocturnal sight, she was far better than me with open sights on the rifle. The remaining vampires instantly disbursed into the night as we pick them off on their retreat one by one.

Their king was dead, their castle burned, and their numbers slaughtered to virtually a handful.

When I could see no more vampires willing to fight. I fired at one more fleeing shadow that screamed out and fell. The slide of my rifle locked back, empty. Feeling safe and so relieved to see her, I neglected to reload as I took a moment to savor the victory and her company.

Abigail, with her better night vision, fired five more shots at vampires who I couldn't see, and I heard responding cries of pain with each of her deadly shots. A few had escaped but we had decisively won the day. There were probably less than a dozen of their coven and they were stupid and leaderless. They wouldn't last long.

She finally set down her rifle and looked at me with a smile, "Now you can hug me."

Overwhelmed with emotion that she had not been turned or shot, I took Abigail in my arms with such gusto that she left her rifle at her feet and returned the embrace. As I lifted her off of her feet, she buried her head in my chest, kissing me on my chest and neck and I graciously kissed the top of her head. I was not even bothered in the slightest that her fangs were at my throat. In fact I loved that sensation of her lips on my throat.

After a moment, the passion died down.

Abigail looked at me sadly and said, "I sense that Jim and his crew got away. We need to find them. As stupid as they are, they have powers beyond my own, even without their king. Jim's and Cindy's psychic control is the only reason they kept fighting after the king died. I really am afraid of them, especially Cindy, and they can quickly turn a bunch of people and vampires into their minions. Within a few weeks, they could be back up and running just as strong even without that damned Sadazar. A part of the king still lives within them."

I shuddered as I heard the guttural but cheery faux English accent from behind me proclaim, "I say, it's Ab-by-gail, my dear girl. You escape. Temporary."

Abigail shook her head violently to clear it. I could see her eyes starting to glaze over.

"Abigail!" I shouted.

Indeed, glory is always fleeting, but the reality and drudgery of mediocrity is painfully eternal

Chapter Eighteen

I watched as Jim walked up to us with a confidence and friendliness that unsettled me. Four other vampires spread out and surrounded Abigail and me. I recognised some of them. One was Cindy who had placed her forehead against Abigail's and had her completely under her power last night. I feared her as much as I feared Jim, maybe more because of Abigail's warning. Another was Tony, a vampire, with a hideous scar on his face.

Abigail tried to sound stern, but I could tell she didn't have much confidence, "Jim, stay away from us. We go separate ways. No need for further bloodshed."

Jim said, "Oh yes there is need for blood, dear Ab-by-gail. You destroyed our home and family. You must replace what you destroyed."

The other vampires giggled, Abigail stepped closer to me so that our shoulders were touching and said, "Fire Eric! Now!"

I lifted my rifle pointing it at Jim's heart, pulled the trigger and swore when nothing happened. It didn't even click. In the excitement of hugging Abigail, I had forgotten to reload. I had celebrated way too early.

I dropped the rifle and immediately drew my sword. I swore some more because I knew I had emptied my handgun in the fight and stupidly neglected to reload that as well. I knew that a bullet's report brought Abigail out from under their control, but they were too close for me to attempt to reload.

I held my sword in front of me. The hilt was at my belt level and I pointed the tip at Jim's eyes.

The vampires circled us on the wider ledge and began chanting in their sickeningly sweet sing-song tone. It was like the tonal scent of sewage to my ears, "Ab-by-gail, Ab-by-gail, Ab-by-gail."

I heard a loud clatter.

I looked at Abigail who had dropped her sword and was staring at something thousands of yards away, in the direction of Cindy, but far beyond. Cindy's eyes narrowed as if focused completely on Abigail's soul.

"Abigail!" I shouted and watched her shake her head to clear it only to stare into the distance again.

"Abigail! Listen to me!" I shouted.

I felt relieved as she stepped back from Cindy and picked up her sword again to fight, but she immediately looked at me from the corner of her eyes with that stare of a great white shark circling its prey.

I let go of my sword with one hand. It went against every fiber of my being, but I backhanded her across the face.

Her face cleared but the vampires kept circling, chanting, "Ab-by-gail, Ab-by-gail, Ab-by-gail."

As they chanted, Jim said, "You must drink the human's blood, Ab-by-gail."

I elbowed her and she stepped back, raising her sword to swing at my head. I squared off against her, keeping my peripheral vision open on the vampires circling us. I was about to be in the fight for my life. I could only go easy on Abigail at my own peril.

"Abigail!" I shouted. "Don't make me defend myself!"

The other vampires laughed as she approached me. Her eyes on my throat. She swung her blade at my head.

"Abigail!" I shouted desperately one last time.

I looked deep in her eyes and pleaded, "Abigail," one more time as her sword whistled at my head for a death blow. I was about to duck and launch a counterattack against her as her attack left her open for me to deliver a counter death blow, but her blade whistled six inches above my head. I knew she had better aim, but her blade sailed well past me. Taking advantage of the opening, I was about to slash at her arm to wound her. However her blade whirled too far around for it to be an accident, and I paused at the last moment of my attack against her. I stopped my razor edged blade a fraction of an inch from slicing through the muscles near her elbow, as I watched her sword slice through Cindy's throat. Then Abigail followed up with a savage slash down as Cindy fell with a split skull. Abigail didn't stop. She yanked the blade out of Cindy and turned that motion into a sword stroke with a vampiric growl. Her blade sank into the skull of another vampire.

Abigail immediately attacked Jim and the deafening ringing of steel on steel resounded through the night as she cried out with the savagery that fueled her attack. With Cindy gone, she seemed to be herself again unless Jim could get inside her mind.

In fear that she might be influenced again, I attacked Tony as his eyes were wide with shock at Abigail's attack on their group. I hacked furiously with my blade. There was no skill that I employed. I simply crashed my sword down repeatedly on Tony's blade as quickly, mightily, and violently as I could. The initial attack took him by surprise and he could only reel backwards in an attempt to right himself before he could launch a counter attack back at me. Once he grew used to my rhythmically telegraphed and mindless attack, he simply kept his sword in place.

I kept that rhythm and then wound up for a savage blow, but just before my sword hit his, I twisted my wrists at the last moment as my sword clashed and slid against his. My blade snaked around his steel, sliced through his wrist, and cleft into the top of his skull. I then lost my mind and hacked him as much as I could to be sure he would never rise again.

I remembered the other two vampires, Jim and Abigail. Fear surged through me as I had my back to them. I whirled around expecting an attack from either one but saw the two engaged fiercely in mortal combat. Abigail continually pressed on Jim so that he retreated step by step.

Abigail didn't appear to need help, and in the past I was brought up to let a one on one fight proceed, but that sense of fairplay had left me quickly after entering this hellhole. I wanted to end this coven so badly that I rushed to flank Jim. He caught sight of me and stepped back quicker and stumbled over a small knee high boulder. Abigail knocked the sword from his hands with hers. The point of Abigail's blade touched his chest at his heart and held it there.

What the hell was she waiting for, I wondered? I sliced down at Jim's throat as he stared at me in horror.

Abigail lifted her sword and blocked my descending slice with a loud clank.

"Stop!" Abigail yelled at me as our crossed swords made an X above Jim. "Don't kill him. Step back, Eric. Jim and I have unfinished business." She looked at him and added, "Right, my mate?"

"What? Does he have psychic power over you?" I asked, thinking she lost her mind in saving him and calling him, "Mate".

"Not with Cindy's reinforcement gone," Abigail replied. "Trust me. I'm of sound mind, but Jim and I have something to discuss."

I had my doubts. Abigail had an odd look on her face. I wasn't sure if Jim somehow influenced her to think that she was safe. I just wanted him dead. Now!

Jim smiled at Abigail with gratitude and smarmy confidence that shook me to the core. I was working hard to hold back from killing the bastard, but I reluctantly trusted Abigail for the moment, at least.

"OK," I said as she looked pointedly at me. I stepped back. The remaining light of bloodlust for my throat was slowly leaving her eyes. In a moment she appeared as a normal woman again. I hoped that she was right that with his crew dead, Jim didn't have control over her mind. I hoped, but doubted. However, I let Abigail do her thing, whatever it was that thing was that she was up to.

"I sorry," she said to me like a failed vampire, and then she smiled seductively at Jim. "So Jim, you wish to be my mate? One of my own kind? Vampires forever?"

He said, "You still be my mate, Ab-by-gail. All will be forgiven."

Her smile faded just faintly as her eyes lit up. He smiled back interpreting her serious demeanor as sexual arousal.

She replied. "OK, take off your cloak, my mate."

He smiled even larger at her, baring his fangs in a toothy smile and started to get up off the ground to take off his cloak, but she placed more pressure on the point of her blade on his chest at his heart.

"Ouch!" Jim said and smiled at her enjoying the pleasure in the pain.

This was getting too weird for me.

"Abigail?" I said letting her name trail off in a question.

She ignored me. Her eyes bored into Jim's with an intent that I couldn't decipher, but he definitely interpreted it as lust for him. Even vampires were fooled by that lustful look that could be the want for a myriad of desires.

"Take off cloak, on knees, like good boy. Striptease. Sexy," she said in the failed vampire's clipped English.

He smiled at her and did a clumsy striptease at her feet. Once the outer garment was off, Abigail instantly dropped her smile from her eyes. Her lips tightened as if welded together. "Eric, grab his cloak," she growled with her fangs barred.

"Ab-by-gail? Ab-by-gail No!!" Jim cried desperately, seeing the sudden deadly intent in her face.

As soon as I took the cloak away, Jim screamed, "Ab-by-gail! No!" as she thrusted the tip of the sword through his heart and immediately decapitated him with savage speed and a light growl.

As I looked at her with confusion, she said to me, "Get cloak. You vampire."

"No," I said, trying to use humor to cover my terror-fueled adrenaline rush, "Me Tonto. You Kimosabe."

"What?" she asked.

I said, "You know, the Lone Ranger TV series from the 1950s?"

She was still confused.

I told her, "Nevermind. It was an old joke and a bad one at that, but you are still using Jim's clipped language."

Her eyes widened with horror, "Really?"

"Yes," I said, nodding with concern. I realized that her use of bad English wasn't just for communication reasons but they had really gotten deep into her psyche.

She looked around as if seeking an outside solution to her internal problem. She finally looked back at me and nodded, saying, "They really got into my head. I've never seen such..." She let her sentence trail off not knowing how to describe what went on in her mind. She said, "I knew there were different types of us vampires that were being experimented on, but I was by far their most successful with psionic abilities in my father Richard's bloodline. But these guys were powerful beyond my understanding. These were morons, faileds, yet idiot savants," her head tilted down and then she looked up at me with sorrowful wide eyes that melted my heart, "I really am sorry, Eric. I didn't mean to attack you. You do know that, right?"

"I know. I experienced what you did. Sadazar took control of me too," I said as I walked up and hugged her with one arm and then quickly reloaded my rifle. I added, "With that damned 'Ab-by-gail' chant, I don't think I will ever call you Abby. Abby will never sound right to me."

"Thank you," she replied with sudden exhaustion in her voice.

I then said, "However, next time you fake a swing at my head to launch an attack at someone else, at least wink or something. I thought I was dead for a moment. I almost attacked you."

She looked deeply into my eyes as she said, "I was trying to kill you at that moment. It was only at the last split second that I changed direction. It was briefly looking into your eyes as you called my name that brought me out. You do know that we have some sort of a connection."

"Yes we do," I nodded and asked, "Will you forgive me for slapping you?"

She replied as she hugged me again, "Fine. Forgive me in advance for when I slap you when you say something stupid in the future."

I chuckled into her hair, "Knowing me, that will probably be in the next minute or so."

She didn't laugh, but just moaned tiredly in my ear.

We embraced tighter and I rested my head in her hair and she rested hers on my shoulder. Our fingers dug into each others' backs as if we feared to ever let go of each other. The desperation of claw and fang did not just apply to fighting but the desire to hold on to the ones you love.

I finally stepped back and asked with dread, "What did you mean by telling me that I was a vampire when you had me take his cloak?"

She said, "When we travel at night, you'll wear Jim's cloak and pretend to be a vampire. That's why I had him take off the cloak before slaying him so as not to bloody it. You don't react well to the blood madness it causes in you when you come in contact with vampiric blood, and let me do the talking if we meet other vampires."

"Do you think that'll work?" I asked.

"It should. Just let me speak. Then, by day, I will wear your red hoodie and I will pretend to be a human. I will let you talk during the day with humans, and I will keep quiet and pretend to be a very submissive wife."

"Submissive? You? That'll be a lot of pretending on your part," I said with a laugh.

"Put it on," she ordered with a smile and a roll of her eyes.

"Not very submissive now, are we?" I joked.

"It's night. I rule," she said with a wink. "Now put it on."

I looked at the garment for a moment as I held it in front of me. It was softer than the rough burlap sensation I was expecting. Of course I had just hugged Abigail who was engulfed in such a cloak, and it was smooth as a silk kimono, but for some reason, I thought of her as a separate entity from a vampire as crude as Jim. I tentatively sniffed Jim's cloak and made a face.

"What?" she asked.

"It smells batty," I said

"You know what a bat smells like?" she asked with a playful yet skeptical smile.

"No, but I am sure that if I did smell a bat, it would smell like this. It's a vampy smell."

She placed her hands on her hips and asked, "Do I smell batty? Vampy?"

I laughed as I put it on, "No. You bathe regularly. You smell like a woman, actually, but this guy needed a ten hour soaking bath."

I flung it over my shoulders and buttoned the top clasp. It was weird. I felt powerful. Like a kid wearing a batman t-shirt.

She huffed as if exasperated but still smiled. "I will wash the cloak as you sleep," she said as she stepped forward and adjusted the collar and the hood of my new cloak. She stepped back cocking her head in a humorous manner as if admiring her work. She looked into my eyes that were like looking into a bottomless pool and she smiled as if she saw my soul through the portals of my eyes.

"There," she said, "You look like the Count himself."

"Count Dracula?" I asked.

"No. DeMoney. Count DeMoney," she said with a coy smile and a playful look in her eyes.

I huffed as if the joke was the most offensive thing in the world before I allowed myself to laugh. I then said, "Let's get the hell out of here."

"Yes," Abigail agreed.

A shudder hit me as I looked at the ground. The bodies of the slain vampires at our feet moved with that unearthly power. I saw Jim's head. His desperate eyes were fixed on Abigail and followed her when we walked away. His lips moved soundlessly saying, "Ab-by-gail. My mate," over and over. I was sure he would continue with this mantra at least until dawn when he'd finally meet the sun's deadly rays and his death. I was too exhausted to slash his skull with a mercy blow. Abigail usually would have delivered such mercy, but whatever he did to her in the castle did not inspire any mercy in her. She turned her back on his animated head with a huff. She wouldn't answer my questions about what happened in the castle, so I let it drop for the time being, but inside, I was worried for her. Despite our earlier joking, I could tell something had shaken her soul.

A few hours before the dawn broke the eastern sky, Abigail and I climbed back down the cliff to check on the two families. We watched the fire in the castle burn down in the safe area of the yard.

The two families were in good spirits as they had more than replenished their bullets from King Sadazar's supply as well as picking up better firearms. Abigail also recovered her pack that I had dragged out into the courtyard before the full collapse of the castle.

With dismay we heard an occasional explosion from a grenade or bullet firing off in the infernal. I wished that we had had a chance to thoroughly loot the castle before it burned.

We used a sturdy rope and helped the family scale the cliff to escape the few vampires, maybe a dozen, who recongregated at the front of the castle, but we didn't worry about those too much.

We thought it would be a good escape route to go over the ridge. None of us wanted to leave through the valley where we arrived. I figured there were still probably a dozen or so vampires left. I didn't think that they would fare well. They weren't very smart, their king was dead as well as Jim and Cindy who were the most powerful in this dim bunch, their daytime roost was in flames, and their morale was gone. I was sure something would get them, the sun, people, or other vampires.

They had a scent on them that other vampires found as repulsive as Abigail found them to be.

At the ridge top, Abigail caught wind of a bear with her keen sense of smell. She lured it to us with her vampiric psionics. She had her fill of its blood and filled up a quart mason jar for the road. I took a big chunk of meat, and let the family have the remaining carcass.

Abigail and I bid farewell to the families and then the two of us left the families to go their own ways. They were still unsettled with Abigail being a vampire after what they went through in the castle. They didn't say anything other than goodbyes and firm handshakes, but it was clear that we were not to stay with them. I was probably more offended than Abigail was. With grace, she seemed to accept that she would never fit in with humanity. That graceful acceptance broke my heart. I feared that if we stuck together, we would never find companionship with anyone else, but I was fine with that. I preferred her company over that with anyone I knew.

However after we parted ways with the family, I realized that they were just as put off by me as they were with her. I wasn't a pleasant person to be around in the Forbidden Zone, especially when I was defending her, but the knowledge that my actions made me as repulsive to humans as an actual vampire really hit me hard. I dwelled on the knowledge for quite some time that despite my initial distrust of Abigail, she, as a vampire, was a much better person than I was.

***

As day broke, Tommy watched the footage from Eric's camera vest in the smoldering ruins, hoping that his friend would reclaim it. Excitedly he watched as the camera was lifted up. He held his breath until he saw the scowling skull face of The Specter/Don Renton glaring into the lens.

Eric was obviously long gone. Tommy wished that he could taunt The Specter. The castle was a place that the big man hadn't dared to enter until Eric had demolished it. Don had beaten up Eric when they first met and considered his friend, Eric, a wuss. Times had definitely changed. Tommy closed his laptop, shutting off the video feed. He went outside for a breath of fresh air.

Tommy accepted that Eric had abandoned the camera. Eric was now on his own with the vampiress. Tommy worried about how he would survive without the main stars of his reality show, but deep down inside he was glad that Eric had ditched the camera that could track his whereabouts.

Chapter Nineteen

We marched for another hour before I told Abigail that it was time for me to sleep. The last good sleep I had was that last day in the Mountain Warriors' camp, and my mind could not remember how many days ago that was because of the exhaustion.

I had worked the night shift in the distant past, but back then, I was surrounded by artificial light. Through this march, I only had the sparse starlight that trickled in through the occasional breaks in the clouds. Abigail was at the height of her energy, but I felt like I had a tiny maintenance man running around the inside of my head turning off every electrical switch in my body, muttering that it was far past closing time.

I could tell she wanted to march on. She was now driven beyond comprehension to make it to Asheville for a cure for vampirism. I remembered Sadazar's words that she would one day acquire his demoniac appearance. I'm sure that he told her the same thing, but she still refused to talk about what had happened to her in the castle.

However, she took pity on me. She sighed and said "OK" at my insistence to stop.

We chose a relatively flat spot far enough from a creek that we had been following. I wanted to camp closer to it for the relaxing bubbling sound, but she nixed that with the argument that the sound of the creek would drown out the noise of an approaching attacker. I agreed and remembered that she was quite a badass and woodswoman long before the zombie apocalypse and even longer before she was a vampire.

Before it all went down, she lived primitively by herself with the goal of becoming a modern female version of Henry David Thoreau. I encouraged her to continue her writing, but she had bitterly given it up because she originally envisioned writing about a more spiritual journey in the wilderness than the mere survival of our current state. I tried to convince her that it still was worth writing about, maybe more so. As one walks the boundaries with death, the physical aspect of survival becomes noticeable on the outside actions while the internal spiritual life becomes more pronounced.

I was happy when she agreed to write about our experience if I got overwhelmed. I had a lot to document. I thought that people needed to hear her voice as well. She had much to say and had a brilliantly unique perspective. Later, she wrote one of the volumes of our travels.

Besides staying away from the babbling creek, she also insisted on making a quick shelter of natural materials over our tent. I had a nice tent but she explained that besides the added insulation of the cover, the color of the tent wouldn't camouflage us and it would let in too much daylight through the translucent fabric for a vampire to sleep. I wasn't thrilled with there being one more step to take because I wanted to go right to sleep, but I agreed. However, I was surprised how quickly she erected a lean-to over the tent. I helped with the frame and then crawled in and almost instantly passed out as she did some finishing touches and then heaped on a ton of leaves for insulation.

She also cleaned my new vampiric cloak in the creek and hung it so it would be dry when we moved on.

There was still a flea's hair worth of time before daylight when she finally crawled in the tent beside me. I was facing away from her and she cuddled up around my back in the small tent. I was grateful for the warmth, however, very few people have ever tried to endure sleeping at night with a nocturnal creature. It reminded me of being a kid with a hamster caged in my room. Abigail didn't just toss and turn, it was like she had that damn hamster's wheel and she was working it furiously next to me on the sleeping pad. We had slept together before, but tonight was by far the worst with her fidgeting. That surprised me because this was by far the safest night that we spent together, and we both needed and deserved our rest after all we had been through.

She was also well fed from the bear's blood and needed to catch up on sleep from our last few crazy days and nights. At that moment, I didn't stop to think what could be arousing her. I was only irritated at the constant interruption of my sleep.

I finally tired of her continuous movement as well as her sighing as if she had something to say. I sharply suggested that she could take care of something outside if she couldn't sleep.

She said that if we were going to start walking by late afternoon, she needed some sleep now and elected to stay beside me.

I sat up and said, "We're leaving at noon, not late afternoon and we are stopping tomorrow at midnight, no later!"

She sat up as well and replied, "We are heading east. I would prefer to walk with the sun at my back rather than in my face or directly above. Don't forget I am a vampire."

I shot right back, "How can I forget that you are a vampire? You're keeping me up all night, for Heaven's sake!"

"I'm sorry," she replied. "How about you wake up at noon, do what you need to do then, then wake me when we must leave and we will hit the trail in the early afternoon."

"OK," I agreed, only to end the conversation.

In the quiet, I quickly went back to sleep, but she had an uncanny ability to wake me just as I drifted off to sleep. I had been entering a dream where I was on a tropical beach when I heard her say, "Colloidal Silver!"

I actually thought that a waitress was offering me an alcoholic drink with an umbrella and colloidal silver mixed in on my dream beach. I shook the pleasant dream from my head.

"What?" I asked.

"Colloidal silver," Abigail repeated.

I blew out a harsh breath.

She continued, "Even if they have nothing to cure my virus at the hospital, Asheville is– was a mecca of natural healers. I'm sure I could get some colloidal silver or herbs or something that could cure me of the vampiric virus."

"That sounds great," I muttered in dismissive agreement and drifted off to sleep again.

I was in a deep relaxing dark void of sleep when I heard, "What about love?"

"What? What about love?" I asked, suddenly totally roused from my sleep.

She explained, "Love. I know it sounds cheesy, but what if love really is the answer? The cure? Not just a cure for me, but this entire crazy and violent world."

"That's impossible," I said, sitting up.

"Why," she asked, sounding hurt.

I replied with a little more compassion as I started to understand her restlessness. It was the same restlessness that I suffered, "You tried to kill me earlier tonight or last night– damn, I can't even tell time anymore... You had me banished from my friends. You're banished from vampires for not turning or killing me. We've risked our lives for each other numerous times. Hell! Think about it, you were literally subjected to crucifixion for me and I almost gave my life rescuing you just this last night."

"And?" she asked.

"And! If either of us had any sense, we'd go as far from each other as possible. On the surface, it's completely ridiculous that we're sticking together."

"You're right," she said miserably.

"So considering that we're ignoring every rational argument, there's only one reason why we're sleeping together, here tonight."

"And what's that?" she asked hesitantly.

I replied as I started to lay back down, "If love was the answer, you would already be cured because we both obviously love each other more than common sense, reason, or even our very own lives. That's the true definition of love. We may not be able to be romantic due to the risk of infection, but we stay together because of our mutually intimate love."

The vampiress cried slightly. She kissed my chest and said, "Thank you, Eric. I feel the same as you."

We held each other tightly.

She rolled over and I turned to face her back. She scooted into me and I could feel her finally drift off into a deep sleep. With my face buried into her hair and my arm around her waist, I laid there wide awake. Despite the relaxation that her steady breathing inspired in me, there was no rest for my mind.

Because of my height, my nose alway seemed to rest on the top of her head as she stood or lay close to me. Something about her, devoid of artificial odors and perfumes, gave off a faint natural scent that was both wild and sweet, redolent of the woods in which she lived and the gracious personality that I saw in her smile and eyes each night and day as I got to know her better.

I felt the steady breathing of her relaxed sleep. King Sadazar was right about one thing. It was now my turn to lie wide awake, full of unreleased passion. It was true. I did love her. I loved her madly with all my heart.

About the Author

R.J.Burle is a former Marine and volunteer firefighter. He has studied and taught a variety of martial arts and is an outdoor survival instructor. He is a chiropractor and writer living in the mountains near Asheville, NC with his wife and children. This is the sixth book in the mountain warrior series. You can find *Outcast, Deadly Ally, March of the Dead, Beneath the Caverns,* and *Unveiled* online and through your favorite bookstore. Visit R.J. at www.rjburle.com and subscribe to his YouTube channel at "R.J. Burle" where you'll find readings of chapters from his novels and short stories.

www.ingramcontent.com/pod-product-compliance
Lightning Source LLC
LaVergne TN
LVHW041753060526
838201LV00046B/987